Look what people are saying about these talented authors...

About Janelle Denison

"Sizzle and romance dance through the pages, making this a truly entertaining read."
—*Romantic Times BOOKreviews* on *That's Amore!*

"I urge you to run, not walk to the store and grab your copy. It is so hot it just may set the store on fire."
—*The Best Reviews* on *Too Wilde to Tame*

About Isabel Sharpe

"Ms. Sharpe has written a story that will have you laughing out loud. There's also tenderness, emotion and hot scorching sex...."
—*Coffee Time Romance* on
What Have I Done for Me Lately?

"Wow, Ms. Sharpe has once again blown us away with a sexy romance that is not only steamy, but full of excitement and fun. A fast entertaining read...sure to bring sweat to your brow and a smile to your face."
—*Coffee Time Romance* on *All I Want...*

About Jennifer LaBrecque

"Jennifer LaBrecque's skill at mixing humor and sensuality is evident in *Really Hot!* (4.5), perhaps her finest book yet."
—*Romantic Times BOOKreviews*

"LaBrecque writes her characters to jump off the pages."
—*The Romance Reader*

ABOUT THE AUTHORS

USA TODAY bestselling author **Janelle Denison** is known for her sinfully sexy heroes and provocative stories packed with sexual tension and emotional conflicts that keep readers turning the pages. She is also the author of the highly popular Wilde series. Janelle's favorite time of year is Christmas, and she hopes that each and every one of you spend the holidays with your own special secret Santa! For information on upcoming releases, visit Janelle's Web site at www.janelledenison.com.

Isabel Sharpe was not born pen in hand like so many of her fellow authors. After she quit work in 1994 to stay home with her firstborn son and nearly went out of her mind, she started writing. Yes, she was the clichéd bored housewife writing romance, but it was either that cliché or seduce the mailman, and her mailman was unattractive. After more than twenty novels for Harlequin Books, and a new direction of women-focused stories for Avon, Isabel admits her new mailman is gorgeous, but she's still happy with her choice. She loves hearing from readers, and what better time than Christmas to spread good cheer? Write to her through her Web site at www.IsabelSharpe.com. Happy holidays to you all!

Jennifer LaBrecque loves romance and Christmas surprises, so she was very excited when the opportunity arose to write a Secret Santa story for Harlequin Blaze. Her work in contemporary romantic fiction has garnered her two RITA® Award nominations, *Romantic Times BOOKreviews* Reviewers Choice nominations, a Maggie Award of Excellence and Notable New Author of the Year Award. Jennifer lives in suburban Atlanta with her husband and daughter, two cats, two greyhounds and a Chihuahua who runs the whole show. She'd love you to visit her at www.jenniferlabrecque.com or drop her a note via snail mail at P.O. Box 298, Hiram, GA 30141.

Janelle Denison
Isabel Sharpe
Jennifer LaBrecque

Secret Santa

A naughty but nice
Christmas collection

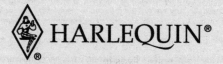

HARLEQUIN®

TORONTO • NEW YORK • LONDON
AMSTERDAM • PARIS • SYDNEY • HAMBURG
STOCKHOLM • ATHENS • TOKYO • MILAN • MADRID
PRAGUE • WARSAW • BUDAPEST • AUCKLAND

ISBN-13: 978-0-373-79296-2
ISBN-10: 0-373-79296-4

SECRET SANTA
Copyright © 2006 by Harlequin Books S.A.

The publisher acknowledges the copyright holders of the individual works as follows:

HE'D BETTER WATCH OUT!
Copyright © 2006 by Janelle Denison.

THE NIGHTS BEFORE CHRISTMAS
Copyright © 2006 by Muna Shehadi Sill.

MISTLETOE MADNESS
Copyright © 2006 by Jennifer LaBrecque.

This edition published by arrangement with Harlequin Books S.A.

® and TM are trademarks of the publisher. Trademarks indicated with ® are registered in the United States Patent and Trademark Office, the Canadian Trade Marks Office and in other countries.

www.eHarlequin.com

Printed in U.S.A.

CONTENTS

HE'D BETTER
WATCH OUT!

Janelle Denison

To my Harlequin editor, Brenda Chin—
Thank you for eight great years of editing,
guidance and friendship. You're one of
the best editors in the business!

And, as always, to my wonderful husband, Don.
You are, and always will be, my Secret Santa!
Merry Christmas!

Prologue

GO AHEAD. DO IT. NO ONE WILL ever find out.

This gleeful goad came from the little devil sitting on Amanda Creighton's left shoulder. Of course Devilish Desiree—the name Amanda had given the more daring part of her conscience—was a figment of her own imagination. Still, the little female devil always seemed to pop up whenever the tiniest glimmer of a naughty thought happened to cross Amanda's mind. With her red sparkly halter top, short miniskirt and matching four-inch heels, Desiree was ready and willing to lead Amanda straight into all sorts of temptation.

Thank God she had Angelic Angie, the prim and proper angel who sat on her right shoulder, to counter Desiree's wicked suggestions. Even now, Angie was fighting to preserve Amanda's integrity.

Don't do it, Amanda, Angie said in that reproachful tone she normally used when Desiree was involved. *You know it's wrong.*

Desiree rolled her eyes and crossed one long red silk-stockinged leg over the other. *Don't listen to her,* she whispered in Amanda's ear. *She's such a Goody Two-Shoes, and that halo above her head is just way too straight and shiny, if you ask me. She's the reason why you never have any fun.*

Amanda leaned back in her office chair and rubbed her temples with the pads of her fingers. She found it hard to argue Desiree's point because when it came to any indecision Amanda might have about right or wrong, or the merest thought about doing something mischievous, Angie's logic and rationale always won out. And that meant Amanda usually did the *honorable* thing, which made her way too uptight and boring, in Desiree's estimation.

It had been that way since Amanda was twelve. Desiree and Angie had arrived shortly after her mother had died, and they'd been with her ever since, playing tug-of-war with her psyche. After the loss of her mother, and as the only child of her workaholic father, she'd spent a lot of time alone, trying to make decisions for herself—which was what had undoubtedly prompted Desiree and Angie's initial appearance. As a young girl, they'd kept her from making bad choices, or succumbing to peer pressure at school.

Even now that Amanda was twenty-seven, they both still believed that they each knew what was best for her and had no qualms about stating their opinions on various matters—from family issues, to the clothes she bought—even the men she chose to date.

Today, it had been a brief "what if" scenario with the office's bad boy, Christian Miller—whom she had a major crush on—that had prompted a visit from Desiree. The impish she-devil had been enthusiastic about encouraging the inappropriate ideas dancing in Amanda's mind, which was quickly followed by Angie and her attempts at damage control.

With a shake of her head, Amanda picked up the neat, handwritten list of names she'd been reviewing before being interrupted by the voices of her conscience. When she'd volunteered to organize this year's Secret Santa list for the executive floor's holiday party, she'd figured it would be a relatively easy and simple task.

Connoisseur, a food and travel magazine that was owned by her father, was a large publishing company that was made up of many different departments and levels—each of which were having their holiday parties on whatever day suited their group the best. The executive floor, which also included accounting, human resources and sales, had taken a vote, and the Friday before Christmas had won out for their get-together and Secret Santa exchange.

As executive editor of *Connoisseur,* and her father's right-hand woman, Amanda had developed a reputation for being well-organized, efficient and dependable, so everyone seemed perfectly happy when she'd offered to be the keeper of the list.

For the most part, coordinating the Secret Santa gift exchange had been just a matter of putting all of the office employees' names into a paper bag, then letting each person draw a piece of paper to find out who they'd be purchasing a gift for. Amanda kept a master list of who picked whom, and went ahead and randomly drew names for the employees who were out for the day. Everything had been going smoothly, until she'd opened the piece of paper she'd picked for Stacey Roberts, the office bimbo, and had read the name *Christian Miller,* the top sales executive for the magazine.

Amanda's pulse had raced, as it always did when it came to Christian. With his pitch-black hair, dark blue eyes and a body made for sin, he was the stuff that made up most of her deepest, fondest fantasies. Adding to his good looks was a charming, flirtatious personality and a smile that had the ability to melt polar ice caps. It was no wonder most of the women in the office had a secret crush on him. Herself included.

As much as she knew that Stacey would love to be paired up with Christian—preferably horizontally if the busty blonde had her way—Amanda couldn't bring herself to give Stacey that kind of satisfaction, which the other woman would undoubtedly exploit to her advantage.

That was when Amanda's thoughts had drifted and she'd fantasized about keeping Christian for herself, and giving Stacey her office archrival slut, Melissa Wintz, instead. The thought of pairing up those two she-cats held a whole lot of appeal and would no doubt add some fun to the gift exchange.

Come on, Amanda, Desiree cajoled. *You know you want to switch those names so you can be Christian's Secret Santa. And why not? You've been attracted to him for the past year. Besides, he's gorgeous, single and hotter than Hades.*

Amanda grinned at Desiree's amusing play on words, until Angie jumped in with her side of things.

He's all wrong for you, she said with a disapproving shake of her head. *He doesn't do relationships and he has a reputation for being a player. Don't you remember when he got caught in the boardroom in a very compromising position with that hussy from production?*

Amanda remembered the scandalous incident very well, which had caused a flurry of office speculation and gossip to run rampant about Christian's sexual prowess. Those juicy, titillating rumors had served to add plenty of spice to the personal fantasies *she'd* had about the man, and also made her wish she had the nerve to be as bold and brazen as the woman he'd been with.

Unfortunately, she also recalled her father's disappointment when he'd summoned the pair into his office the very next day to deliver a reprimand, along with a warning to keep their hands, and other body parts, to themselves during work hours. Luckily for Christian, the issue had become a moot point when the production assistant had quit two weeks later.

He's a ladies' man and a philanderer, Angie went on with determination. *He has more notches on his bedpost than you have designer shoes in your closet.*

Gorgeous stilettos that rarely see the light of day, I might add, Desiree said as she admired her own red heels that did amazing things for her legs. *It's a crime not to wear all those amazing shoes you buy.*

Leave it to Angie to use her one guilty pleasure to press her point home, and Desiree to mourn the fact that Amanda's huge shoe collection went unappreciated. Amanda definitely had a weakness for sexy shoes, with Jimmy Choo and Manolo Blahnik topping as her favorite designers. They were all openly displayed in her walk-in closet for her to look at, touch and even slip on her feet occasionally.

But Desiree was right—she didn't wear them outside of her house. Four-inch heels weren't practical for everyday wear, and those fun, sexy shoes didn't exactly go with the business suits and modest outfits she wore at the office. At least not without attracting a whole lot of attention, including her father's scrutiny.

Amanda had long ago decided that as some women collected porcelain dolls or rare figurines that they displayed for their viewing pleasure, she did the same with designer shoes.

Your shoe fetish aside, being a womanizer isn't necessarily a bad thing, Desiree stated, bringing the conversation back to Christian and all the reasons why Amanda ought to consider having a fling with him. *And so what if he doesn't do relationships? What more could a girl want for Christmas than a holiday dalliance with someone who is built like a God and knows what he's doing in the sack?*

Amanda winced at that last remark. Desiree was obviously referring to her last steady boyfriend, whom she'd referred to as the one-minute wonder because of his lack of stamina when it came down to doing the deed. Once in, once out, and he was done for the night, leaving Amanda to her own devices if she wanted an orgasm.

But it hadn't been just the bad sex that had brought their relationship to an end. Like most of the men who wanted to date Amanda, he'd been more attracted to her name, wealth, and what her very powerful publisher-father could do for him and his own career.

Lips pursed, Angie smoothed a hand down her immaculate white gown. *Christian is all wrong for you, and after that fiasco in the boardroom, your father would hardly approve of him as a suitor.*

Suitor? It's not like she's going to marry the guy. Besides, Daddy wouldn't ever have to find out that she's getting some on the side from the office stud. A sly grin curved the corners of Desiree's lips. *Don't forget, he's been quite respectable the past eight months or so. He's cleaned up his act and been quite focused lately.*

Only because there's a promotion on the line, Angie argued pointedly. *He has his eye on that promotion to sales director. He wants to impress Amanda's father by proving that he's a responsible, reliable team player now instead of the cad he was back in the boardroom.*

True, Desiree agreed as she glanced at her fire-engine red painted fingernails. *But he can't remain a monk forever, and that could certainly work to Amanda's advantage.*

The banter in her head was making Amanda crazy. "Arghhh! Stop already," she ordered the two of them in a firm tone, grateful that her office door was closed so no one could hear this bizarre conversation she seemed to be having with herself. "I never said I wanted to have an affair with him."

Desiree leaned close and whispered in her ear. *You might not have said it out loud, but you've thought about it plenty. I would know since I spend a lot of time in that head of yours.*

Way too much time, Amanda was beginning to realize. And when had this discussion gotten so out of hand? She'd only pondered the idea of switching names to be Christian's Secret Santa—*secret* being the operative word—and it had blown into a full-fledged attack on her lack of a love life.

Amanda inhaled a deep, calming breath. "I'm *not* going to have a fling with him."

The halo above Angie's head shone brightly as she cast the red devil on Amanda's shoulder a triumphant smile. *Good girl.*

Desiree shook her head in disappointment. *You're going to die without ever experiencing true passion and mind-blowing sex.*

Amanda couldn't take it anymore. "Go away, both of you," she muttered.

But...

"Go. *Now.*" Amanda shut her eyes and forced the two troublemakers out of her head with a deliberate mental block. When blessed quiet reigned for a good long minute, she slowly opened her eyes and thanked a higher power for the silence.

Biting her lower lip, she glanced at the gift-exchange list again, this time contemplating her idea without any extraneous input from the distracting duo. All she wanted was to feel like a seductive, sexy woman and a bit of a bad girl—and know that she was capable of attracting the interest of a man like Christian, even if it was in a secret way.

With confidentiality working in her favor, she could be a little reckless and purchase him a gift that would seduce his mind and body. She could watch his reaction as he opened the present without fear of him ever finding out that she was the one who'd given him something so provocative. It would be like having her own private, sexual interlude with Christian, but without any emotional or physical involvement.

Being his Secret Santa would be safe and fun, for both of them, she thought with a smile. He'd no doubt enjoy the attention and thrill of temptation that came with the present he opened, but like all of his previous relationships, she had no doubt the initial intrigue would eventually fade and he'd forget all about who might have sent him the suggestive holiday gift. And ultimately, no one would ever have to know what she'd done.

Excitement and anticipation blossomed within her, and she had to admit that she liked the sensation that came with being impulsive and adventurous. Before she could change her mind, or Angie and Desiree could reappear with their opinions on the matter, Amanda picked up her pen and jotted Christian's name down on the Secret Santa list.

Right next to her own.

1

CHRISTIAN HUSTLED DOWN the corridor toward the office of Douglas Creighton, the owner and publisher of *Connoisseur* magazine. He'd been summoned by the big boss, and since there was a promotion dangling on the horizon, he wasn't about to keep him waiting any longer than necessary.

Christian had spent the past eight months trying to repair his tarnished reputation after the disastrous incident with Maureen Bowen in the boardroom, and that meant dodging advances from other women in the company who believed he was an easy catch, especially Stacey Roberts, who'd made it her mission to end his oath of celibacy.

He'd worked hard ever since Maureen's departure from the company, dedicating long hours at the office coming up with new and innovative sales strategies that had catapulted him to the number-one sales executive for the past six months in a row. He'd instantly turned down invitations to join his buddies at the local hot spot for a few drinks and an evening of hitting on willing women. He no longer took two-hour pleasure lunches, and the only phone calls he received at work were strictly business. Even his friends were calling him a monk because it had been months since he'd gotten laid.

No doubt about it, he'd cleaned up his act and kept his focus on the job and the possibility of snagging the sales director promotion he wanted so badly. In a few weeks, after Christmas and the first of the year, he'd finally find out if his drive, dedication and respectable way of living had paid off.

As he made his way through the executive floor toward

Creighton's wing of offices, he passed a maze of cubicles dominating the center of the twenty-seventh floor of the Jackman
Butler Building in New York City, where employees were busy
at work. The outer offices flanking the cubicles had amazing
views of Manhattan and were reserved for the higher-ups in the
company. It was Christian's ultimate goal to earn one of those
coveted offices for himself, with floor-to-ceiling windows,
paneled walls to hang pictures, and a cherrywood desk large
enough to spread out his work without feeling cramped.

He returned his gaze back to where he was going just as
Stacey stepped out from her cubicle and deliberately into his
path. Her sudden appearance in front of him forced Christian to
come to an abrupt halt or collide into her Double Ds, which were
one breath away from spilling out of the fur-trimmed bodice of
the sexy Mrs. Claus costume she'd worn for the department's
holiday party that afternoon. The red velvet minidress was form-
fitting, way too short and no doubt had most of the males in the
office fantasizing about getting lucky with her for Christmas.

Unfortunately, Stacey had her sights set on *him*, and he wasn't
interested. He'd thwarted her advances more times than he could
count, but she gave the words *determination* and *persistence* new
meaning. She was just too easy, and despite his own bad-boy
reputation, he realized that he'd changed over the past eight
months. He'd become more particular and discriminating, and
less promiscuous. Somewhere along the way, he'd developed
standards and overly assertive women like Stacey no longer
appealed to him.

Still, he smiled at her because there was no sense in making
an enemy out of the woman by outright telling her how he felt.
He did, after all, have to work with her every day. "Cute outfit,
Stace. I'm sure you'll be a big hit at the party today."

"I'm glad you like it," she said as her fingers toyed with the
white furry ball hanging from the tip of her red velvet Santa hat.
"Care to jingle my bells?" She jiggled her breasts, and the two
little silver bells attached to the bow barely securing the front of
her dress made a light tinkling sound.

He wasn't about to touch that double entendre. "Uh, sorry, but I'll have to pass. If I don't hustle, I'm going to be late for my meeting with Douglas."

"You're no fun anymore, Christian," she said, her cherry-red lips forming a sultry pout. "You know what they say about all work and no play…"

Yeah, it would hopefully give him the promotion he was after. "I'm sure I'll have fun at the holiday party this afternoon."

She brightened considerably at the mention of the department's get-together. "That's right. We're exchanging Secret Santa gifts." She ran her index finger down the front of his tie and leaned in close. "If you'll let me be your secret Santa Claus, I promise to give you a gift guaranteed to blow your mind, among other things," she added suggestively.

Jee-suz. Could the woman be any more forthright? At one time her blatant approach might have interested him, but now he just felt trapped. The need to escape, and fast, overwhelmed him. "Uh, thanks, I'll remember that."

"Ummm, be sure that you do."

Before she could proposition him again, he stepped around her and made a quick getaway. Only then did he notice that they'd had an avid audience who'd witnessed the entire exchange.

Great. Just great.

The guys in the department were shaking their heads in disappointment, as if they couldn't believe he'd turned down a sure thing. And then there was Drew, who was openly gay, and was grinning at Christian in that flirtatious, come-to-daddy way of his.

Christian shuddered. He wasn't homophobic and worked with Drew without any problems. He even considered him a friend, of sorts. But he was uncomfortable with the other guys' jokes that if Christian ever decided to stray to the *other* side, Drew had first dibs on him.

No way. No how. Christian was heterosexual all the way, and he was just on hiatus from dating at the moment to focus on his career. Who knew being celibate would be so difficult, and would compromise his manhood in the process, for crying out loud?

Shaking his head, he beelined it down the long corridor that led to the executive suite that was Douglas Creighton's office. He walked past a long panel of glass on the right-hand side, which framed Amanda Creighton's office and mini-suite—a great perk for being the executive editor of *Connoisseur* and heiress to one helluva lucrative publishing company. The floor-to-ceiling window afforded her a modicum of privacy in her inner sanctum, yet allowed her to keep an eye on what was going on outside her office. From what he'd seen, the double doors behind her large desk led to a room furnished with a couch, sitting area, bathroom and even a small kitchenette.

But even though Amanda had been born with the proverbial silver spoon in her mouth, she wasn't a prima donna as most people assumed, based on the first impression Amanda usually gave—of composed sophistication with a reserved personality all wrapped up in a staid, button-up designer suit or outfit. Instead, she was a woman who actually involved herself in all aspects of the company, including contributing her own monthly column, involving herself in various projects and assignments, and generally making sure that everything ran smoothly. She had a way of pitching in without offending anyone, and in the process earned the respect of her co-workers.

Christian came to a stop at her open door. She was standing to the left of her desk at her tall cherrywood filing cabinet, and he lifted his hand to knock just as she pulled out a lower drawer and bent over at the waist to retrieve a file. His hand stilled as he took in the sensual curve of her hips and the sweetly shaped bottom in a pair of tailored black pants.

Awareness hit him hard, and his lower body stirred. The reaction that Stacey had been after made its presence known now—a purely sexual response that reassured him that he was an all-American male who enjoyed women.

But being attracted to the boss's daughter was another thing entirely. Despite how much he might desire this woman, he put the brakes on his thoughts and that glimmer of attraction warming him in private places that had been cold and dormant for too long. Sure, Amanda was very pretty and everything soft and feminine, but there were certain lines in business that a smart man didn't cross. And she had always been one of them. Because her office was also on the executive floor and she was so involved in all aspects of the company, they talked and interacted, but he just never allowed himself to treat her as anything more than a colleague, even if he wished otherwise.

Having found whatever it was she'd been after, Amanda pushed the drawer closed, straightened and turned around holding a file folder in her hand. Her gaze landed on him as he stood in the doorway, and she gasped in surprise.

"Christian," she said, her tone breathless and her face flushed as she pressed a hand to her chest. "I didn't hear you behind me."

Christian never would have considered a turtleneck sweater as a sexy piece of clothing, especially considering how much skin it covered—from beneath her chin, down her arms to her wrists, and all the way to her waist. But that was before he'd seen one on Amanda.

The stretchy knit fabric clung to her upper body like a second skin, and without his permission his gaze dropped briefly to her breasts to take a moment to appreciate the lovely shape of those full, lush mounds outlined to perfection. The bright, festive red color of her sweater complimented her shoulder-length brown hair and made her eyes seem much darker and greener than normal—just as he imagined they'd look in the throes of passion.

What the hell am I thinking?

He mentally shook himself out of his trance and lifted his gaze back to hers. "Sorry about that," he said, unsure if he was apologizing for sneaking up on her, or for ogling her breasts. "I didn't mean to startle you. I was just about to knock. I'm here to see Douglas."

"Oh, of course." She set the file folder down on her desk and appeared as professional and polished as always. If you didn't count the fact that her nipples had tightened and were pressing against the front of her sweater like twin laser beams. An interesting reaction considering it wasn't at all cold in her room.

"He said for you to go on into his office when you arrived," she said, as if her body's response hadn't betrayed her. "He's expecting you."

He nodded. "Great. Thanks." He turned to go, then something stopped him and he turned back around. "Are you going to be at the holiday party this afternoon?" He had no idea why he asked, or why her answer mattered so much. Maybe it was the attraction he'd always felt toward her, or maybe the hormones that still had his body in an aroused state that were talking for him.

"I wouldn't miss it for anything." She sat down behind her desk and met his gaze with an easy smile. "It should be fun."

Fun. There was that word again. "I was just accused by Stacey of not being any fun, so I better make sure I have a good time at the party."

She laughed lightly, probably because it was a known fact that Stacey had made it her mission to show him her version of fun. "With the Secret Santa gift exchange, the party is bound to be full of surprises."

He leaned casually against the door frame and tipped his head curiously. "So, whose name did you get?"

She lifted a brow, making him feel like a naughty boy for asking. "You know I can't tell you that." Amusement laced her voice.

"You could, if you really wanted to." He pushed his hands into the front pockets of his trousers and grinned persuasively. "It hardly seems fair that you know who everyone else has for a Secret Santa, but no one knows who you have."

Her pretty eyes sparkled mischievously. "Ahhh, that's one of the perks of being in charge of the list. And, I've always been good at keeping secrets." Then she pointed across the way to the big double doors behind Christian. "I do believe Douglas is waiting for you."

He immediately straightened and silently reprimanded himself for getting so caught up in the conversation, for getting so caught up in *Amanda,* that he'd forgotten his original reason for being there.

What the hell had that been all about?

Refusing to analyze that particular question, he turned around and made his way toward Douglas's office. He took a brief moment to collect his composure and thoughts, then knocked twice and entered the spacious room.

The other man glanced up from where he was sitting behind his desk. Douglas was in his mid-sixties, but he was one of those lucky men who had the kind of ageless features and thick, salt-and-pepper hair that belied his age and gave him a distinguished look. His eyes were the same green shade as his daughter's, and held a wealth of wisdom and shrewd intelligence.

Christian closed the distance between them. "You wanted to see me, sir?"

"Yes, I did." Douglas took off his wire-framed glasses, set them on a pile of papers, then waved a hand at the chairs in front of his desk. "Have a seat, Christian."

It wasn't often that he was summoned to Douglas Creighton's office, and considering the last time he'd paid a visit to the big boss had been for scandalous reasons, Christian was hoping this meeting would end on a more positive note.

Settling into one of the seats the other man had indicated, he forced himself to relax. "What can I do for you, Mr. Creighton?"

"Actually, it's what I'd like to do for you." Douglas leaned back in his chair and regarded Christian in that direct manner of his. "I was just reviewing your most recent employee evaluation, and I'm very impressed with your sales performance review, as well as the initiative you've taken lately in various creative approaches that you've used to increase advertising sales in the magazine."

So far, so good, Christian thought. "Thank you."

"It seems you've really put that talent and drive I've always known you possessed to good use. Your hard work, along with all the long hours you've put in at the office has been duly noted." Withdrawing an envelope from the top drawer of his desk, Douglas handed it to Christian. "Here's a holiday bonus based on your review."

The flap wasn't sealed, and Christian took a quick peek at the check inside. He swallowed hard, bowled over by the amount of his bonus. "That's very generous. Thank you."

Douglas nodded. "I always knew you had potential, Christian, given the right incentive and direction. And I want you with the company for a long time to come. You know that the sales director position needs to be filled, and there's a few of you I'm considering for the job. Keep up the good work and we'll see how things go after the first of the year."

Excellent. Now, all Christian had to do was keep himself on the straight and narrow for the next two weeks, and one of those outer offices with a view of Manhattan might just be his after all.

FESTIVE AND *FUN* DEFINITELY described the department's holiday party later that afternoon. Considering how Christian's meeting had gone with Douglas, he was in a fantastic mood and ready to enjoy himself for a few hours.

Everyone on the executive floor was gathered in the reception area where a small three-foot Christmas tree had been placed. The fake green branches were weighted down with silver tinsel, swags of garish garland and bright ornaments. Beneath the tree was a slew of gaily wrapped presents waiting to be opened.

A table had been set up with holiday sweets and potluck style offerings, and Christian had already indulged way past his normal limit. Eggnog, hot spiced cider and lively conversation flowed freely, mingling with lots of revelry and good cheer. An abundance of mistletoe that someone had hung in strategic places around the room added to the entertainment, but Christian steered clear of those sprigs of trouble. He had no desire to get caught in a compromising position with Stacey, or anyone else for that matter.

Then there was comedic Drew, who'd attached a sprig of mistletoe to the front of his slacks as a joke, but as yet no one had taken him up on the offer to plant a kiss there. When Drew crooked his finger Christian's way, he merely laughed and shook his head at the other man's outrageous humor.

"Okay, everyone, take your seats," Stacey announced excitedly, clapping her hands to get the group's attention. "It's time for the gift exchange."

Christian found an empty chair and sat down across from where Amanda was seated. They exchanged smiles before Jason, the guy sitting next to her, said something and she started talking to him. That was okay with Christian because it gave him a few moments to watch her interact with the other man. His gaze took in her profile and the classic features that made up her lovely face. He watched her sensual lips as they moved, the way her green eyes sparkled with genuine sincerity, and the breathy, lighthearted way she laughed.

He felt that familiar tug of awareness and glanced away before it slipped beyond his control. For the past five years that he'd worked with Amanda, Christian had always found her attractive in a very soft and subdued way—quite the opposite of the bold and willing women he'd hooked up with in the past. But in his head, he'd always known that she was way out of his league. She still was, considering who her father was, and he'd do well to remember that before he did something incredibly stupid—like ask her out on a date.

Yeah, like someone of her caliber would be interested in a playboy like you!

He pushed the thought from his mind and returned his attention to the party. Someone had brought a CD of holiday songs, and strains of "Here Comes Santa Claus" filled the reception area. Christian looked up and saw *Mrs.* Santa Claus, coming straight toward where he was sitting with an I'm-going-to-eat-you-up smile on her lips. She bent low, giving him a unwanted view of her ample cleavage, and flashed her white ruffled panties to everyone behind her as she handed him the long, slim wrapped box she was delivering.

"This present is for you," Stacey said, licking her lips in a way he found much too tawdry for his taste. "And just so you know, you can unwrap me anytime, anywhere."

She walked away with a deliberate sashay of her hips, and he groaned, certain she was his penance for his own past promiscuous behavior. The good news was she made him realize that he had no desire to go back to that shallow, superficial way of living.

The gift exchange began, with everyone taking a turn to open their presents. Jason received an engraved money clip, and Drew was thrilled to get the DVD gift set of his favorite movie, *Brokeback Mountain*. Someone gave Amanda a set of her favorite Victoria's Secret bath products, and Stacey wasn't at all ashamed to show everyone the racy G-string panties her Secret Santa had bought for her. In fact, Christian was surprised that she didn't offer to model the barely there undies for everyone to see.

Before long, it was Christian's turn. He ripped the wrapping paper off his gift, lifted the lid and found a nice, dignified blue-and-gray striped tie inside. Nothing wild and crazy or embarrassing, thank God. Tucked between the tie and tissue paper was a small white envelope, and he picked it up. Undeniably curious, he withdrew the plain white note card inside and read the typed message.

At first glance, this tie may seem like a respectable gift.
And it is, if you wear it to work. But if you were my lover,
I'd use this gift to tie you up so I could do all the things
I've fantasized about doing to you for a long time now.
I want to tease you, and please you, and make you lose
control. Will you let me do those things to you?

Hell, yes. He was so caught up in the moment that the answer came way too easily. Oh, yeah, he was definitely intrigued.

Realizing that the note had actually aroused him, in more ways than one, he kept the box on his lap and dared to glance up. A dozen pairs of eyes were watching him, and he realized that there were only a couple of people in this room that he could think of who would have the nerve to send him such a suggestive note.

"Mmmm, nice tie," Stacey said appreciatively, and he had no doubt that *she'd* tie him up given the chance.

"I agree," Drew said, adding his fashion sense to the conversation, along with a wink at Christian. "Blue and gray look good on you and really bring out the color of your eyes."

Oh, God. Had Drew fantasized about gazing into his eyes while Christian was tied to his bed? Had he just gotten turned on by a gay guy's propensity for bondage? The notion shriveled his arousal.

Desperate for answers, he searched other faces for some kind of clue, but most everyone's attention had moved on to the next person who was opening their gift. Everyone but Amanda, who looked at him with amusement and was trying not to laugh at Drew's girlie comment.

At least, that was what he assumed until a sudden realization dawned on him. Amanda was the list keeper, the one and only person who knew exactly who'd given him the gift. And he knew he was going to drive himself insane trying to figure out who his secret admirer was. Because there weren't many people in this room that he wanted to get down and dirty with, and now that he had this tie and provocative note hanging over his head, he was going to be constantly second-guessing certain people's motives, comments and suggestions.

He couldn't afford that kind of distraction right now, not with the promotion and corner office almost his. No matter what it took, he had to get Amanda to reveal who his Secret Santa was.

2

WELL, THAT WAS CERTAINLY interesting, Desiree said, appearing on Amanda's left shoulder to make her opinion known.

Amanda carried a few empty bowls from the potluck into the break room in an attempt to clean up after the party, as well as to escape the speculative stare Christian had been tossing her way for the past half hour. She had no idea why he was watching her so intently, but his attention was starting to unnerve her.

Interesting was definitely one way to describe his reaction to her gift. When he'd first opened the present she'd bought for him, he'd looked relieved that he hadn't received some kind of outrageous gag gift. Then he'd read the note she'd tucked between the tissue paper and the tie. From across the room she'd watched his expression shift from pleasant surprise to fascination. She had to admit that the slow, sexy smile that had curved his lips as he'd read her intimate message had given her a small thrill. Oh, she'd definitely managed to get under his skin, until he glanced up, scoured the room with his gaze and his initial excitement gave way to full-blown panic.

Amanda set the bowls in the sink and filled them with warm, soapy water. She had no idea what had triggered the latter response, and now, for some reason, he had *her* set in his sights. So, she figured the best thing to do was hide out until the party was completely over. Already, employees were heading back to their cubicles and offices to pack up for the weekend, so it was only a matter of time before Christian left, as well. With luck, the naughty note she'd sent to him would no doubt be forgotten by Tuesday morning, after Christmas had come and gone.

I don't have a very good feeling about this, Angie said, wringing her hands anxiously in her lap.

Stop being such a worrywart. Desiree scowled at her nemesis for putting a damper on the fun. *Christian loved the gift and sexy note. Now, if only Amanda had the nerve to follow through on that little fantasy of hers, she'd be one happy and very satisfied woman, I'm sure.*

Annoyed with the bickering, Amanda shook her head as she turned off the faucet, then grabbed a towel to dry her hands. "Go away. The two of you are driving me crazy."

"Who is driving you crazy?"

Startled by the sound of Christian's voice behind her—the second time in the same day, no less—Amanda spun around to face him. He stood just inside the break room, looking gorgeous as always with his tousled hair, intense blue eyes and lean, honed body she'd imagined naked far too many times. A small frown creased his dark brows as he waited for her to answer his question.

God, he's so hot. Desiree sighed and fanned herself with her hand. *If you're not going to take advantage of all that studliness, introduce me and I'll do it for you.*

If Amanda had the ability to knock the cheeky devil off her shoulder, she would have. Instead, she ignored Desiree and her outrageous request. "Uh, nobody. I was, uh, just talking to myself."

"Oh." He pushed his fingers through his already disheveled hair, his expression troubled, which wasn't something she'd ever associated with Christian, who was always the epitome of self-confidence. "Look, I need to talk to you."

That doesn't sound good at all, Angie said, much too nervously for Amanda's liking. *I warned you that sending him that gift wasn't a good idea!*

Amanda pushed Angie and her ominous words out of her head, refusing to allow her guardian angel's apprehension to become her own. Placing the terry towel on the counter, she smiled at Christian as if nothing was wrong. "Sure. What's up?"

He released a tension-filled breath. "I need to see the Secret Santa list."

Uh-oh, Angie muttered.

Amanda kept her outward composure cool and calm, but inside she had to admit to her first little niggle of uneasiness. "Christian, you know I can't show you the list."

His lean jaw clenched. "Then I need to know who had my name."

She shook her head. "I can't tell you that, either."

Gaze narrowed, he walked across the break room, slowly closing the distance between them. "Yes, you can."

"No, I can't." She took a step back and let out a small squeak of surprise when her back connected with the edge of the counter behind her.

Finally, he stopped in front of her—a respectable distance away for two colleagues engaging in a discussion, but his nearness affected Amanda on too many levels anyways. She could smell the warm, male scent of his cologne and feel the heat emanating from him. Her keen awareness of him as a man, not to mention those sensual lips of his, did crazy things to her hormones and made her weak in the knees.

Thinking fast, she changed the direction of the conversation. "Is there a problem with your tie? Because I can ask the person who gave it to you for a gift receipt so you can exchange it for something else."

"No, the tie itself is fine."

"Then what's wrong?" she asked, but knew exactly what had set him off—her written fantasy.

He hesitated a moment, then shoved his hands into the front pockets of his trousers before saying, "There was a note that came with the gift, and I need to know who wrote it."

Her heart beat so hard and fast in her chest, she was surprised it didn't show against her sweater. "Was the note offensive?" It was hard to believe that an experienced guy like Christian would be repulsed by the provocative message she'd penned for him, so she was guessing that he was just out to appease his curiosity.

But how far would he go to satisfy his need to know? she wondered, and felt a tiny shiver course down her spine.

"It all depends on who wrote it," he said, frustration deepening the tone of his voice. "There are two people who seem the most likely, and well, let's just say that if I know who sent me that note I can at least watch my back."

The innuendo in his comment, along with the slight bit of humor curving the corner of his mouth told Amanda that one of those people he suspected of writing the note was Drew. And, undoubtedly, the other was Stacey because the office bimbo had made her interest in Christian openly obvious over the past few months.

Laughter and voices traveled into the break room from the reception area, and Christian cast a quick glance over his shoulder to make sure they were still alone before returning his attention back to Amanda. He leaned close, his gaze holding a hint of desperation as he pressed his advantage in low, urgent tones. "I swear, if you tell me who my Secret Santa is, I'll keep the information to myself. No one will ever know that you told me anything."

She really had shaken him up with that note, more than Amanda had ever believed was possible. Now, it was more imperative than ever that he never find out that she was the one who'd penned the fantasy because it could make things awkward between them and ultimately change the dynamics of their working relationship.

I hate to tell you that I told you so, Angie whispered in her ear, *but I did tell you so!*

Feeling trapped between the counter, Christian's gorgeous body and her own deceit, Amanda felt the overwhelming need for space and breathing room. Forcing her feet to *move,* she stepped around the man in front of her.

"I'm really sorry, Christian. Everyone trusts me with that list, and it's up to each individual person to decide whether or not they want their recipient to know they were their Secret Santa." She gave him her best apologetic look. "I just can't break confidence that way."

As if finally accepting that she wasn't going to cave to his request, he exhaled a deep breath and gave up the fight. "Fine." The one word was rife with exasperation, but there was a determination burning in his gaze that contradicted his acquiescence.

Without another word, he turned and left the break room, and that uneasy feeling in the pit of her belly grew.

Wow, you really did a number on him, Desiree said with a proud smile on her red lips. *I didn't think you had it in you. I'm very proud of you, girl.*

Amanda placed a hand on her churning stomach, trying without success to calm that unsettling sensation spreading through her. She'd wanted a reaction out of him, and she'd gotten that, and probably a whole lot more than she'd bargained for. Lord help her if Christian ever discovered that she was the one responsible for the gift he'd received and the tantalizing note that had piqued more than just his curiosity.

The Lord has nothing to do with this mess you and Desiree made of things, Angie said primly as her halo gleamed a bright, shiny gold over her head. *I really do think you're on your own with this one.*

Amanda was afraid that Angie was right.

CHRISTIAN WAS BEGINNING to think that Amanda wasn't ever going to leave for the evening, and he was starting to feel like a stalker considering the way he was staking out her office from the meeting room across the way. The light was off in the room he was in, and he was able to remain out of sight while keeping an eye on Amanda through the glass partition. Still, he'd been in there for an hour, and he was quickly growing impatient and restless.

However, he had to admit that he was enjoying being able to watch Amanda on the sly. Believing she was completely alone in the office after six o'clock on a Friday night of a holiday weekend, she was very relaxed and at ease. The reserve and poise that surrounded her during business hours was now stripped away, revealing a woman who was much softer and more laid-back than she let anyone at the office see.

As executive editor and the daughter of a publishing mogul, she had to keep up a strong and competent front with her co-workers, to prove she could handle the pressures and stress of the job, as well as everyone else. And she managed the feat quite well because no one ever questioned her dedication, or the fact that she deserved to follow in her father's footsteps. Her commitment and loyalty, as well as her ability to handle any crises with finesse, spoke for itself.

But as she moved around her desk with a natural grace, he had to admit that this open, unconstrained side to Amanda tempted him. As did the stunningly sensual curves of her body, and that rich, brown hair that looked so soft and inviting beneath the lights in her office. When she absently ran her tongue across her bottom lip, his mind veered off on a tangent of its own, imagining that sweet mouth beneath his, all hot and damp and eager just for him.

From there, the scenario spun out of control, taking him places he had no business traveling with Amanda, even if it was all in his mind. Places like his bed, and having her gloriously naked and wonderfully wanton in it. With him restrained by a blue-and-gray striped tie and Amanda teasing him, pleasing him and making him lose control…

The words from the note he'd received with his gift earlier today played into his fantasy, giving him a much needed jolt of reality and reminding him why he was hiding out in the meeting room. And it wasn't because he'd suddenly become a voyeur, though the erection straining against the fly of his slacks begged to differ.

After confronting Amanda in the break room and getting nothing for his efforts, he'd decided that there was only one thing left for him to do. Sneak into her office after everyone was gone for the night and find that damnable Secret Santa list.

Jesus, he was so pathetic. And desperate to discover who was yanking his chain with that provocative note.

Forever seemed to pass before Amanda finally tossed a few things into her briefcase, snapped it closed, then put on her black wool coat, leaving it unbuttoned despite the evening chill awaiting her. Grabbing her purse and briefcase, she locked her office door, switched off the main lights, then headed for the elevator that would take her down to the private garage where she parked her car.

As soon as the elevator door closed behind Amanda, Christian made his move. Jimmying her office door open was ridiculously easy since it wasn't a bolt lock. A slow, careful slide of a thin credit card released the latch, and that easily, he was in.

He turned the light back on and began searching her desk for the list, feeling a tad guilty for breaking and entering, not to mention shuffling through Amanda's things. To ease his conscience, he didn't linger on any one thing and kept his focus on his search.

Everything was neat and tidy, like the woman herself, making the task of looking for the list a quick process. Unfortunately, what he was looking for wasn't to be found in her desk drawers. Frustration got the best of him, and he swore out loud, refusing to admit defeat just yet.

Hands on his hips, he glanced around the office, and his gaze came to a stop on the filing cabinets. Figuring it was worth a look, he checked the private files under *S* for *Secret Santa,* and laughed out loud when he found one labeled with that exact title. Leave it to Amanda to be so predictable.

Tucked inside was the handwritten list he'd been after. Feeling triumphant, he withdrew the paper and his gaze immediately zeroed in on his name, which was right beside the name of the one person he never would have suspected of doing something so bold.

Amanda Creighton.

"Jees-uz," he muttered beneath his breath, unable to believe that Miss Prim and Proper had penned such an arousing and seductive fantasy—to him. Knowingly. Deliberately. And with the certainty that he'd never discover the truth. Was it no wonder that she wouldn't let him take a peek?

Now he understood why, and her involvement certainly put an interesting and unexpected twist on things. It also made his attraction to her very real because the desire was obviously reciprocated on her end, as well. Try as he might, he couldn't ignore the warm flare of arousal that had begun to radiate through him at the mental image of Amanda tying him up for their mutual pleasure and satisfaction.

The big question was, what was he going to do about the incriminating information he'd just uncovered, as well as the tie and brazen note she'd given him? If he was a smart man, he'd slip the Secret Santa file right back into the cabinet, pretend he never saw that list, and forget about Amanda and her erotic, mind-blowing fantasy involving him.

"What do you think you're doing?"

The sound of Amanda's indignant question jarred Christian out of his thoughts and made him jump from her unexpected presence. Still holding the list in his hand, he turned around to face the woman standing in the doorway of her office. Her eyes were wide as she stared at him, and the flush sweeping across her complexion combined shock, panic…and a flash of guilt.

So much for being a smart man and getting out while the getting had been good. Now, he didn't have that option. Caught red-handed with no escape, Christian figured there was only one thing left for him to do—confront Amanda with the evidence he'd unearthed and teach her a little lesson about what could happen when you teased a man beyond his limits.

OH, YEAH, NOW THIS IS GETTING good! From Amanda's left shoulder, Desiree rubbed her hands together and her eyes sparkled with anticipation, taking obvious delight in the recent turn of events.

Amanda, on the other hand, was mortified to find Christian in her office—the Secret Santa list clutched between his long fingers. She'd definitely startled him, but he didn't look at all worried about being caught in the act. In fact, there was a certain smugness about him that caused a frisson of awareness to take hold.

And judging by the satisfied look in his eyes, there was no doubt in her mind that he was now well aware that *she'd* given him that very intimate note.

What did you expect? Angie scolded, like the mother Amanda had lost at such a young age. *When you play with fire you're bound to get burned.*

If that's the case, then burn me, baby, Desiree said in a low, sultry purr that was directed Christian's way.

Ha! Angie crossed her arms over her chest. *You're so used to the heat, you have no idea what it's like to be burned!*

You're just jealous that I like it hot. Desiree smirked.

Stop, both of you! Amanda gave her head a hard shake. *I can't think straight with the two of you squabbling in my mind!*

The voices went quiet, but Amanda knew the reprieve was only temporary. Neither Angie nor Desiree was about to miss this showdown between her and Christian.

When Amanda had gotten down to her car and realized she'd forgotten a file for an article she planned on editing over the holiday weekend, she'd never have imagined that a quick trip back up to her office would turn into a confrontation she had no wish to have with Christian. But other than ignoring the fact that he'd broken into her office and gone through her personal files, she didn't have much choice.

She just hoped and prayed that she'd be able to get out of this very awkward situation with her pride intact.

"I asked you what you were doing in here," she said, lifting her chin in a show of authority.

"Well, now, that should be obvious," he said in a slow, lazy drawl that had way too much of an effect on Amanda's sorely neglected libido. "I'm getting the answer that you weren't willing to give me earlier in the break room. With good reason, it seems, considering *you're* my Secret Santa."

Despite that truth, there was no way she was going to let him get the upper hand. Squaring her shoulders, she strode into the room and right up to Christian, focusing on a more condemning issue that involved him. "You broke into my office. I could have you written up for that, or even fired."

An infuriatingly sexy smile curved up the corner of his lips. "But you won't do either."

She arched a brow. "And what makes you so sure about that?"

He leaned a shoulder against her file cabinets, making himself comfortable. "For starters, I have a list right here in my hand showing that you're my Secret Santa."

Unimpressed, she shrugged. "So?"

"I also have a very suggestive note from you, which if brought to light, could be misconstrued in many ways."

Hearing the idle threat in his words, she narrowed her gaze. "Such as?"

"Let's see," he said, taking a moment to think as his eyes glimmered with amusement. "There's always sexual harassment."

She opened her mouth, then snapped it shut again. He was toying with her, just as she'd toyed with him. And he was enjoying every minute of it. "Oh, that's a rich claim, coming from the office bad boy."

"Hey, I've been a very good boy for months now," he said, affecting a virtuous look that would have made Angie proud. "And I'm quite sure that your father would be absolutely appalled to find out his daughter wrote such a naughty letter to me."

"Ohhhh, you're a rat!" Her hands clenched into fists at her sides, even though she knew that she was to blame for riling him in the first place with that tie and note. This whole entire mess was her fault, but that didn't mean she was going to let Christian have any kind of advantage over her.

"Give me that list." She held out her hand.

"Nope." He folded the piece of paper in half, then in another half, making a tidy square. "It's my security deposit. You get me for breaking and entering, and I have the Secret Santa list and a very sexy note to go with it."

She gasped in shock. "That's blackmail."

"Hmmm." He grinned shamelessly and winked at her, exuding way too much charm for her peace of mind. "Sure, if that's what you want to call it."

She made a quick grab for the folded paper, but he was quicker. He held it just out of her grasp, and unless she wanted to plaster her body against his to reach the list, she was out of luck. It was an appealing thought, but she didn't want to end up in a wrestling match with him, no matter how much Desiree would enjoy being a spectator to that sport.

"Give it back, Christian." She used a firm, no-nonsense tone that usually got her exactly what she wanted.

Not today and not with Christian. "If you want it that badly, you'll have to get it yourself." He slid the folded list down the front of his pants, his gaze brimming with a wicked challenge. "That is, if you dare."

Stunned by his audacity, she gaped at him, though she couldn't deny that the tips of her fingers tingled at the thought of chasing after that paper. Heat flushed across her cheeks and down her body, making her wool coat feel suffocating and un-bearably warm.

He laughed, a low, rich chuckle that slid down her spine like a silky caress and increased her awareness of him. "I didn't think so. Afraid you might just get more than you bargained for?"

Oh, yeah. "You're a cad."

"I've certainly been called worse." He crossed his arms over his chest and regarded her with mild curiosity. "But you, Ms. Creighton, are a tease. What was that tie and note about, anyway?"

The shocking truth lodged in her throat, and thankfully a quick, logical explanation popped into her head. "It was a joke, okay?" One that had taken a turn she never would have anticipated.

"A joke," he said, repeating her words and looking as though he were mulling over her response. "Was it because you wanted to get me all hot and bothered?"

Her heart skipped a beat at his too-accurate guess. "Of course not!" she managed to sputter. For a woman who always kept her emotions in check, especially at work, this man had a way of flustering her from head to toe.

You wouldn't be in this situation if you'd just listened to me, Angie whispered. *But nooo, you were weak and let Desiree lead you over to the dark side.*

"Well, just in case you're curious, it did get me all hot and bothered," he said, humor and something far sexier lacing his voice. "That is, until the possibility crossed my mind that either Stacey or Drew had given me such a provocative gift." He shud-dered for effect, telling Amanda without words how he felt about those two scenarios.

A burst of laughter escaped her before she could stop it, relieving a bit of the nervous tension pulling tight within her. In a way she'd never admit to him, she now better understood his desperate need to find out who his Secret Santa was.

"You find that funny?" He tried to appear stern, but couldn't hide the mirth flickering in his gaze.

She pressed her fingers to her lips to hold in her laughter, but couldn't stop another residual chuckle. "It really is funny when you think about it. Especially with Drew."

"I'm glad you're so amused." Pushing away from the file cabinet, he moved toward her and stopped less than a foot away. "As for me, I'm much more intrigued by the fact that you sent me that tie, and wrote me that note." Lifting his hand, he grazed his thumb along the line of her jaw, while his fingers dipped just inside the high collar of her sweater and caressed the side of her neck. "Why did you do it, Amanda?" he asked huskily.

Her pulse tripped all over itself at his sensual touch, and her nipples tightened into hard peaks, aching for the same kind of intimate attention. She inched backward to break the contact, and her bottom connected with the edge of her desk.

"I told you, it was a joke," she said lightly. "A gag gift."

"Liar," he chided softly. Slowly, he closed the distance between them once again, and she knew just by looking into his dark, determined eyes that he wouldn't let her escape him so easily a second time. "I think you're secretly attracted to me."

Instinctively, she pressed a hand to his chest to hold him off, and immediately realized her mistake when she felt the solid heat and strength of his body beneath her fingers. Her *attraction,* the one she was just about to deny, flared into full-blown desire. She struggled to breathe, and when she finally did manage to inhale, she drew in the heady scent of sandalwood and aroused male.

She swallowed back a needy groan. Feeling her physical response to him slipping a few critical notches, she kept her hand splayed on his chest and grasped for control. "Don't flatter yourself, Casanova," she said with a sassy toss of her head. "Attraction has nothing to do with it."

"Oh, really?" A too-perceptive smile eased up the corner of

his tempting mouth as he slipped his hand inside her coat and boldly settled his large palm on her hip. "If you're not attracted to me, then why are you trembling?"

She rolled her eyes, pretending indifference, which wasn't an easy feat when everything about Christian made her acutely sensitive to just how alone the two of them were in the office building. "You're obviously imagining things."

"Am I?" He tipped his head, studying her like a man who had all the time in the world, and planned to use every minute to make her squirm. "Maybe we ought to put the attraction theory to a little test."

She frowned, immediately wary. "What kind of test?"

Instead of responding verbally, he used the slow, gradual press of his body against hers to make his point, proving he was a man of action rather than words when it came to getting a woman's attention. Their hips and thighs met, and the curve of her bottom caught on the edge of her desk. Sliding the fingers of his free hand into her hair, he cupped the back of her head in his palm. He gave a small, light, arousing tug on the strands tangled around his fingers, forcing her face to tip up toward his.

His gaze was hypnotic as it stared into hers. Dark and hot, and filled with all kinds of sinful intent.

The heat alone was enough to make her melt from the inside out. Between the hard, powerful body aligned against hers like a familiar lover, and the strong male hands anchoring her even more securely to the spot, she felt breathlessly excited, and a whole lot out of her element when it came to this kind of situation.

"What…" Her voice rasped, and she swallowed to clear her throat, though it was impossible to steady her erratic pulse. "What are you doing?"

"That should be obvious." His lashes fell half-mast over his eyes, and his mouth eased into a slumberous smile, making him all the more sexy and appealing. "I'm putting your 'I'm-not-attracted-to-you' claim to the test. So far, you seem to be failing."

He lowered his head toward hers, and a swell of panic rose within her. She curled her fingers into the fabric of his shirt, knowing that if his lips so much as touched hers, she'd be a goner. Putty in his hands to do with as he wished. She knew he was just playing with her, attempting to get even for the gift and note she'd given him, and that was reason enough to put a halt to this crazy situation.

"*Christian,*" she said firmly, trying to put him off, except a soft, sultry, telltale moan followed his name.

His lips skimmed along her cheek to her ear, and nuzzled that sensitive spot beneath the lobe that made her shiver and increased the rapid beat of her heart. "Shhh," he whispered, his breath feathering warm and damp against her skin. "This test won't hurt a bit. I promise."

That was what she was most afraid of—receiving too much pleasure only to have him leave her craving so much more.

Go for it, Amanda. Desiree urged, her enthusiasm unmistakable. *You know you want to.*

Oh, yes, I do. So why was she fighting what she wanted so badly? Who cared that he was out to extract a bit of retribution, especially when he was offering such an erotic form of revenge? Tossing aside any last misgivings, she decided to seize the moment, enjoy the kiss and whatever else Christian was willing to give.

Closing her eyes, she turned her head, seeking the warmth of his mouth with her own. Their lips met, his firm and sensual as they claimed hers and took control of the kiss. Reaching up, she tunneled her fingers into his thick, silky hair and opened to him, to the dampness and heat and the slow, deep stroke of his tongue.

The hands on her hips tightened as he pressed his lower body closer, harder, against hers in a slow, grinding thrust that made her moan deep in her throat. Shamelessly, she strained beneath the delicious assault, and as if knowing exactly what she needed, he slid his hands around to her bottom and lifted her so that she was sitting on the surface of her desk. He nudged her knees wide apart and moved in between her legs, branding her with the unmistakable pressure and friction of his rock-hard erection rubbing against the sensitive place between her thighs.

His mouth slanted across hers in a more provocative, dominating kiss, dragging her deeper under his spell and possessing her in a primitive, sexual way that was new and exciting to her. She was used to polite, courteous sex, not this explosion of aggression and heat that threatened to consume her.

She wrapped her legs around the back of his thighs and embraced the electrifying sensation. Desire began to flow through her veins, liquid and hot. Down to her aching breasts. Swirling in her belly. Making her sex weep for the pulsing, driving force of him sliding deep, deep inside her. Seemingly of their own accord, her hands slid down his chest and grazed the belt buckle securing the front of his pants.

Abruptly, he broke the kiss and jerked back, his expression stunned. He was breathing hard, his eyes dark and glazed with lust, and it took extreme effort on Amanda's part not to pull him back and make him finish what he'd just started.

From her left shoulder, Desiree applauded her efforts. *It's about time. I was starting to worry about you.*

Christian swore beneath his breath and stepped farther away from Amanda, breaking all physical contact and leaving her sitting on the desk. A dark, troubled frown creased his brows and a muscle in his jaw ticked. In a carefully controlled voice that still held an underlying rasp of arousal, he said, "I need to get the hell out of here before we do something we'll both regret."

With that, he turned and walked out of her office, leaving her alone and very confused about what had just happened between them. Considering their working relationship, and Christian's love 'em and leave 'em reputation, she ought to be grateful that at least he'd been thinking clearly enough to stop things before they'd escalated to the point of no return.

But she wasn't grateful. She was disappointed.

Wow, the man certainly knows how to kiss, among other things, Desiree said breathlessly.

Even Angie fanned herself, a pink blush sweeping across her cheeks. Despite that, she still managed to put everything back into perspective, as was her job as Amanda's guardian angel. *Of course he does. He's had a whole lot of experience.*

Experience is a very good thing, Desiree retorted with a sly smile.

Amanda dragged a shaky hand through her hair and stood on less-than-steady legs. "Yeah, well, it doesn't seem to matter now. He got exactly what he wanted, and now it's over."

He'd taken the list for safekeeping, and a kiss for revenge. An erotic, bone-melting kiss that would haunt her dreams for a long time to come.

3

CHRISTIAN SLID the blue-and-gray striped tie between his fingers as he paced a restless path in his living room and thought about what had happened between him and Amanda just a few hours ago, a kiss that had literally rocked his world and left him wanting her with an intensity he couldn't shake.

He'd only meant to teach Amanda a lesson. To show her that when you teased a bear with something he wanted, you were bound to get bitten. But instead, all he'd managed to do was unleash a desire that she clearly felt as well, and it had taken every ounce of strength he possessed not to take her right then and there on her desk.

Lord knew, she'd been soft and warm and more than willing. Just remembering the way she'd wrapped her legs around his hips and responded so wantonly to their embrace made him rock-hard all over again.

The big question was, what was he going to do about their mutual lust? *Absolutely nothing,* should have been his immediate response. He'd walked away from her earlier with every intention of never touching her again. He'd meant what he'd said about regrets, and they did have their working relationship to consider, not to mention his promotion that was still up in the air.

But now, after rereading her sexy note and contemplating all the sensual pleasures the two of them could no doubt share, he couldn't help but wonder if making love to Amanda, and taking her up on her Secret Santa gift, was worth the possible risks.

Yes. That particular answer came much too easily, and he wasn't about to refuse something he wanted so badly. After all, they were consenting adults and were completely capable of indulging in a brief, private affair outside of the office. Judging by Amanda's attempt to keep her gift to him a secret, he was certain she'd welcome a mutual agreement to keep their relationship just between the two of them.

For the first time in hours, Christian grinned, feeling like a man on a mission. Amanda wanted to tie him up and have her way with him? No problem, he thought, as he slipped the tie she'd given him around the collar of his shirt and secured it into a loose knot against his throat.

He was up for any kind of erotic, sexual games she wanted to play.

IT REALLY IS FOR THE BEST that Christian walked away before things went too far between the two of you.

Neither Angie's voice of reason nor the pint of Ben & Jerry's Chocolate Fudge Brownie ice cream she was spooning into her mouth could console Amanda and her dismal mood. Even the new, sexy, bright red Jimmy Choo heels she'd slipped on after a long, hot bath did nothing to lift her spirits. More depressed than before, she tucked her legs beneath her on the couch so she didn't have to stare at the pretty strappy shoes that would most likely never see the light of day. Just like all the others in her collection.

She closed her eyes and groaned. If Ben & Jerry's and a beautiful pair of expensive shoes couldn't cure Amanda's blues, she was in worse shape than she'd realized. Sure, she'd been devastated when Christian had kissed her senseless then dismissed the incident because he was afraid of regrets, but she never would have imagined that she'd feel so rejected. So alone and wondering if any other man would ever live up to that amazingly seductive kiss.

Even now, hours after the fact, she still felt on edge and restless in a way that would no doubt keep her tossing and turning for the entire night. Christian had started a craving in her, then had left her aroused and wanting more. More of his drugging kisses, his sensual touch, his strong, hard body pressed against hers. Preferably with both of them completely naked.

But that wasn't going to happen, she knew, and shoveled another bite of chocolate fudge brownie into her mouth. He'd made his feelings about the situation abundantly clear, and just like every other woman he tangled with, she was yet another casualty of his charm.

Well, that was what she got for ignoring Angie's warning and sending Christian that Secret Santa gift in the first place. She truly had no one but herself to blame for the entire fiasco.

Her apartment phone rang, interrupting her thoughts. The distinct ring tone told her it was the doorman downstairs calling. Picking up the extension on the end table next to the couch, she answered with the most upbeat voice she could muster. "Hello?"

"Good evening, Ms. Creighton," William replied in his normal businesslike tone. "There's a gentleman by the name of Christian Miller here to see you. Shall I send him up to your place?"

Shocked by the unexpected announcement, Amanda's mind spun. He'd obviously gotten her address from the company roster, but after the tense way they'd parted company at the office, she couldn't begin to imagine his reasons for being at her place now. To apologize, maybe? To return the tie he had no intention of ever wearing?

"Ms. Creighton?" William prompted after too many silent seconds had passed.

She shook herself from her stupor and replied. "I, uh, yes, of course. Send him on up."

She hung up the phone, not sure what to do first. She had about a minute before he arrived. Quickly, she took her Ben & Jerry's back to the kitchen and put the rest of the pint into the freezer. Then she ran her fingers through her still-damp and tousled hair, wishing she'd dried it tonight. Wishing, too, that she had more time to prepare herself, mentally and physically, for Christian's spontaneous visit.

But she didn't. Her doorbell rang and a dozen butterflies took flight in her stomach as she headed toward the entryway. The heels of her Jimmy Choos clicked on the marble floor, and she groaned when she thought about how odd she probably looked in her drawstring pajama pants imprinted with bright red lips, a matching cotton camisole top ... and a pair of racy red shoes with a four-inch heel.

The doorbell rang again, followed by a brisk, impatient knock, leaving her no time to unfasten the double straps wrapped around each ankle to take the shoes off. So, she opened the door and faced the man who'd rejected her just a few hours before.

He stood on the other side of the threshold, looking incredibly gorgeous, with his dark, disheveled hair and those deep blue eyes that took in her pajamas in a slow, sweeping glance. The sensual heat in his gaze made her toes curl in her Jimmy Choos. He'd changed into a pair of fitted jeans and pale blue knit shirt, and it didn't escape her notice that he was wearing the tie she'd given him, which not only looked ridiculous with his informal outfit, but it also added to her confusion as to why he was there.

When she continued to stare at him, he tipped his head and offered her a friendly smile. "Can I come in?"

Amanda's curiosity prompted her to step back so he could enter her apartment. "Sure."

He walked past her and into her living room, and she followed behind with a resounding *click, click, click* of her heels on the floor, which made her acutely aware of how equally ridiculous *she* looked in her pajamas and heels.

He took in her upscale Manhattan apartment and contemporary furnishings, then turned back around to look at her. "Nice place."

"Thanks." Unable to bear a string of polite chitchat, she decided to get right down to business. "Christian...what are you doing here?"

He casually slid his hands into the front pockets of his jeans, but his expression reflected something far more direct and purposeful. "I'm wearing the tie you gave me."

"I see that." The big question in her mind was *why* was he wearing the tie? To tease and torment her, no doubt. "I'm glad you like it."

"I do like it," he said, his voice dropping to a husky pitch as he stroked the strip of fabric with his fingers in a too-seductive caress. "Very much."

She swallowed hard, unsure of where this conversation was heading. She wasn't about to assume anything at this point. "And you're here because...?"

A slow, bad-boy smile kicked up the corner of his mouth as he stepped toward her, closing the distance between them. "I came here tonight to collect the other part of my Secret Santa present."

An electrifying jolt of awareness surged through Amanda, making her feel jittery. Nervous. Uncertain. And good God, even hopeful. Her throat went dry, making speech impossible at the moment.

Lifting a hand, he lazily traced the thin strap of her camisole top, down to the low scoop neck, and she bit her bottom lip to hold in a soft gasp. As he watched, her nipples tightened into hard knots against the cotton material, telling him without words how much she wanted him.

He raised his gaze back up to hers, satisfaction and a deeper, darker desire glimmering in the sapphire depths. "I believe the note you gave me with the present said something about being your lover and using the gift to tie me up so you could do all the things you've fantasized about doing to me. *That's* what I'm here for, Amanda."

Desiree chose that moment to make an appearance on her left shoulder. *Wow, he certainly has a way with words, doesn't he?*

Oh, yes, he most definitely did. Amanda was already unraveling inside, her body softening, growing warm and damp in feminine places. Still, that cautious, insecure part of her personality wanted to be sure he wasn't just toying with her. "Are you serious?"

In response, he placed his hands on her hips and moved even closer, forcing her back a few steps until her shoulders came into contact with the wall and his lower body pinned her there, as well. The unmistakable length of his erection pressed against her lower belly, which started another chain reaction of carnal desire to ripple through her.

Their faces were mere inches apart, so close that they shared each breath they took. "Now that you know my answer, how serious were you about the note you wrote to go with the tie?" he murmured. "Or was it all a joke, like you said?"

The air between them was thick and ripe with awareness, and her heart pounded an erratic rhythm in her chest. "No, it wasn't a joke," she whispered.

Lifting his hand, he slid his fingers along the side of her neck and used his thumb to tip her face up higher. His gaze searched hers with an unnerving amount of scrutiny. "Why did you write the note, Amanda?"

She'd never expected to have to explain herself or her motives behind the sexy note, and answering his question meant baring a part of her soul, which was something she'd never done with another man. In the past, she'd had physical relationships with the men she'd dated, but the emotional component had always been missing. That visceral connection that went beyond the sexual attraction or the appeal of her last name and everything that came with it.

Despite his reputation as a playboy, she felt that deeper level of intimacy with Christian and refused to spoil the moment by questioning why. There was something about him that made her feel secure, and ultimately, she trusted him with her secrets.

"I wrote you that note because I've always been attracted to you," she admitted, and looked deep into his eyes before finishing. "I wanted to do something bold and sexy that would get your attention."

"You didn't need the note or tie for that," he said as he tenderly caressed the line of her jaw with his thumb, while his other hand slipped beneath the hem of her top and his fingers brushed along the curve of her waist. "I've *always* noticed you."

She attempted to laugh, certain he was flirting with her, or trying to make her feel good. And she had to admit that the hand stroking her bare skin felt very, very good indeed. "I'm hardly your type," she pointed out, just to keep things in perspective.

"I know. And that's why I'm so attracted to you *now*." A

crooked smile canted the corners of his mouth, right before he lowered his head and gently rubbed his cheek against hers. "I can't get you, or your note, out of my head," he whispered raggedly into her ear, the defeat in his voice unmistakable. "I want you so badly, Amanda, that I can't think straight anymore."

She closed her eyes and bit her bottom lip to hold in a moan as he touched his mouth to her neck. Despite the tingling sensation unfurling deep in her belly, she thought about how he'd left her high and dry at the office earlier, and his reasons for doing so. Knowing she wouldn't be able to bear being rejected by him a second time, she had to ask, "What about regrets?"

He lifted his head from hers and both of his hands came up to cradle her face in his palms. She opened her eyes, stared into his, and saw nothing but hunger and pure carnal heat. For *her.* Her pulse quickened and she suddenly felt breathless.

"No regrets. I swear." A sinful grin transformed his features, and with a roll of his hips he branded her with the heat and impressive length of his erection confined behind the zipper of his jeans. "Just a whole lot of mutual pleasure. I promise this weekend will stay just between the two of us. But ultimately, it's up to you."

He wasn't offering her any kind of promises, but she knew better than to expect anything beyond this moment from a carefree guy like Christian. This was all about sating long-denied desires between the two of them, nothing more. And after so many years of being a good girl and a dutiful, virtuous daughter, she was ready to break free of those restraints and enjoy this one night with him, guilt-free.

She smoothed her palm down the tie he was still wearing, excited by the thought of fulfilling her fantasy with him. "Yes," she whispered, and sighed when he dropped his mouth to hers and surprised her with a deep kiss infused with lust and an exciting amount of aggression. A demanding kiss that left no doubt in her mind how badly he wanted her.

Oh, yeah, Desiree cheered gleefully. *We are* so *getting lucky tonight, and it's about damn time!*

Amanda couldn't help but feel the same way.

After a while, Christian gentled the kiss. "God, you taste good," he murmured against her lips. "I just want to eat you up."

The image of him doing something so wicked caused a surge of heat to settle in her stomach like fine cognac, making her feel dizzy and drunk on this man's brand of seduction. "It's Ben & Jerry's chocolate fudge brownie," she felt compelled to say.

He chuckled, then shook his head. "No, I'm absolutely certain the taste is all you," he said and resumed the kiss, stealing her breath and what little was left of her sanity.

His hands left her face and moved to her neck, then lower, gliding across her shoulders until his fingers hooked into the straps of her camisole. He dragged the thin straps down both of her arms, to her elbows, effectively causing the front of her top to follow in the same direction. Cool air rushed across her bared skin, making her shiver. Instantly, a large, warm palm cupped one of her breasts, and he gently squeezed the plump flesh as his thumb rasped over the hard, aching tip. Her sensitive nipple stiffened even more, and his appreciative male groan vibrated against their still-fused lips.

She moved restlessly against Christian, rubbing her hips against his in search of a more intimate touch. As if sensing exactly what she craved, he skimmed his free hand along the curve of her waist, then tugged the waistband of her pajama bottoms lower, until he was able to easily slip his hand inside her pants. His long fingers stroked her lower belly, traced the elastic band of her panties down to the apex of her thighs, then finally, *finally,* dipped beneath the damp silk fabric of her panties.

He wrenched his mouth from hers, buried his face against her neck and growled deep in his throat, the sound raw and primal. "God," he breathed. "You are so soft here. So hot and wet."

Those erotic words made her melt even more.

His touch was delicate at first, teasing her with soft, feathery caresses that only built her need and anticipation for more. Then he pushed deeper inside her, filling her exactly where she needed to be filled, and stroking her with his thumb exactly where she needed to be stroked. And if his expert caresses weren't enough to send her spinning out of control, he lowered his head and took one of her breasts in his mouth, his tongue licking and swirling over her tight nipple.

She sucked in a quick breath as everything within her clamored for the release he was coaxing from her. She was so aroused, so ready to indulge in the sensual pleasure he was creating with his mouth and fingers. Closing her eyes, she threaded her fingers through his hair, clenched the soft strands in her fist. She let her head fall back against the wall, and knew she was about to surrender her body, maybe even a piece of her heart and soul, to Christian.

Once you cross that line, there will be no going back to the simple, uncomplicated way it was between the two of you. Are you sure that's what you want?

Jarred out of the sensual fog consuming her, Amanda's eyes blinked open, and she prayed that she hadn't just heard Angie's prim and proper voice in her head. Not now, when her decision about Christian and making love with him was already made.

Shhhh! This forceful hush came from Desiree, confirming that the duo had reappeared to wreak havoc with Amanda's conscience. *You're so killing the moment for Amanda.*

Angie's chin lifted determinedly. *Well, someone has to think sensibly before—*

Heaven forbid, she has an orgasm? Desiree cut in, her sarcasm unmistakable. *She's so due, you know!*

The feel of Christian's mouth on her breast, and his fingers working the best kind of magic elsewhere clashed with the bickering, distracting voices in her head. Finally, Amanda just couldn't take it anymore.

"Oh, stop already!" she muttered firmly. *"Please!"*

Everything went silent and still. Including Christian. His hot, heavy breathing wafted across the dampness on her breast, and the fingers inside her, along with the pressure and friction of his thumb against her clitoris, immediately stopped.

Oh, God. She couldn't believe that she'd actually spoken out loud. She waited for Christian's reaction to the words she'd accidentally blurted out in frustration. Slowly, he lifted his head and looked into her eyes, searching deeply. His own gaze was a dark, smoldering shade of blue, and a concerned frown creased his brows.

"You want me to stop?" he asked gruffly, and judging by the tense set of his muscles, she knew he'd bring the encounter to a halt if that was what she really, truly wanted.

But, the last thing she wanted him to do was stop, and was certain she'd die if he didn't finish what he'd started. She'd been so, so close, and it wasn't going to take much more to send her soaring over that edge of release.

"No, I didn't mean you," she said and inwardly cringed at the way that sounded, as well as the confusion etching his features. Knowing there were no words to explain what had just happened that didn't make her seem like a crazy woman, she grabbed the tie hanging from around his neck and tugged his head back down to her breasts.

And just in case there were any last doubts or concerns lingering in his mind, she brazenly whispered her desires in his ear. "Make me come, Christian. Please."

With a ragged groan, he picked up where he'd abruptly left off as if he'd never stopped. His teeth grazed her nipple, followed by a soothing lap of his tongue, and between her thighs, his hand and fingers moved in a slow, provocative rhythm designed to heighten the tension pulling tighter and tighter within her.

Ahhh, that's much better, Desiree sighed.

Go away! Refusing to let Desiree and Angie be voyeurs and ruin what was going to possibly be the best sex of her life, Amanda banished them completely from her mind. With the two of them gone, her sole focus became Christian, and her own shameless desires.

The man was a master, and when he'd teased her to the point of exquisite torture, he finally gave her body what it ultimately needed. A slick, deliberate stroke along her flesh. A slow, deep thrust of his fingers. The suction of his mouth on her breast that seemed to spiral all the way down to her sex, then snapped free in a burst of sensation.

The orgasm that swept through her was pure, unadulterated

ecstasy, like a full-body climax, touching on every erogenous zone she possessed, and some she didn't even know existed. Her toes curled in her Jimmy Choos, her blood rushed to her head in a dizzying surge, and she cried out and shuddered against the pulsing sensation buffeting her entire body.

When the incredible pleasure finally ebbed and she came to her senses moments later, Christian was kissing and nuzzling her neck, his breath hot and damp on her skin. He eased his hand out of her pajama pants and lifted the straps of her camisole back up to her shoulders, covering her tender, swollen breasts.

Confusion trickled through her, clearing the passionate fog from her mind. He couldn't be done—he was still hard as a rock and she was ready and willing to give him just as much sensual satisfaction.

"Christian?" Tangling her fingers in the hair at the nape of his neck, she gently tugged his head back so she could look at his face and search his gaze. "What about you?"

"God, I want you, Amanda," he said, the heat and unquenched lust in his darkened eyes backing his claim. "I want to know the sexy, uninhibited woman who wrote me such a provocative note and promised to tie me up and have her way with me. All you have to do is say yes if you want this to go any further."

Emboldened by the strength of her desire for him, and eager to be the bold, brazen woman Christian wanted, her answer didn't require a whole lot of thought.

"*Yes,*" she said, and taking his hand in hers, she led him back to her bedroom.

4

As Amanda switched on the lamp on the nightstand, Christian took a quick glance around her spacious master bedroom. He smiled to himself, thinking the furnishings and decor reflected just how soft and feminine Amanda was beneath that no-nonsense facade she presented at work.

He liked what he saw. A whole lot. A cream-and-lavender floral comforter and ruffled pillows covered her mattress, and matching curtains framed the windows. The bed frame was a rich antique iron, with bars and scroll accents. The wallpaper in the room was textured, and the dresser and armoire were white-washed and elegant in design.

As he continued to scan the room, a framed picture on the wall of a man, woman and child caught his attention. It was an older photograph, depicting a much younger version of Douglas Creighton, a woman he assumed was Amanda's mother and a little girl of about ten who possessed the same features as the beautiful woman Amanda had become. It was a family portrait, obviously taken long ago, and it made him realize how little he really knew about Amanda outside the office, other than the fact that she was an only child.

He wanted to know more. About her family. Her past. Her childhood. And even what she saw for herself when she contemplated her future. That notion startled him, considering how intimate and personal his own thoughts had become when it came to Amanda. It also made him realize how deeply he was into her, despite all the potential complications of getting involved with the boss's daughter. Yet, even knowing what was at stake, he couldn't bring himself to turn around and walk away from her, and this night together.

Then his troubling thoughts scattered as she strolled back toward him, a sultry smile on her lips, her gaze bright with seductive intent. He was helpless to resist this sweet, sexy woman who'd sent him such a tantalizing Secret Santa gift. A woman who clearly wanted him as much as he ached for her.

Stopping in front of him, she reached for his tie and pulled it free of its knot. "I'm going to be needing this in just a few minutes," she murmured huskily and tossed the long scrap of material onto the bed behind him for safekeeping. Then she tugged the hem of his shirt from his pants and pulled it over his head and off.

She ran her hands over his chest, sighing appreciatively as she slowly skimmed her palms downward, touching and caressing her way to the waistband of his jeans. But before she could reach the snap securing his pants, he playfully pushed her hands aside, knowing one firm stroke of her fingers could easily set him off, and that would be the end for him.

"Not just yet," he said and hooked his own fingers into her pajama bottoms. He pushed them down, over the curve of her hips, along her slender thighs, then let the soft cotton pants drop to her ankles.

She tried to step out of the bottoms, but the material got caught around her feet and she laughed a bit self-consciously. "I need to take off my shoes."

The last thing he wanted was her removing those high heels she was wearing. At least not yet. "I'll help you out." Crouching down, he gently eased one foot, then the other, out of the pants while she held on to his shoulders for balance.

Slowly, he stood back up, trailing his fingers along her legs, her hips, her waist, as he took in the entire length of Amanda's gorgeous body. Finally, he straightened to his full height, as did his cock. There was something so damned erotic about Amanda Creighton standing in front of him, her hair tousled around her face and wearing nothing more than a skimpy camisole top, silky panties and bright red four-inch heels. He'd noticed those shoes earlier, mainly because they were the exact opposite of the prim, conservative pumps she always wore at the office.

She shifted on her feet and bit her bottom lip. "Umm, you forgot to take off my shoes while you were down there."

He grinned rakishly, thinking of a few other wicked things he could have done while he'd been kneeling in front of her. "Be patient, sweetheart. I'm getting there." Sitting down on the bed, he patted the mattress between his spread legs. "Put your foot up here for me and I'll take care of those shoes for you."

Doing as he asked, she lifted her leg and braced her foot right where he indicated. Her toenails were painted a daring red, he noticed, as he slipped a thin strip of leather through the tiny buckle wrapped around her ankle.

"So, what's with wearing the dress-up shoes with your pajamas?" he asked, glancing up at her face as he took that high heel off and started in on the other.

A warm flush of color rose in her cheeks, probably because she was just as aware of the fact that she'd never worn such provocative shoes to work before. "I just bought them and I was trying them on to see how they fit when you arrived."

"Well, I like them." He unfastened the second strap and let the shoe drop to the floor, but kept his fingers circled around her ankle to keep her foot in place on the bed between his thighs. "They make your legs look longer and sexier than they already are." To prove his point, he slowly, leisurely skimmed his fingers over her calf, behind her knee and along the inside of her smooth, silky thighs.

Her skin quivered beneath the stroke of his fingers, and her nipples tightened against her cotton top. Loving her reaction to his touch, and wanting a more physical contact with her, he put her foot back to the floor and stood up. Then he wrapped an arm around her back and brought her body flush to his, from her soft breasts all the way down to her supple thighs.

She felt incredible in his arms. Incredibly *perfect*. More so than any woman he'd ever been with.

His hand wandered downward, following the slope of her spine and over the sweet curve of her ass. He squeezed her bottom, and wished he'd gotten rid of her panties when he'd had the chance. "Do you know what men call shoes like the ones you were wearing?"

Placing her hands on his bare chest, she smiled up at him with an innocent bat of her lashes. "Dress-up shoes?" she replied cheekily.

He chuckled, then dipped his head close to hers and whispered his scandalous answer in her ear. "No, they call them 'fuck me' shoes, because that's what it makes a man think of when he sees a woman wearing them. And that's exactly what I want to do to you."

His intent made her shiver, and she laughed softly against his cheek. "Tonight, it's going to be the other way around."

He groaned, this assertive side to Amanda heightening his excitement, along with the need to be inside of her. Soon. "Lucky me."

She leaned back, her eyes sparkling with desire. "Well, I do need to make good on the Secret Santa gift I gave to you, now don't I?"

"Oh, yeah," he growled. Letting her go for a moment, he reached into the front pocket of his jeans and pulled out half a dozen foil packets. "I came prepared." He grinned sheepishly.

An amused smile curved her lips. "And you're obviously very confident and feeling quite ambitious, considering how many condoms you brought."

He shrugged unrepentantly. "Hey, a guy can hope."

She took the packets from him and tossed them onto the pillow with the blue-and-gray striped tie. Then she pushed him back until he was sitting on the bed again. "Move up toward the headboard," she said, and he did as she ordered.

Settled in the middle of the bed, precisely where Amanda wanted him, he watched her kneel on the mattress by his feet. She removed his shoes and socks, then crawled her way upward, between his spread legs, and went to work on the button and zipper on his pants. She caressed and squeezed him through the denim, making good on her promise to tease him to distraction before finally skinning his jeans and briefs down his legs and off.

He was stripped bare. She stared at his thick, aching erection and licked her lips. He imagined her mouth on him, sucking him deep, and his cock twitched and strained for any kind of attention she was willing to give. Unfortunately, she bypassed his hard-on and instead crawled up the length of his body until she was sitting astride his chest—so close that the scent of her arousal made his head spin. He was tempted to grab her thighs and pull her up higher, so he could taste her with his mouth and tongue and make her come again.

Frustrated that she was still wearing her top and panties while he wasn't wearing a stitch of clothing, he raised his gaze from the crux of her thighs, all the way up to her face. "You know, I'm feeling at a distinct disadvantage being completely naked, while you're still dressed."

"Semi-dressed," she corrected him, and reached for the tie on the pillow beside his head. "Besides, you had your chance to get me naked. But don't worry, I'll get there, too."

"I seriously can't wait." His stomach tightened as she wove the strip of silk between her fingers in a slow, erotic show of seduction and possession. Sitting on his chest with that *I'm-so-going-to-do-you* look in her eyes, she was his every fantasy come to life.

She leaned over the upper half of his body to secure his wrists together, then fastened them to one of the iron rods with a firm, inescapable knot. Her breasts were literally in his face and he nuzzled the soft, lush weight before turning his head and gently biting one of her nipples through the cotton T.

She gasped in shock and sat up straight, then narrowed her gaze playfully. "You are *so* going to pay for that."

"God, I hope so." He grinned.

She grabbed one of the condoms, but instead of getting right to business, she scooted her bottom down a bit, until his erection met the damp barrier of her panties. Face-to-face now, she lowered her mouth to his and kissed him—a slow, hot, deep kiss that made him hungry for so much more. Her damp lips traveled leisurely to his neck, down his throat, to his chest. Her soft hands followed, caressing and stroking his skin, and he groaned when her tongue flicked over one taut nipple, then sucked in a quick breath when her teeth scraped across the sensitive tip.

He felt her smile against his chest that she'd gotten even with her own love bite, then that incredible mouth and wet tongue of hers was forging a path of erotic pleasure down his stomach, until she was kneeling between his legs.

At the first delicate touch of her tongue on the tip of his cock, his entire body shuddered and his hands clenched around the bonds securing his arms to the headboard. Her lips parted over the head, and he growled deep in his throat as she took his entire shaft into her warm, wet mouth and stroked him deep. The silky strands of her hair brushed across his thighs, adding to the sensual sensations, and just when the tension inside of him started to spiral toward the breaking point, she pulled away and tore open the foil packet.

He realized he was panting for breath, and he hadn't even come yet. He glanced down toward the foot of the bed, watching as Amanda rolled the condom on him, using both hands to do it, her own erratic breathing reflecting just how excited and eager she was, as well.

Once she had him sheathed, she sat back and peeled off her top, her full, lush breasts bouncing gently now that they were unbound. Then she shimmied out of her panties and tossed them aside. Gloriously, beautifully naked, she straddled his hips, took his cock in her hand, and eased him inside of her. She slowly, gradually lowered herself, prolonging the moment, until he found himself deep, deep inside her.

Splaying her palms on his lower belly, she raised her heavy-lidded gaze to his, her mouth lifting in a purely female smile as she set out to drive him crazy with need. She moved her hips in small circles that eventually gave way to sexier, more uninhibited strokes that increased the pleasure and friction between them. And with each breath-stealing glide of her body against his, he slid deeper, and grew impossibly harder, inside her.

He automatically tried to reach down to caress her breasts, her belly and thighs, but the ties on his wrists reminded him that he was a slave to her desires. God, he wanted to touch her in the worst way, and he would, *next* time. And there was no doubt in his mind that they *would* make love again, because he was coming to realize that having her once wasn't going to be nearly enough for him. He wanted more…more of Amanda and everything that made her the incredible woman she was.

It didn't take him long to realize that he didn't need to touch Amanda at all. She knew exactly what she wanted from him, what moves aroused her the most, and she didn't hesitate to do whatever felt good. That in itself was a huge turn-on for him, and as her climax escalated toward that ultimate sexual bliss, so did his own.

With a soft, ragged moan, she dropped her head back and arched into him, shamelessly grinding against his groin as her orgasm rippled through her. Her inner contractions milked his shaft, and the tight, slick grip unraveled the last of his restraint in a hot and potent release that wrung him dry and ripped a strangled cry from his throat.

She collapsed on top of him and buried her face against his neck, her breathing warm and damp against his skin. She sighed softly, languidly, and he had the thought that this woman knew exactly how to tease him, please him and make him lose control, just as her note had suggested.

He smiled to himself. This night with her was, by far, the best Secret Santa gift anyone had ever given him.

CHRISTIAN TURNED ONTO his side and reached his arm across the bed, but the warm, soft female body he'd slept with, and made love with the entire night, was gone. He came awake slowly, the scent of Amanda and sex filling every breath he inhaled. It was a great way to wake up, and that's all it took to rouse his senses, and other parts of his anatomy.

A sleepy glance at the clock on the nightstand told him it was 8:24 in the morning on Saturday, and his completely sated body confirmed that last night hadn't been a dream, but a vivid, provocative reality. One that had sent his life as he knew it spinning in a direction he never would have anticipated.

He rolled to his back and stretched, a smile easing up the corners of his mouth as erotic memories flooded his mind. Who would have thought that cool, poised Amanda Creighton was such a temptress in private? Who would have thought that Amanda Creighton would become the one woman he wanted more than just a casual fling with?

Startling, but true. Sure, he'd always been attracted to her, and while sex with Amanda had been phenomenal, there were so many other things about her that intrigued him, so many contradictions that made him curious to know her on a deeper, more emotional level. It wasn't a smart move, all things considered. Like the fact that she was the boss's daughter. Like the fact that he'd worked damn hard to get that coveted promotion that Doug Creighton had the ability to give, or take away.

Still, knowing all that, he wasn't quite ready to end things with Amanda. And with that thought in mind, he hauled himself out of bed so they could make the most of their day together. That was, if she didn't already have plans.

He heard noises from another part of the apartment, and judging by the clattering sounds, he guessed she was in the kitchen. Perfect. With her busy, it gave him time to take a quick shower before greeting her. As he crossed the room, he glanced at an open door and realized it was her closet. A *huge* walk-in closet, and he switched on the light, curious to see what was inside.

Lots of clothes, obviously, and he couldn't help but grin at the way they were all hung up in a neat, orderly fashion by pants, blouses, dresses, then sorted by color. There were drawers and cubbyholes filled with purses and belts and those sensible shoes she wore to work, but what drew his attention was the custom-built, floor-to-ceiling rack displaying dozens of colorful, sexy, high-heel shoes. The strappy, traffic-stopping kind she'd worn last night with her pajamas.

"Well, I'll be damned," he murmured in amusement. It appeared that Ms. Creighton had a shoe fetish of some sort. One she kept private for some reason, because he sure as hell hadn't seen her wearing any of those hot, seductive shoes before. And they were just too provocative for any man not to sit up and take notice if they had been on her feet.

This secret side to Amanda was yet another intriguing facet to her personality.

He continued on to the bathroom and noticed that she'd left a brand new toothbrush on the counter for him, which he appreciated. He took a quick hot shower and got dressed, sans the tie this morning. After finger-combing his damp hair, he strolled barefoot down the hall, following the scent of coffee and something else that smelled delicious, according to his rumbling, empty stomach.

He stopped at the entryway into the kitchen, where Amanda was standing at the stove cooking breakfast. Choosing just to watch her for a few minutes without making his arrival known, he leaned against the doorjamb and took in the long-sleeve pink sweater she was wearing and the crisp, new-looking pair of designer jeans that hugged her curves, including that fine ass of hers that he'd held in his hands more than once last night. Much to his disappointment, on her feet were practical leather loafers, instead of one of those pairs of sexy, flirtatious shoes in her closet.

He was going to have to do something to change that.

He heard her say something, and thinking she was talking to him, he lifted his gaze from her feet back up—and realized that she was still facing away from him as she buttered some toast, still unaware of his presence. She was carrying on a one-way conversation with herself, and it wasn't the first time he'd caught her doing so. There was that time in the break room yesterday, and again last night when he could have sworn she'd asked him to stop touching her and she'd tried to explain it away with a strange "no, not you" remark.

"Yeah, yeah, yeah," Amanda said with a sigh. "I have to admit it was pretty damn good. The best sex I've ever had."

He grinned. Male ego aside, Christian liked the fact that he'd given her something no man ever had before, and knew he felt the same way about her. "Me, too."

She abruptly whirled around, a butter knife in her hand and

her eyes wide with surprise. "I didn't know you were out of the shower already."

Pushing off the doorjamb, he strolled across the kitchen toward her. "It would have taken much longer, and been far more enjoyable, if you would have joined me." She blushed, and he kissed her soft, parted lips, lingering just long enough to let her know that last night meant something more to him than a one-night stand. "Good morning."

"Morning," she replied huskily, and absently licked her bottom lip before turning back to her task. "Would you like some coffee?"

"Sure, I'll get it." There was already a second mug on the counter for him, and he poured himself a cup before glancing at the two plates of food on the counter. "Breakfast smells terrific."

"Good." She cut two slices of toast in half and added them to their dishes. "I made you a vegetable-and-cheese omelet. I hope that's okay."

"It's certainly better than the bowl of Cheerios I usually eat in the morning, and it's very appreciated. I'm starved." Picking up his mug of coffee, he took a sip as she carried their breakfast to the small kitchen table. "So, do you talk to yourself often?" he asked.

She stiffened ever so slightly, seemed to regain her composure, then turned toward him again. She shrugged, but surprisingly didn't deny her penchant for personal conversations. "It's an odd habit of mine," she said, waving dismissively as she went to the refrigerator and pulled out a pitcher of orange juice.

Odd, yes, but also endearing. And since it was clear that the topic embarrassed her, he switched to a different, but equally intriguing, one. "I do have a curious question for you."

She poured two glasses of OJ and cast him a cautious, uncertain glance. "Okay."

"You know those shoes you wore last night?"

She looked away, but not before he saw yet another flush of pink sweep across her cheeks, as if she were remembering what he'd said about those high heels he'd taken off for her. "Yes."

"Well, I couldn't help but notice that you have a whole closet full of them." She lifted a brow as if to ask what he'd been doing in her closet, but he wasn't about to let her sidetrack this conversation, too. "How come you never wear any of those shoes to work?"

"Because they aren't appropriate for the office," she said and set the two glasses of orange juice on the table.

Her answer came much too easily, as if she'd spent years convincing herself of that fact. What she didn't realize, however, was that he'd seen that quick glimpse of insecurity in her gaze before she'd masked it with a nonchalant reply.

He tipped his head, daring to challenge her. "Says who?"

"It's not exactly the image I want to portray at work," she tried to explain, but he sensed her reasons ran much deeper than that. "Besides, it's more of a hobby for me than anything else."

"Collecting designer shoes?" he asked incredulously.

She came up beside him and topped off her own mug with the steaming coffee. "Hey, we all have our quirks."

Hers were just a bit more eccentric than most. Who spent hundreds of dollars on shoes that they didn't wear and enjoy? "You really ought to put them to good use and wear them." He reached out and brushed the backs of his fingers across her smooth cheek. Her gaze softened, and something very near to the vicinity of his heart gave a distinct *thump* of emotional awareness. "Those shoes change the way you look, the way you carry yourself. They make you look damn sexy and very confident."

Laughing lightly, she flitted away from him and headed to the table with her mug in hand. "Well, I'm sure I'd shock everyone, including my father, if I came strutting into work in four-inch strappy heels."

Ahhh, her father. He wondered at their relationship outside of the office, if he'd been a strict parent with her, or if being so reserved was all her own doing. "Maybe the first day, yes," he agreed as he sat down next to her. "But honestly, who cares? Why not wear them because they make *you* feel good?"

She picked up her fork and smiled at him. "I *do* wear them."

"In private. At home." He grinned wryly. "Wow, you're such a rebel."

She wrinkled her nose at him, but didn't reply to his comment, choosing instead to let the entire subject slide, which she was very good at, he was coming to realize.

"So, what are you doing for the holidays?" she asked brightly.

His stomach growled hungrily, and he dug into his omelet. "I'm driving to my parents' house in Boston tomorrow afternoon."

"You're not flying?" she asked, surprised.

He shook his head. "It's only a three-hour drive and I do it all the time. My whole family will be there tomorrow for Christmas eve, and then stay until Christmas morning to open presents. It's a yearly tradition. What about you?"

She ate a bite of her breakfast and chased it down with a drink of orange juice. "I'll be spending Christmas with my father and his wife and a few of their friends. Nothing too exciting."

Her father's *wife*. So, Douglas Creighton had remarried at some point. "And your mother? Do you get to spend time with her?"

She wiped her mouth with her napkin, a bit of sadness coloring her eyes. "Actually, she died a long time ago."

"I'm sorry to hear that." He placed his hand over hers on the table and gave it a gentle squeeze. "Is she the woman in the picture hanging on the wall in your room?"

At the mention of the portrait, her gaze warmed again. "You noticed that?"

He was beginning to notice everything about her. "Yes, but only for a quick moment before you distracted me for the rest of the night." He winked at her.

She laughed at his playful comment, just as he'd intended. "Yeah, that's my mom," she said, tucking a stray strand of silky hair behind her ear. "It's been a long time since she passed away. I was only twelve when she died, and there are times I really do miss her. Especially around the holidays."

He could only imagine how difficult this time of year was for her, considering both of his parents were still alive and he had enough siblings to turn the holidays into one big party. Suddenly, he didn't want her spending the weekend alone when she could be spending it with him. At least until he had to leave for Boston.

Finished with his breakfast, he pushed his plate aside. "Hey, what are you doing today?"

She thought for a moment. "Not much."

So far, so good. "Any last-minute Christmas shopping you have to do?"

"Not really. I'm done. Everything is bought and wrapped."

"Why am I not surprised?" he teased, certain she'd finished her Christmas shopping a month ago. "As for me, I'm one of those last-minute holiday shoppers, and I sure could use some help picking out gifts for my sisters and nieces. Care to join me?"

She stared at him as if he were insane. "Are you crazy? It's less than two days before Christmas. Isn't it a madhouse at every store out there today?"

"Of course it is." He grinned persuasively. "You just haven't fully experienced the spirit of Christmas until you've been in the midst of holiday shopping twenty-four hours before Christmas eve."

"Okay, you are crazy," she said and laughed, her eyes sparkling merrily. "But what the hell. I'm game."

"Good." Now came the good part—a little nudge from him for her to embrace that sensual woman he'd been with last night. "*But,* there is one condition if you want to join me."

Her gaze narrowed with amused suspicion. "And what kind of condition would that be?"

He took a long drink of his coffee, drawing out the moment and letting her imagination take flight before he said, "I want you to wear one of those pairs of designer shoes in your closet."

"You've got to be joking." She sat back in her chair and shook her head. "In case you haven't noticed, it's winter in New York and it's freezing outside."

There was no way he was going to let Amanda talk her way out of this one. "I saw a few pairs of sexy high-heeled boots among all those opened-toed shoes, and I'm sure any one of them would keep your feet warm and toasty." He leaned closer, and before she could go on about practicality, he tossed out a little challenge he was certain she wouldn't be able to resist. "Unless, of course, you're afraid of getting them scuffed."

She opened her mouth, then closed it again, clamping her lips together. After a moment, she let loose a soft peal of laughter. "You are so—"

"Irresistible?" he offered.

"Actually, I was thinking more along the lines of *manipulative*," she grumbled good-naturedly.

He took the playful insult in stride. "Hey, whatever it takes to make you live a little on the wild side, sweetheart."

She sighed in exasperation, which contradicted the smile threatening to spill across her lips. "Okay. Fine. You win."

He grinned triumphantly. "Yeah, I usually do."

5

AFTER A LONG, EXTREMELY FUN day of hitting most of the big department stores in Manhattan, and being a part of the Christmas craze, Amanda was exhausted. Christian, with his last-minute gift-buying energy, gave the expression *shop till you drop* new meaning. But, Amanda had to admit that she'd had a great time and enjoyed assisting Christian in picking out gifts for the females in his family.

Once he'd crossed the last person off his gift list, he'd taken her to dinner for Italian fare at Puttanesca. Feeling very mellow after consuming two glasses of wine over the course of their meal, he'd taken advantage of that fact by cajoling her into coming back to his place to help him wrap the dozens of toys and gifts he'd purchased. Not that she would have refused him under any circumstances, but she didn't want to appear easy and preferred to make him work for her assent.

Now, they were sitting cross-legged and barefoot in the middle of his living room, with the coffee table pushed out of the way to give them room to spread out. The floor was littered with tape, scissors, rolls and rolls of Christmas wrapping paper, and dozens of bright, colorful ribbon and stick-on bows. After Christian had sheepishly confessed his lack of talent when it came to wrapping packages—and confirmed it as well when his first attempt looked as though a five-year-old had done the job—they decided that he'd stick to the kid's presents and she'd take care of the adults. Their system had worked very well, and two hours later they were nearly done with the huge pile of gifts.

Finished wrapping his mother's crystal tapered candlestick

holders, Amanda pulled a long stream of ribbon from the roll and went to work giving the package a pretty finishing touch. She glanced at Christian and hid a smile as she watched the intense way he was concentrating on attempting to fold the wrapping paper around an oddly shaped box that held a Tonka truck for one of his nephews. He came up short on one end and let out a growl of frustration that made her laugh.

"I'm so glad I'm able to amuse you," he said wryly.

She curled the hunter-green ribbon on the present with the sharp end of her scissors and added a name tag. "You know, it's really not that difficult if you just take your time and make sure you fold the ends a little more neatly."

He rolled his eyes humorously as he taped a strip of wrapping paper where he'd fallen short, giving the package a patchwork look. "I'm not putting that kind of effort into the kids' presents. They're going to rip into them without even noticing the wrapping job."

"That's why you're in charge of their gifts, and I'm doing the grown-ups." She set his mother's present with the rest that she'd wrapped, and grinned as she noticed the big difference between her pile of lavishly decorated gifts and his stack of haphazardly wrapped packages. "Do you think they'll be able to tell you had help?"

"Definitely." He returned her grin with one of his own. "Yours are way too fancy. But they look great. Thank you." He leaned over and showed his gratitude with a warm, soft kiss on her lips.

Such a simple touch between them, but it was enough to start a slow burn of desire for him. "It was my pleasure," she murmured when he finally pulled away. And truly, it was. She only had a few gifts to wrap each year, and she loved the whole relaxing, creative process of choosing just the right holiday paper, ribbon and bows to embellish a present.

"You certainly have a huge family," she said, taking in all the gifts they'd bought and wrapped—all in one day, no less. While they'd been shopping earlier, then at dinner, he'd regaled her with tales about his siblings—two older sisters and a younger brother—along with a small passel of nieces and nephews he seemed to absolutely adore. "It must be crazy on Christmas Day."

He topped off the Tonka truck with a pre-made, stick-on bow, and added a name tag with his nephew's name on it. "Yeah, it's loud and boisterous and a whole lot of fun."

She could only imagine, and could easily see Christian on the floor playing with his nieces and nephews. As an only child, she'd never have those experiences, and envied him that. "You're very lucky to have a big family."

"Try telling me that when I was a teenager and fighting my two sisters and brother for the bathroom in the morning before school," he griped, but there was a sincere fondness for his siblings in his gaze.

"At least you had siblings. It was very, very quiet in my house." And incredibly lonely at times, too, which always gave Desiree and Angie the opportunity to keep her company.

Christian rummaged through one of the bags from a department store and pulled out a silver box with a matching satin silver ribbon tied around it. "Hey, look what I found," he said in mock surprise. "One last gift."

She eyed the box, trying to remember when and where he'd bought that particular present, but her mind came up blank. "Luckily for you, it's already wrapped. And very elegantly, I might add. How did you manage that?" she teased.

"I can't claim responsibility for this one. I had the clerk at Sak's take care of this gift on the sly." He handed the box to her, his gaze a dark, intimate shade of blue. "It's for you."

"Me?" She was shocked, mainly because a present of any sort from Christian was the last thing she expected. For that matter, her weekend with him was all the gift she wanted, and needed. "When did you manage to buy this?"

He shrugged. "When you were picking out a perfume set for my sister."

Ahh, now she remembered. He'd asked her to choose what fragrance she thought one of his sisters might like, while he'd ventured over to women's accessories, which was where she'd found him fifteen minutes later. Obviously, he'd accomplished a lot in that short span of time.

She fingered the satin ribbon, and though she was secretly pleased that he'd thought of her, she didn't want him to think a gift was necessary. "Well, you really shouldn't have."

"I wanted to. Besides, I couldn't resist. Really." He winked at her, a wicked gleam in his eyes. "Go on, open it up."

Unable to stem the excitement and curiosity rising within her, she untied the bow and pulled off the ribbon. She opened the lid, peeled away the signature tissue paper and gasped when she saw something silky in the brightest, most gorgeous jewel-toned shades she'd ever seen. There were purples, pinks, blues and greens in an abstract design, the kind of rich and vibrant colors that gave her such a rush of pleasure.

Uncertain exactly what it was, she lifted the luxurious fabric out of the box and realized that it was a silk scarf. And an expensive, high-end, Emilio Pucci one at that. The man certainly had great taste.

Stunned, knowing that the hand-picked gift had to cost him a small fortune, she swallowed hard and glanced back at Christian. He was watching her intently, waiting for her reaction, and she knew deep in her heart that there was more behind Christian's reason for giving her this gift than it just being a designer scarf.

"It's absolutely beautiful," she said, her voice raspy with emotion.

He reached out and touched the line of her jaw then smoothed his thumb down to her lips. "When I saw that scarf, it immediately reminded me of all those colorful, sexy shoes you have in your closet. You were meant to wear bold, sensual things, Amanda."

She hugged the scarf to her chest, holding it for the cherished, insightful gift it was. "I love it. Thank you." Her words felt so inadequate for what he'd given her.

She was so incredibly touched because no one had ever given her something so intimate and meaningful. It occurred to her that in just one day together he'd proven to her with this gift that he knew her better than her own father or friends did. That beneath her practical and staid clothing and personality there was a woman who ached to be confident and daring enough to wear those colorful designer shoes in her closet, and the jewel-toned scarf he'd bought for her.

And she was beginning to think that maybe, just maybe, she could be that woman after all.

Overwhelmed by the onslaught of indescribable emotions she was feeling for this man, she leaned over and *showed* him how grateful she was for everything he'd given her this weekend. More than just sex and a good time. More than just a scarf. He'd given her a sense of self and quite possibly the confidence to embrace her inner vixen. And wouldn't Desiree be pleased with that?

Her lips met his, and she kissed him with hunger, passion and a soul-deep longing that rocked her to the very core. She touched her hand to his stubbled cheek, and his fingers tangled in her hair, tipping her head just so to deepen the connection of their mouths, and the erotic swirl and slide of their tongues. The kiss quickly turned wild and hot, to the point that she was seriously contemplating tearing off his clothes and having her way with him right in the middle of all the wrapping paper and bows. But before she could follow through with that plan, it was Christian who slowed things down a bit.

"You know," he whispered against her lips as he continued to tease her with soft, damp kisses, "I have to admit when I first saw that scarf I thought about all the different ways you could use it."

"Really?" Despite feeling light-headed and breathless, and getting hotter by the minute, she managed a smile against his mouth. "Why do I get the impression that you're not thinking about it accessorizing an outfit?"

"Maybe because I'm not." He chuckled, the low, sinful sound causing her breasts to swell and her nipples to tighten into hard, sensitive knots that ached for the touch of his fingers. The warm, wet suction of his mouth.

Remembering what she'd done to him with the tie, she pulled back so she could look into his eyes, which had grown dark and smoky with desire. "You want to tie me up with the scarf?"

"Oh, yeah," he growled sexily. "That, and a whole lot more."
He stood up and held out his hand to her. "Care to find out
exactly what I have in mind?"

She glanced up, unable to miss just how aroused he was, or
the heat and seductive promise in his eyes. Helpless to resist this
one last night with him, she stood up, too. Then she put her hand
in his and let him lead her to his bedroom…and straight into
temptation of the sweetest kind.

AMANDA STEPPED OUT of Christian's shower, grabbed the big,
fluffy towel hanging on the wall hook, and dried off, including
her wet hair. Once she was done, she wrapped it around her body
and tucked the end between her breasts to keep the towel secured.

She'd taken a nice, hot, relaxing shower while Christian had
gone down to the corner café for coffee and pastries for breakfast, and now the bathroom was filled with fragrant steam, which
made it difficult to use the mirror since it was completely fogged.
She cracked open the door to let a bit of cool air in, and used a
hand towel to wipe off a spot on the mirror so she could see her
reflection.

She was unexpectedly greeted by Angie, who was sitting on
her right shoulder, her gaze narrowed in concern as she took in
Amanda's features and the warm flush of her complexion. *Oh,
no, you have* the *look,* she said and pursed her lips in disapproval.

Amanda sighed as she picked up the wide-tooth comb on the
counter and pulled it through her damp hair to the ends. She'd
managed to keep the distracting duo out of her head yesterday
and last night, but it appeared they were back to cause their
brand of havoc with her conscience.

Of course she has the *look,* Desiree replied with a sly,
knowing grin. *It's the glow of a woman who's enjoyed incredible,
mind-blowing sex with a hot stud.*

Amanda couldn't deny the truth. "Yeah, the sex was pretty
incredible, *again,*" she murmured.

If she'd thought that Friday night's pleasurable escapade and
her multiple orgasms had been a fluke, then last night had con-

firmed that there was enough chemistry between her and Christian to set the sheets on fire. He'd used the silk scarf in ways she never would have imagined and, coupled with the fact that he was a master with his hands and mouth and fingers, Amanda had spent hours indulging in the kind of sexual bliss she'd only fantasized about before now.

No, it's more than that, Angie fretted and wrung her hands anxiously in her lap. *I'm afraid she's falling for that bad boy!*

"No, I'm not," Amanda said, but the denial lacked any real conviction. Probably because Angie had hit too close to the truth.

Desiree leaned forward and peered intently at Amanda's features in the mirror. Her eyes widened and she abruptly sat back on Amanda's shoulder. *Uh-oh,* she said with a hint of worry in her tone. *Angie just might be right. For once.*

That comment earned Desiree a sharp glare from her nemesis, who always thought she knew best.

The comb caught on a tangle of wet hair, and Amanda gave it a forceful tug out of pure frustration—and lost a few extra strands in the process. "Well, it can't happen," she told Desiree and Angie, as well as herself.

I think it already has, Angie said in that maternal way that Amanda couldn't ignore.

Amanda frowned at her reflection. "Okay, so maybe it has," she admitted, and knew by the pounding of her heart in her chest that she had, indeed, fallen harder for Christian than she'd ever intended.

Oh, yeah, she was halfway in love with him.

She inhaled a slow, deep breath, and grabbed the counter for support as the truth of her feelings smacked her in the face. As did a good dose of reality. No matter how great their brief time together had been, she knew better than to expect anything beyond this affair. They'd both agreed upon no regrets, and Christian had made no promises that even so much as hinted at a relationship after today.

In all honesty, this fling of theirs had all been a product of the Secret Santa note and gift she'd sent him. It had given them both permission to act on their attraction and desires and, without that bold and daring move of hers, they never would have traveled down this particular path.

So, she accepted their affair for what it was, and just hoped to God that she didn't compare every guy she dated after this weekend to Christian. Ha! Fat chance, she thought. Because despite her little pep talk, she knew deep in her heart this was a man who could have been *the one* for her.

Oh, Amanda, Angie said softly, consolingly. *I'm so sorry.*

Amanda appreciated her guardian angel's empathy, especially since Angie had been so against her involvement with Christian from the beginning. For good reasons, obviously. It appeared that Angie did know best after all. "Hey, it was a one-shot deal, and we both knew it going into this weekend."

More like five or six shots, Desiree said, using a bit of innuendo in her attempt to lighten the mood. *But really, who's counting?*

Amanda laughed and shook her head. "Obviously, *you* are."

The door behind Amanda slowly pushed open, and she glanced into the mirror to find Christian standing there, looking incredible sexy and gorgeous. He was wearing a soft gray, New York Mets pullover sweatshirt and a pair of jeans, and his thick hair was tousled around his head, as if the wind had combed his hair this morning. She had no idea when he'd returned from the café, or what, if anything, he'd overheard.

He tipped his head and grinned at her. "You talking to yourself again?"

She felt a surge of heat travel up her neck to her face, and didn't bother to try and evade his question. "Umm, guilty as charged."

He casually leaned a shoulder against the doorjamb, settling in for the moment. "You know, it really does sound as though you're talking to someone, and not just yourself." There was an abundance of curiosity in his gaze, along with something deeper that told her he suspected there was more to her one-way conversations than she was letting on.

The man was too perceptive, and she turned around to face him. "Actually, I kind of am talking to someone else." She didn't know what possessed her to make that confession to him, but once it was out, she couldn't take it back. Besides, he'd caught her muttering to herself so many times that he was probably beginning to think she was a little psychotic.

"One of those invisible, imaginary friends from childhood?" he guessed, amusement dancing in his eyes.

She'd come this far, and figured what the hell. "There are two of them, actually."

She truly expected him to burst out laughing at her elaborate tale, to tell her to stop pulling his leg, but instead he played along. "Really? Care to introduce me?"

He crossed his arms over his chest and didn't seem inclined to move from guarding the door—which kept her pretty well trapped in the bathroom. She stared at his expression, judging his sincerity, and couldn't miss the genuine interest in his eyes.

She'd never, ever told anyone about the duo, not even her father. But in a very short span of time she'd come to trust Christian, and knew that just as he'd understood about her array of colorful designer shoes, he'd understand this particular quirk about her, as well.

"Well, there's Angie on the right, who is the angelic side of my conscience," she said, pointing to her right shoulder, even though she knew Christian couldn't see anyone sitting there. "And then there's Desiree on the left, who is the more daring side. Angie keeps me in line and makes sure I'm doing the *right* thing, and Desiree is the one who is constantly trying to tempt me to be more adventurous."

He chuckled. "I think Desiree and I would get along just fine."

Amanda didn't doubt that for a moment, given his own badboy reputation. "They've been with me since I was twelve."

His humor fled, replaced by a serious, tender expression. "When your mother died?" he asked.

She was amazed that he'd made that connection, which proved just how much he'd paid attention during their conversation yesterday. "I went through a really tough time after my mother passed away, especially since she was a stay-at-home mom. All of a sudden, I was coming home to an empty house after school until my father got home from work. So, I felt as though I had to make a lot of decisions on my own."

A small, knowing smile curved the corner of his mouth. "And that's where Angie and Desiree come in?"

Nodding, she leaned back against the bathroom counter, suddenly aware of the fact that she was still only wearing a towel. But, it was obvious that Christian wasn't letting her go anywhere until she finished explaining.

"Whenever I had an issue with peer pressure, or something came up with a friend that I didn't know how to handle, Angie was there to try and guide me in the right direction, while Desiree did her best to coax me into trouble. But, in the end, Angie usually won because I didn't want to give my father any reason to be disappointed in me, in any way."

"I think your father is very proud of the woman you've become," he said, as if he knew for certain it was so.

"I think so, too," she said and smiled. "But who knows how I would have ended up without Angie and Desiree's influence."

"You would have ended up just as you are. An incredibly smart and beautiful woman, inside and out." He pushed away from the door and closed the distance between them. Placing his hands on the curve of her waist, he leaned into her, intimately close. "*You're* the one who made all the right decisions and choices throughout the years, Amanda. And if it helps you to believe that you had a bit of assistance along the way, well, there's nothing wrong with that."

She reached up and placed her palm on his cheek, and swallowed past the surge of emotion crowding in her chest. "Thank you," she whispered, wondering if he realized just how much his words meant to her. It was as if he understood how insecure and vulnerable she'd been after her mother's death, and now that she'd finally talked about that time in her life, she suddenly felt lighter. Stronger in both mind and spirit. It was an awesome, overwhelming feeling, one she wholeheartedly welcomed.

And she owed this man for setting a part of her free and for giving her such a precious gift.

"But you know what?" he said as a seductive, mischievous

gleam entered his eyes, changing the mood from serious to playful. "I have to agree with Desiree. You really do need to be more adventurous."

She thought about the shoes he'd asked her to wear, the things they'd done with the tie and scarf that even now made her blush. She'd stepped out of her comfort zone with Christian numerous times, and had loved every minute of it. "Don't you think I've been plenty daring this weekend?"

"Eh," he said, the one word sounding much too doubtful as he lifted her so she was sitting on the vanity and her spread legs bracketed his hips. "Honestly? I think you still need a few more lessons before you're fully qualified as daring."

She lifted a brow and shivered as his hands slipped beneath the hem of her towel and up her bare thighs. "Oh, really?"

"Oh, yeah," he replied before dipping his head and nuzzling his face against her neck.

His palms skimmed over her hips and around to her bottom, causing the knot securing the towel at her breasts to unravel and fall to the sides, baring her naked body and inviting his gaze, his touch, and anything else he wanted to do to her.

"So, what did you have in mind?" she asked breathlessly. A stupid, ridiculous question considering his mouth was already traveling down to her aching breasts.

His hands cupped her bottom and pulled her to the very edge of the counter, until his jean-clad erection pressed insistently against her damp, sensitive flesh. "Ever had slow, hot sex on a bathroom vanity?"

Her stomach muscles clenched in anticipation. "I can't say I have." He flicked one of her nipples with his tongue, and she tangled her fingers into his silky-soft hair, dropped her head back and moaned.

"Well, then, there you go," he said and smiled against the curve of her breast while his hands went to work unfastening his jeans and releasing his shaft. "Another brand new adventure for you to enjoy."

Somewhere in the bathroom cabinet he found a condom and

slipped it on. She gasped as the head of his erection glided through her slick, feminine folds, then oh-so-gradually pushed into her, until he was all the way in and filling her completely. With a low, primitive groan, he crushed his mouth to hers and kissed her, as deeply and slowly as he made love to her body. She whimpered as sensations built upon sensations, as the lazy thrust and agonizingly slow retreat of his hips made her desperate to feel the hot length of him driving harder and deeper inside her.

But he didn't give in to her impatience and instead took her on a long, erotic journey that escalated into a sexual inferno between them one last time. When he finally allowed her explosive orgasm to crest, he was right there with her, both of them shuddering with the most exquisite, sublime pleasure she'd ever known.

CHRISTIAN CAME TO A STOP at a red light and glanced at Amanda, who was sitting in the passenger seat of his car. Ever since they'd left his place, she'd been talking nonstop, barely even giving him a chance to respond to anything she had to say. It was just a long stream of inconsequential conversation on her end, and it was making his head spin.

This sort of fidgety behavior was so unlike the poised, in-control Amanda he'd once known, and it had taken him longer than usual to figure out what was wrong. But, once he'd pinpointed where the change in her had begun, the shift from calm and relaxed to anxious and uncertain all made sense to him.

Everything had been fabulous between them after their escapade in the bathroom, and even during breakfast. The shift had come when he'd told her that he needed to take her home so he could get on the road to Boston for Christmas eve with his family. At first, she'd grown quiet, then once they were in his car she'd started talking…and hadn't stopped since.

The light turned green, and he continued down the street toward her place, recognizing her endless chatter for the diversion it was, along with the false brightness in her tone. She was nervous, and he was guessing that she didn't want to deal with a *weekend-after* kind of conversation before they reached her apartment. The kind of discussion that would put an end to their temporary affair, allowing them to go their separate ways without anyone ever knowing what had transpired between them.

The funny thing was, despite promising her that their weekend together would stay just between the two of them, he didn't want this blossoming relationship to end, and he couldn't remember the last time he'd ever felt that way about a woman. It was true that he'd gone into this affair with Amanda with the sole expectation of finally getting her out of his system. But despite those not-so-noble intentions, during the course of their two days together something had changed, and he knew she felt it, too. Beyond the physical pleasure they'd shared, they'd connected on a deeper, more intimate level.

She'd become so much more than just the boss's daughter to him. So much more than a co-worker he'd been attracted to. She'd become a woman he cared for very deeply. A woman who struck an emotional chord in him and made him think about the future, and a series of *what if* questions he'd never contemplated before.

He contemplated them now with Amanda.

Her building came into sight, and he pulled into the circular drive by the front entrance. "I'll walk with you up to your place," he said.

"You don't need to do that," she said, much too cheerfully. "I'll be fine, really. You need to get on your way to Boston."

No, he really didn't. Whatever was between them was far more important. He hesitated, then decided to get it all out there in the open. "Amanda, about this weekend—"

She placed her fingers on his lips, stopping him mid-sentence. She shook her head and managed a smile that was far too fragile. "Please don't say anything, okay?" she pleaded in a voice brimming with what sounded like tears. "I had a great time with you. Thank you for everything."

Okay, the last thing he wanted was her gratitude, and he hated that she was brushing him—and their time together—off. "Amanda—"

This time it was her lips that cut him off, along with a quick, hot kiss that felt way too vulnerable and bittersweet. Finally, she broke the kiss and moved back to her side of the vehicle.

"Merry Christmas, Christian," she said, then bolted out of the car before he could say or do anything to stop her.

He sat there in front of the entrance for a good five minutes, debating whether or not to go up to Amanda's apartment or leave her alone for the time being. After mentally grappling with both scenarios, he finally decided to put the car back into gear and head toward Boston.

Judging by her actions, she wasn't ready to hear anything he had to say, and was obviously under the assumption that she was just another notch on his belt. Without a doubt, he had the reputation to back up those thoughts, but it appeared that his life was about to take a different direction, and she was the reason.

Okay, so she needed more time to calm down and let him explain. Fine, he'd give her that bit of space while he was in Boston. But once he returned, they were going to talk, even if he had to tie her up to force her to listen to what he had to say.

6

"So, how's work going, Christian?" one of his older sisters, Kathy, asked as she walked into their parents' living room from the kitchen and handed him a cold bottle of beer. "Last we all heard at Thanksgiving you were still the number-one sales executive and working toward the sales director position."

"I still am." He thanked his sister for the beer and took a drink, watching with a smile as his youngest nieces and nephews chased each other through the house, despite the fact that their mothers had already warned them to quit being so wild and rambunctious. "It should be decided after the holiday."

"Well, you deserve it," his other sister, Diane, said as she set a tray of ham-and-cream-cheese roll-ups on the coffee table for everyone to enjoy. "We all know how hard you've worked toward this promotion."

"To the point that he's become a confirmed bachelor, instead of settling down like the rest of you have," his mother complained from her position on the couch across the room.

Christian rolled his eyes because this was a scenario he relived every time he came home for a visit. His mother's greatest wish was to see all her children happily married with a family of their own. So far, he was the only one who hadn't conformed to her expectations. "Now, Mom…"

"You know it's true," she went on and looked to their father for confirmation, but he wisely remained quiet. "How many times have you told me that you're just too busy furthering your career to settle down?"

"Too many times to count," Kathy offered before Christian

could reply, and laughed. "Don't worry, Mom. It'll happen. He just needs to meet the right woman for him, and once he does, I can guarantee he'll change his way of thinking."

A greater truth had never been spoken, Christian thought. He hadn't been looking for Mrs. Right, but she'd happened along anyway, and he wasn't about to let her slip from his life, if he could help it.

He'd been at his parents for a few hours now, and his thoughts were never far from Amanda. In fact, he'd already pulled his cell phone from his pocket five times with the intention of calling her to talk things through, but managed to restrain himself. After the way she'd scrambled from his car earlier, he knew she wasn't ready to hear what he had to say, and he hoped to God that a few days apart might help his cause and make her listen to reason.

"Christian, I'm thinking you must have paid a small fortune to have those presents you brought with you wrapped," Diane teased, pulling his attention away from his troubling thoughts to yet another topic that made him think of Amanda and the time they'd spent together over the weekend.

"I have to agree," Kathy commented from her seat close to the Christmas tree and the gifts piled beneath. "They look like they were professionally decorated."

"Sorry to disappoint the two of you, but they weren't wrapped by a professional, and it didn't cost me anything." Grinning, he reached for one of the delicious stuffed mushrooms his mother always made as a holiday appetizer and popped it into his mouth.

"Well, we all know that *you* didn't wrap them," Diane said, the curiosity in her tone unmistakable. "Wrapping presents is so not your forte."

His younger brother, Brian, who was sitting next to him on the couch and had been quiet up to this point while he chowed down on the appetizers, finally had something to add to the conversation. He slapped Christian on the back in male camaraderie and said, "He's probably dating a gift-wrap clerk over the holidays and that's just one of the perks of their fling."

"She's not a fling," Christian said automatically, then realized too late how defensive he sounded.

Everyone else noticed, though, and the adults in the room went quiet. Now, they were all staring at him with open interest and speculation.

"Whoa, you're really dating a gift-wrap clerk?" Brian asked around the ham roll-up he'd just stuffed into his mouth.

"Since when have you had a serious relationship?" Diane asked in shock.

His mother didn't hesitate to chime in, as well. "And if it's *that* serious, why haven't you told *us* about her?"

He sighed, and tried to explain. "Because it just *recently* became serious."

Brian stared at him incredulously. "Holy shi—"

"Watch your language," his wife, Sarah, said, cutting off her husband before the words were out of his mouth. "The kids can hear you."

"Holy *cow*," Brian said as he slanted Sarah a wry look before glancing back at Christian. "I do believe my brother is finally whipped."

Christian just smiled, knowing that his silence, and the fact that he didn't argue, spoke volumes.

An excited gleam entered his mother's eyes. "So, when do we get to meet this woman?"

He rolled his beer bottle between his palms and shrugged. "Just as soon as I can convince *her* that it's serious between us."

Brian let out a loud guffaw. "Oh, man, it's so sweet to finally see the invincible love 'em and leave 'em playboy on the other side of the fence."

Despite the truth of his brother's statement, Christian wasn't the least bit amused. "Her name is Amanda, and she's my boss's daughter," he said, just so everyone knew exactly what he was up against.

That earned him a gasp from his sister Diane, whose expression had softened considerably. "Oh, Christian, that can't be good for your upcoming promotion."

That particular concern had crossed his mind, as well, during the drive to Boston, because the possibility did exist that Douglas might not take too kindly to the fact that Christian wanted to pursue his daughter, considering his past indiscretion at the office. But Christian had come to a very important decision, and he shared it with his family.

"When I get back home, I plan to talk to Amanda and try to convince her to give us a chance," he said. "My job is very important to me, and I do care about the promotion, but if push comes to shove and I have to make a choice, I care about Amanda more."

As for her father, somehow, someway, he'd make Douglas Creighton understand just how much Amanda meant to him.

EXCITEMENT WELLED UP inside of Amanda as she surveyed the floor-to-ceiling rack in her closet displaying all the bright, colorful designer shoes she'd bought over the years. They all looked shiny and brand new, with nary a scratch or scuff to mar the closed-toe shoes or the expensive leather straps on the high heels.

Now that she'd decided to put the shoes to *real* use, it was like having a sweet tooth and being set free in a candy store to gorge on all your favorite treats. But the difficult part was which treat did she indulge in first?

She bit her bottom lip and glanced down at the new outfit she'd bought yesterday at a department store's day-after-Christmas sale. Her father had given everyone an extra day off from work to enjoy the holiday weekend a little longer, and Amanda had spent the day shopping and updating her wardrobe to reflect the new her.

She'd replaced her practical, businesslike suits with ones that were more feminine. She'd added lace to her tops, chosen bolder colors and went a few inches shorter on her skirts. Instead of long, double-breasted jackets, she'd selected a few cropped, fitted ones that showed off her figure, rather than hid her curves. She'd implemented subtle, sensual changes in her choice of clothing, and today she was wearing a fitted suede jacket in a gorgeous color of azure-blue, a pretty cream-hued camisole beneath and an A-line black skirt that ended a few inches *above* her knee, instead of below. Now, all she needed to do was pick out a pair of shoes to complement the outfit.

After much deliberation, she finally settled on a pair of Manolo Blahnik sling-back heels with colorful, sexy straps that crisscrossed over her foot. She carried them into her bedroom, and with an undeniable burst of exhilaration she slipped them on, then turned to face her reflection in her dressing mirror to finally check out the end results.

So, you're really going to wear those shoes outside of the apartment?

"Yeah, I am." Amanda smiled at Angie, who'd appeared on her right shoulder and was taking in all the new changes in Amanda's appearance. Despite the slight concern creasing her guardian angel's brows, there had been no censure or scandal in her voice. Just an acceptance of the decisions Amanda had made over the past few days. "I'm going to wear those designer shoes to work, and to dinners, and anywhere else I can."

Well, good for you, Desiree piped in and applauded Amanda's new attitude.

"Thank you very much." Amanda gave the cheeky devil a slight bow for her praise. "In fact, all my old, sensible pumps are getting dropped off at Goodwill since I won't be needing them anymore."

Oh, yeah! Desiree punched her first in the air triumphantly, her voice infused with pride. *You go, girl!*

Laughing at Desiree's enthusiastic response, Amanda walked toward her dresser and picked up the scarf that Christian had given her for Christmas. A gift that had so much thought and meaning behind it. She slid the vibrant silk through her fingers, and a huge lump gathered in her throat when she thought of their last moments together, and the paralyzing fear that had gripped her.

When Christian had dropped her off on Sunday and started his goodbye with the dreaded *about this weekend* phrase, she'd been so certain that he was going to try and let her down gently, or remind her that their time together was only a two-night deal. She'd been so afraid of being rejected after the most incredible weekend of her life that she hadn't given him the chance to say anything at all. She didn't want to hear the words that would pierce her heart, and it had been so much easier for her to be the one to walk away first, rather than be devastated by a brush-off.

But now that she'd had a few days alone to think about her behavior, she realized just what a coward she'd been. And how unfair, too. She hadn't given Christian any opportunity to say what was on his mind, and had anticipated the worst—even after he'd been so caring and understanding with her. She'd been very wrong to assume anything, and knew that good or bad, she needed to hear whatever Christian had to say to her.

The old Amanda would have gone to work and pretended nothing had ever happened between them. But this new Amanda, the woman in the mirror who felt so confident and sexy because of Christian's encouragement, was going to face issues head-on and take the kind of risks she'd avoided in the past. Risks like telling Christian how she really felt about him. She hoped that he felt the same. And if he didn't, well, at the very least she'd like to think they could be friends.

Are you going to be okay?

She knew that Angie was concerned about her emotional state after her weekend with Christian, but Amanda truly couldn't have felt more optimistic about her future, regardless of the outcome with Christian. "I'm going to be fine. More than fine," she reassured Angie with a genuine smile. "In fact, there's something I need to tell the two of you."

Desiree and Angie grew somber, as if they both knew what she was going to say.

"You two have been in my life for so long, but it's time for me to be on my own." Being with Christian had made her realize that she needed to make her own choices, that she no longer needed the emotional crutch of having Desiree and Angie around. She now understood that it was all about her letting them go. Not the other way around.

You're right. Our work is done here, Desiree said, and Amanda could have sworn she saw a glimmer of moisture in the she-devil's eyes.

Yes, you're ready to be on your own, Angie agreed softly, and with pride.

When Amanda glanced back into the mirror, the duo was gone. But, surprisingly, she didn't feel as though anything was ending. Rather, it was the start of a new beginning.

CHRISTIAN WAS NERVOUS as hell, and that was saying a lot since he was normally so cool, calm and collected even under the most stressful of situations. But, it wasn't every day that he put his heart, and his job, on the line for a woman.

He'd arrived at work early so he could catch Douglas Creighton before everyone started arriving at the office. But now that he was sitting across from his boss, his stomach was in knots because he couldn't even begin to anticipate the end result of this conversation.

He exhaled a deep breath and jumped right in. "Thanks for seeing me so early. There's something important I'd like to talk to you about."

"Sure," Douglas said easily. "What's on your mind?"

There was no sense in beating around the bush, and he got right to the point. "I want to see your daughter."

The older man frowned, clearly confused. "You see her every day at the office."

Christian shook his head and chuckled, releasing the tension that had been tightening his chest. "Okay, maybe I need to be more specific. I want to *date* your daughter. Exclusively."

This announcement was met with silence and a narrowing of Douglas's gaze. Before the other man could launch himself across the desk and strangle Christian for even suggesting such a thing, he figured he might as well get everything out in the open and really give Creighton a reason to kill him.

"I spent some time with Amanda over the weekend, and I want to continue spending time with her without sneaking around," he said on a rush of breath. "I wanted to be honest with you so you would know my intentions right up front."

Douglas leaned back in his chair and stared at Christian for what seemed like hours, when in fact only a minute had passed before the older man rubbed a hand along his jaw and finally spoke. "I certainly respect your honesty, but given your past indiscretion here in the office, I can't help but be a bit concerned about Amanda's reputation."

"I understand," Christian said, knowing that Douglas's worries were valid, all things considered. "But I do care for her, and I wouldn't be in here, risking my promotion to be with her if I didn't feel she was worth it."

"Yes, I suppose you are putting that promotion on the line." Douglas studied him again, and Christian wished he knew what the other man was searching for. "You know, Amanda has had trouble in the past with men wanting to date her to get to me. They were more interested in what I could do for them than they were in her."

"No, I didn't know that," Christian said, but realized how this situation must look to Douglas. However, he could only prove his sincerity over the course of time. *If* he walked out of here with Creighton's blessing.

"However, I can honestly say that none of those other men had the guts and integrity that you do, to come to me and risk your job as you have."

"Thank you, sir," Christian said, hoping his candor counted for something in the end. "I think finding the right woman makes all the difference in the world."

"Ahhh, that they do," Douglas said with a smile. "You do know that behind every great man is an even greater, stronger woman, right?"

Christian grinned. "So my own father has said, numerous times."

"Smart man, and he's passing some good, solid advice on down to his son." Douglas sat forward in his chair again, his gaze direct and all business. "Now, about that promotion. I had every intention of giving it to you. However, after this conversation—"

Christian held up a hand to stop his boss, disappointed, but knowing he could better deal with the loss of the promotion if he didn't actually hear the words out loud. "I completely understand."

Douglas tipped his head and clasped his hands together on his desk. "Do you?"

Christian nodded. "You want to make sure I'm not like all those other guys, and I'm not out to use your daughter for a promotion, or anything else for that matter."

"Actually, I already know you're not like all those other men she's dated." The confidence in Douglas's voice rang true. "You've proved yourself within the company, and again today, right now, that you're a man who's loyal and values honesty. I can't ask for more than that. The sales director position is yours, Christian."

Stunned, it took a few extra seconds for the reality of Douglas's words to sink in, and when they did, Christian stood up and shook his boss's hand. "Thank you," he managed to say, still dazed.

"You're welcome. You've earned it. I was going to wait until after the first of the year to announce the promotion, but I figure there's no better time than the present."

Christian sat back down in his seat, trying to take it all in.

"Back to my daughter," Douglas said, redirecting the conversation to what Christian had originally come into his office for. "I met her for breakfast this morning, and now I know why she looked so sparkly, bright and alive. *You're* the reason."

Sparkly and bright? Christian frowned in confusion over those words. "Excuse me?"

Douglas laughed in amusement. "Ahhh, you obviously haven't seen her yet today, have you?"

"No. I wanted to talk to you first."

Creighton glanced at his wristwatch, noting the time. "Well, she should be in her office by now. And since we're done here, I suggest you don't keep my daughter waiting any longer."

Christian grinned. "Yes, sir," he said and hightailed it out of there.

RIDING ON A HUGE HIGH of adrenaline, Christian headed toward Amanda's office, and felt a surge of disappointment when he realized she wasn't inside sitting behind her desk. As he cast a quick glance around, he noticed that the double doors connecting to the private room behind her office were opened. Hearing noises from within, he stepped into the room and quietly closed and locked the doors behind him.

Moving deeper inside, he caught sight of her in the kitchenette making a pot of coffee. Her back was to him, and he waited patiently for her to finish. Finally, she turned back around and started for the doors, then came to an abrupt halt when she saw him standing there.

"Christian!" she said, her eyes wide and startled. "I didn't hear you come in."

He opened his mouth to reply, then snapped it shut again as he took in her outfit. Now he understood what her father had meant by sparkly, bright and alive. That was exactly how Amanda looked to him now. The stunning changes in her showed in her eyes, the way she carried herself and those telltale heels she was wearing on her feet that made her legs look so damn long and sexy. Then there was the scarf that he'd given her that she'd tied loosely around her neck and tucked into the lapels of her jacket. The dazzling colors looked so good on her, and a part of him wondered why she'd worn the scarf when it held so many provocative memories for the two of them.

"Wow," he finally said around the knot in his throat. "You look *amazing*." So much so that he ached to touch her, kiss her and feel her all soft and warm in his arms. They'd only spent a few days apart, and he truly missed everything about her.

"Thank you." She accepted his compliment with a smile and strolled toward him. "I'm glad you're here, because I want to talk to you."

He shook his head. "No, I want to talk to *you,* and this time you're going to listen to me. I even locked the door so you couldn't bolt on me again."

She laughed, but he didn't know what he'd said that she thought was so funny. "That really wasn't necessary."

"Yeah, well, I'm not taking any chances this time." With that said, he took her hand and led her across the room. He was glad when she didn't try and pull away because he was fully prepared to do whatever it took to make her listen to him.

When they reached the couch, he sat down, then pulled her onto his lap. She gasped, surprised by his bold move, but let him have his way and remained sitting on his thighs. A slightly amused smile tugged at her mouth, and he had no idea why she wasn't taking all this more seriously.

He made sure he had her full attention before getting started. "What I have to tell you is very straightforward and simple. When we agreed to get together this past weekend, I never thought it would be anything more than a brief affair. I also never expected that I'd fall so hard for you. But I did."

A slow breath eased out of her, and her gaze softened as she lifted her hand and touched the tips of her fingers tenderly to his jaw. "I did, too," she whispered. "I'm halfway in love with you."

Relief shuddered through him. Oh, God, he felt like the luckiest guy in the world, and he grinned like a fool. "Looks like we'll have to work on that other half, now won't we?"

She laughed huskily. "Don't worry, I have a feeling it won't take much at all for me to fall totally and completely in love with you."

He wrapped an arm around her waist and pulled her closer, so that she was pretty much plastered against his chest. "So, you'll date me?" he asked and placed a soft, teasing kiss on her lips. "You'll be my girlfriend and turn down any guy that shows even a glimmer of interest in asking you out? Because I have a feeling that those sexy shoes of yours are going to attract a whole lot of attention."

She framed his face in her hands, her eyes shining with affection and adoration, and a whole lot of happiness. "The only attention I care about is yours."

"Good answer," he said and kissed her fully and deeply, until they were both breathless and aroused. "I'm so crazy about you,

Amanda. I want to be with you. I want you to meet my family. And I really, really want to take your clothes off and make love to you, right here and now."

She shivered at his words, but the desire heating her gaze gave way to a bit of concern. "We need to tell my father about us."

"I already have." A huge grin spread across his face. "He gave me his blessing, and the promotion. I'm now officially the director of sales."

"Congratulations!" she said excitedly. "That's incredible!"

"No, you are." He touched the scarf around her neck and looked into her eyes, needing to know something. "Did you do all this for me? Wear the scarf, and the shoes, and your new outfit?"

She shook her head. "No, I did it for *me*. It was time for a change. Past time, really."

Her answer was exactly what he wanted and needed to hear. "Then you did it for all the right reasons."

She threaded her fingers through the hair at the nape of his neck. "And I have *you* to thank for making me realize who I really am deep inside."

He placed his hand on her bare knee and slowly skimmed his palm upward, loving the feel of her soft, smooth skin beneath the tips of his fingers. "Ummm, it was my pleasure."

She raised a brow. "I do believe if you continue in that direction, the pleasure is going to be all mine."

"Yours, mine, ours." He shrugged. "It's all the same."

Before she could issue a comeback, he gently, playfully tumbled her back onto the couch and pushed the hem of her skirt up to her hips. With a purely wicked grin he dipped his head and gave the inside of her thigh a love bite, which he immediately soothed with his tongue.

"Oh, yes," she moaned softly.

A thought occurred to him, and he stopped and lifted his head so he could look up at Amanda. "Uh, are Angie and Desiree here?" Now that he knew about the two, he didn't care to have them as voyeurs every time he made love to Amanda.

She laughed, obviously knowing why he'd asked that particular question. "No. They're gone. It's just you and me and no more interruptions."

"Thank God," Christian said with a laugh, then set about finishing what he'd just started.

THE NIGHTS BEFORE CHRISTMAS
Isabel Sharpe

To my sons, two of my best friends, who keep Mom young and always make her proud.

1

"OH MY GOD, Cathy, you're not going to believe this. Listen to your horoscope today."

Cathy glanced over and continued making her lunch to take with her to work—smoked ham, natural cheddar, light mayo, brown mustard and lettuce on whole-grain bread. Sometimes she went wild and put in a pickle. "Okay, let's hear it."

Her roommate, Melinda, was holding up the *New York Post,* which she devoured every morning before she went off to her waitressing job at iCi Restaurant on DeKalb Avenue, a couple of miles from their Brooklyn apartment at Eighth Street and Fifth Avenue. Melinda treated horoscopes as predictions of biblical importance.

"'A surprise gift today will lead you straight to true love.'" She lowered the paper with a jerk and stared at Cathy, her already big blue eyes even bigger. "Not only is this exactly what Madame Cassandra predicted, but today is your office's Secret Santa party!"

"Imagine that." Cathy dried the apple she'd washed and added it to her blue insulated lunch bag neatly printed with her name in permanent marker. Melinda had dragged Cathy to one of her psychic advisor appointments and insisted Cathy get a reading, too. Not to burst Melinda's bubble, but in "Madame Cassandra's" outer office, Cathy had seen an apparently overdue parking ticket addressed to Cass Brown, which made the woman seem a lot less exotic and not at all clairvoyant. Shouldn't she have foreseen getting that ticket?

Granted, occasionally Madame Cass's intuition was eerily

accurate, but most of the time Cathy could trace her "sight" back to hints and subtle signals Cathy was providing in spite of herself. Fascinating stuff, but fakery.

How hard was it to predict that in December she'd receive a gift from a loved one? Madame Cassandra had said from a man, but, hey, her Dad was a man and she loved him. Ditto her brother.

"I'm serious, Cathy. Madame Cassandra is the real deal, and this horoscope only confirms it." Melinda slapped the paper on the table and jumped up. "Let's revisit your closet. You have to look incredible today."

"Nothing wrong with this." She gestured to her olive pants and beige patterned top, which she'd ironed and laid out the night before. No way would she change her outfit because some news-paper column said—

"What if it's Quinn?"

Cathy felt a blush spread over her cheeks and knew Melinda would pounce on it. Big mistake to confess her silly crush to someone who imagined love lurking under every glance or sigh. "Be serious. Even if Quinn picked my name for Secret Santa, true love is not going to happen there."

"Why not?" Melinda's stare went on so long, Cathy wanted to clap her hands in front of her face to make her blink.

"Because he's not my type."

"How so?"

"Let me count the ways. For one thing, he's *Quinlan… Jussstin…Alexaaander.*" She drew the words out in a low, dreamy lilt, then pitched her voice high and brisk. "And I'm CathyAnnJohnson."

"What does that—"

"He's international playboy, I'm girl next door. He's calendar pinup, I'm digital photo snapped by Grandma. He's caviar and champagne, I'm PB&J and a glass of cold milk. Both good, but they don't belong together."

"I still don't—"

A familiar tap-tap-boom knock sounded on their door. Cathy's heart jumped—with relief, for one thing, to get away from Melinda's off-target matchmaking skills. And, well…Jake, their new neighbor across the hall, was very…she could definitely…

Well, mmm. And he'd been showing a lot of interest in the few weeks he'd lived here. Seemed a guy could think of a lot of reasons to drop in on his single female neighbors when he wanted to.

She let Melinda get the door and heard her chatting comfortably with Jake. Melinda could chat with anyone. She'd be her same sunny, curious, slightly flaky self talking to the Queen of England. *Hey, there, Elizabeth, great hat. So what's your sign?*

Footsteps approached. Cathy folded over the Velcro flap of her lunch bag and tucked it carefully into her black leather tote, trying to appear oh-so-nonchalant.

"Hi, Cathy. How's it going?"

"Hi, Jake." She stepped out of their kitchen and was very glad she did. He must have just gotten out of the shower; his dark hair had curled from the wet, making him look even more boyish and appealing. "How are you liking life in the ugliest building in New York?"

"Not bad. At least we don't have to look at the exterior from in here." He smiled and rocked back and forth on his heels, glancing at Melinda a couple of times. "So, Cathy, are you on your way out?"

She checked her watch. She didn't have to leave for seven minutes. "Not just yet."

"Oh. Okay, well, I was going to walk with you…." He glanced at Melinda again. "So we could talk."

"You know what?" Melinda grabbed her newspaper and winked up at Jake, who topped her by about two feet. "I have a sudden urge to go to my room. See you later."

Cathy's heart started to thumpa-thumpa; she tossed back her hair to cover her nerves. "What's up?"

He grinned and his eyes got warmer than she'd ever seen them, which caused warmth to spread over her cheeks again, darn it. Blush, blush, blush. Embarrassing how easily she flustered.

"You look very pretty today."

Cathy laughed. "You say that every time you see me. One of these days you'll drop by and I'll be unwashed and horrifying and then you won't be able to."

"I doubt that." He looked her up and down in a way she usually hated men doing, but this time…okay, she still hated it. She never knew if they were lusting or tallying up her figure flaws. "You know, Cathy, there is nothing more wonderful than waking up on a Saturday morning before Christmas, rolling out of bed and going out to brunch. Don't you think?"

"I…well, sure, yes." Blush-blush-blush. *Stop it!* She'd been asked out plenty of times but had yet to find a way past the awkwardness surrounding a first date. "It sounds really nice."

"Yeah?" He took a step closer. "You want to do that with me tomorrow?"

"What, roll out of bed?" She grinned at her joke, but instead of laughing, Jake looked startled and then…enthusiastic.

Um, no. Get to know each other first, sex after. "I was kidding…"

"Oh. Right." He lifted one shoulder in a half shrug. "A man can always hope. Just brunch then?"

"Brunch definitely." A great start to the holiday weekend. She liked Jake a lot.

"Excellent." He backed away a few steps, then jerked his thumb toward the door. "You coming?"

"Oh. Yes." She picked up her bag and coat, considered stepping into her warm, waterproof but extremely unsexy boots and changed her mind. Most of the snow had melted. The sidewalks wouldn't be that bad.

"Cathy?" Melinda chose that moment to burst out of her room. "Hang on a second, you forgot your…um…"

She glanced around wildly, found nothing—since Cathy always got everything ready the night before—and frowned. "Can I talk to you a sec?"

"Sure." Cathy turned apologetically to Jake. "Meet you downstairs?"

"I'm on it." He gave a sexy boy-next-door grin, waved to Melinda and left.

"So? So? So?" Melinda rushed over, blond curls bouncing. "Tell all!"

"Honestly, Melinda." Cathy shoved her arm into her coat. "I'm going to be late."

"Did he ask you out?"

Cathy's smile ruined her perfect exasperated attitude. "Yes. Brunch tomorrow."

"Ooh! I knew it! I knew it! I'm totally jealous. He is supremely hot." She patted her chest as if to calm her heart. "So, okay. He just has to give you a present today and—"

"For crying out loud." The exasperation sailed back in. "He does *not* have to—"

"Yes, he does. That way you'll know if it's true love or not. If it's not, can I have him?"

"Melinda." She used her mother's let's-get-this-straight voice, then sighed and gave up. "I'm going to work. See you later."

She met Jake in the tan minimalist lobby of their bizarrely shaped building famous for having been built without right angles. Undoubtedly the architect considered it a masterpiece of design. She'd like to point out that he hadn't chosen to live here. But in this city, if you were lucky enough to find affordable, clean and comfortable, you didn't worry about aesthetics.

They strode down Eighth Street together toward the Fourth Avenue subway, Cathy nearly running to keep up in her low heels, toes rapidly chilling, wishing for her unsexy warm boots. "How do you like living in New York?"

"It's different." He dodged to avoid a pedestrian and veered back next to her. "I miss Boston. But when your boss says, 'An opportunity has arisen that we'd like you to take advantage of,' you don't say, 'No, thanks.'"

"What do you like better about Boston?"

"Easier to negotiate. A big city with a small-town feel. Brooklyn is nearly like it, but downtown—" he gestured in the direction of Manhattan "—is deadening."

"I hear you." She told herself it meant nothing that they both took the same view of New York. Like millions of other people didn't feel that way? "I moved here five years ago from Chicago—where I went to college—to be closer to my family. Sometimes I miss the relative calm of the Midwest."

"I bet."

"Would you go back to Boston if you got the chance?"

"Right now? In a heartbeat. There's another management consulting firm there I'm pretty sure would snap me up if I went back. But I've been with Bronson and Company for seven really good years and I haven't been here long enough to give New York a fair shot. Ask me again in six months?"

"I will." She liked thinking about him still being around in six months. Horoscope notwithstanding, maybe this *was* the beginning of something really good….

They reached the Fourth Avenue subway at Ninth Street and clambered companionably down the stairs and through the turnstile. Cathy would take the F train to Times Square and Jake the R train to Wall Street. "Have a good day at work."

"You, too." Jake raised his eyebrows. "Hope Secret Santa brings you something you really like."

She gaped. "How did you hear about that?"

"Melinda."

"I should have known." Cathy laughed uncomfortably, wondering what else Melinda had been telling him. "She's obsessed with that astrology stuff."

"I gathered. It can be pretty interesting. So I'll see you tomorrow morning, if not before." He touched her shoulder and cleared his throat awkwardly. "I…hope before."

"Oh." She got the sudden feeling he'd been about to say something else, but she hadn't a clue what. "Me, too."

"Have fun at your party." He winked and lifted a hand in farewell.

"Thanks." She let their eye contact linger, and started off toward her train with the feeling he was standing watching her. Luckily she avoided tripping, though she didn't go so far as to risk a seductive wiggle.

Jake seemed perfect for her in a lot of ways, and she was happy he was interested. Fireworks weren't going off between them, but she was probably being stupid expecting so much when they hadn't even gone out yet. Her mom and dad had been happily married for thirty-five years, and Mom told her fireworks hadn't started until their fourth or fifth date.

Even if fireworks never showed up, there was more to life and love than instant chemistry. More important things to build a relationship on.

Still, she couldn't help hoping something would start sizzling as they got to know each other better. Didn't have to be big-bang, cover-the-sky-with-stars fireworks. Bottle rockets would work. Even a couple of good-size sparklers...

She did manage to daydream about Jake and get fluttery over their date all the way to Times Square. Then out of the train into the sea of jostling, rushing bodies, up the stairs and onto the sidewalk trimmed with dirty snow, heading for the glass-and-steel Jackman Butler Building, where she'd been photo coordinator for the food-and-travel magazine *Connoisseur* for the past five years. Then through the revolving door into the sleek black-and-white marble lobby where shoe and boot heels clicked and thudded and murmured conversations echoed. Then through security, nodding to the guards, past the company's Christmas tree, flawlessly decorated as usual, this year in red and gold.

At the elevator, she exchanged greetings with a woman from the HR department and stood waiting in the small crowd of employees, many already holding steaming cups of coffee as if they couldn't even last the trip up to their offices without a chemical boost.

The gold doors opened, bodies piled in; the elevator began its stop-and-start ascension. Cathy got off on the twenty-sixth floor, where the photo department lay in the southeast corner of the building. Her first month, she'd gotten lost nearly every time she'd come to work and had spent several panicked minutes every morning striding purposefully through the maze of clustered cubicles and offices, trying to look as if she knew where she was going.

The magazine had completed its holiday issue months

previously—they were now working well into spring—but in the offices, Christmas and Hanukkah reigned. Her department's three-foot tree had been funkily decorated with photographs, plastic eating utensils, tiny kitchen gadgets, corks, Pepto-Bismol tablets, used boarding passes and foil-covered chocolates.

Neatly piled around it, the colored, ribboned stack of Secret Santa presents. Cathy casually rummaged in her tote for her gift of flavored coffees and a hefty Starbucks gift certificate for Bill, the senior photo editor and resident java addict, plunked it down and beat a hasty retreat to her desk, located on the short side of a nearby L-shaped grouping of cubicles.

On the Friday before a major holiday, the mood was festive, and thoughts of Jake and the Secret Santa party—and, okay, even the dopey horoscope—made work nearly unbearable. She could honestly say she got nearly nothing accomplished all morning, most likely along with everyone else. Now, pleasantly full from lunch, staring blankly at her computer screen, she just needed to kill a little more time until the party started. Maybe she could do some research on—

"How is Cathy Johnson today?"

She started and looked up into the square-jawed, clean-shaven, blue-eyed face of staff photographer *Quinlan…Jussstin…Alex-aaander,* who was looking at her as if he really wanted to know how she was instead of just hurling the question out as a greeting. He'd been in the office quite a bit over the last two weeks and had been coming to chat nearly every day, be still her heart. Clearly he needed more to do with his time. "She's fine. And how are you?"

"Fine, huh?" He picked up a pen and half sat on her desk, next to the neat stack of folders Bill had asked her to pull and the picture of her family on a ski vacation in New Hampshire. "Would you tell me if you were miserable?"

"Probably not." She grinned stupidly. "But you haven't told me how you are, either."

"Me?" He quirked an eyebrow and gave her a devilish look that was so sexy she had to do deep breathing to keep herself from blushing. "I'm fine."

Cathy laughed too loudly and stopped herself too abruptly. Why couldn't she be at least somewhat collected around Quinn the way she could be around Jake? "Glad to hear it."

"What are your plans for the holidays?"

"I'm going to my parents' house. As usual. In Westchester. My brother is coming, too. With his family. What about you?"

"Same, only Princeton, not Westchester." He tapped the pen against his palm, looking at her much too intently for her comfort. But then, he looked at everyone that way. She'd seen him reduce Bianca, their no-nonsense art director, to outright giggles. "And I've got two brothers to your one. Much older."

"Oh." She nodded rapidly, her mind infuriatingly blank of appropriate follow-up questions. "That sounds fun."

"It is—for about two hours." He gazed off across the office. "Until Dad and my brothers start making snide remarks about my job, since I'm not a CEO or a surgeon."

"Ow." Cathy winced. "That doesn't sound fun."

"Nope."

She waited eagerly, in case he felt like telling her more personal details.

Which apparently he didn't. "And then you're leaving for London on Tuesday for the year?"

"Yes, Cathy. A whole year. I'll do my last assignment for *Connoisseur* there. Then I'll be studying photography at Sotheby's Institute of Art and sharing a studio with my friend John." He turned back and eyed her gravely. "Can you live without me that long?"

In spite of the double backflip her heart executed, she managed to look equally grave. "I'm not sure, but…I think so."

"If you can't, let me know. Or, better yet, catch a flight and come—"

"Oh, what, you're hitting on Cathy now? Honestly, forget *one* girl in every port, this guy's got dozens." Sandra Dentyne, beautiful, sexy, supremely annoying office slut, sidled up to Quinn and ran her hand down his arm. "You like it that way, huh?"

"What's not to like?" He shrugged innocently.

"You're depraved. *And* you're wanted at the party, so gather up your latest sweet young thing and come on." Sandra sauntered off, giving Quinn a look of pretend exasperation she undoubtedly meant to be flirty.

Blech.

"Well, then, let's go." Quinn grinned as if he and Cathy were sharing an unspoken joke and flipped the pen back onto her desk. "This'll be my first Secret Santa event. Usually I'm out of town."

"Oh, right. You are. Usually." She sighed. Could she sound *any* stupider? "It's pretty fun."

Great, Cathy, *fun* again. This was *fun* and that was *fun* and, whee, she was coming across as soooo sophisticated. Not that it mattered, really, except for her own self-esteem. But you'd think since he'd come over to her desk fairly regularly over the past two weeks that she'd be able to react with a few more of her brain cells functional.

"So, Cathy, tell me." He leaned in closer, tousled sandy hair falling forward, dark blue eyes making her want to gasp and move back. "Are you my Secret Santa?"

She shook her head and let out a nervous burst of laughter.

"Darn." He sat up straight again and winked. "I was hoping you'd buy me something sexy and outrageous."

"Oh." Okay. Blush. Big-time. She couldn't help it. Why he was flirting with her, she hadn't a clue. Maybe he was bored. The past two weeks must have been pretty dull for him. He was used to travel and adventure and hot babes all over him. She just wasn't sure why, in a building bursting with tall, skinny, elegant women, he'd bother landing on her desk. She wasn't tall, skinny *or* elegant, though she did manage to be a woman. "Well...I..."

"Sorry." He slid off her desk. "Didn't mean to embarrass you. Let's head over."

"No. It's fine." *Aw, hell.* She got up and walked with him toward the central area where the tree stood. She had to salvage this before he thought she was a complete loser prude. "I was just picturing what I could get you."

"Oh?" He turned, that sexy amused look on his face again. "What?"

Good question. But she was *not* going to freeze up and act the idiot again.

"How about…" Inspiration struck. "One of those thongs with the strategically placed elephant head. Where it's your job to provide the trunk."

There. Now please don't let him be horrified.

He wasn't. He threw back his head and laughed so loudly other members of the staff gathering for the party stopped talking and looked over.

"What's the joke?" This from Ron, tall and reed-thin with out-of-control hair dyed black, easily the nosiest person on the planet.

"None of your business." Quinn winked at Cathy, still chuckling. "But I'm starting to think this woman has a side she doesn't show at work."

"Naturally." Cathy attempted an air of mystery and escaped to join the party. She chose a chair at one end of the tight semi-circle around the tree and tried to control her disappointment when nosy Ron sat next to her, and Quinn took a seat opposite. Oh, how mature. She was all whupped up hoping to bump shoulders with him. What a dorky crush. She'd just agreed to go out with Jake this morning and here she was drooling over someone else. What was wrong with this picture?

The last employee—workaholic Bill—showed up and chose a seat, and the present opening started. Big laughs over the practically soft-porn Working Men calendar for openly gay Dan. Big oohs and aahs over the CD of famous arias for music-loving Glenda. Appreciative *mmm*s for the coffee selection Cathy bought Bill. And then it was her turn. A flat box shoved into her lap, a half circle of attentive faces.

She slid the ribbon off, started to carefully loosen the tape, then gave in when the staff protested and ripped the paper off. Up came the top of the box, and she rummaged in the tissue to find—

Oh, jeez. A bright red lingerie set made of lace and…more lace, trimmed with white marabou, like something Mrs. Claus would wear to get down and dirty with Santa. Very tiny. Very sexy. And embroidered in white across the panties: *Seduce me*.

Ron caught sight immediately and let out a lewd yell.

"Hold it up!" Dan shouted.

Face burning—what a surprise—she held it up, and the room erupted into howls and teasing.

"Look!" Ron snatched a red envelope out of the box that had *Private* written in big block letters and ripped it open, yanking out a card with a giant bouquet of red roses on the front. "*Ooh. Let's see who it's from.*"

"*Ron.*" She grabbed the card back and sat on it. No more mortification. Whoever had given her this totally personal and fairly inappropriate gift wanted the card read when she was alone. No way was she letting anyone else see.

Whoever had given her this…

A gift. Today. As her horoscope predicted her true love would, even though, of course, she didn't believe in that stuff.

Who?

She perused the circle of boisterous faces and came to a sudden stop when she locked eyes with *Quinlan…Jussstin… Alexaaander.* Who wasn't laughing or making rude remarks but sitting quietly, watching her with that amused half smile that made her a little crazy.

And before her stunned brain could even begin to formulate another thought concerning the circumstances…

He winked.

2

CATHY EXITED THE revolving door of the Jackman Butler Building and stepped out into the darkening neon-lit chaos of Times Square. The temperature had dropped sharply during the day and a biting breeze sent pedestrians scurrying for warmer destinations.

Bring it on. She was still so overheated and flustered and dazed and whatever else she was that a little icy edge might cool her off and bring her back to reality.

As soon as the furor in the office had calmed, teasing stopped and partying started, she'd slipped away to the bathroom, the only place she could be sure to read the card accompanying her gift in private.

Surprised to get this at the office? You shouldn't be. Necessity is the mother of invention, and I need to get to know you a lot better—you've probably figured that out by the signals I've been sending lately. Come over tonight, eight o'clock—I don't have to tell you the address. Whether you wear the lace or not, whether you want to talk or do a whole lot more, I'll be waiting. Guess Who.

That same card was now in the bottom of her practical black bag, along with the, er, unpractical gift. She'd read the note probably twenty times. Surprised? Um, yeah. Signals? Well, Quinn had been coming by fairly frequently and, yes, flirting. But she never imagined he'd been doing anything more than killing time. In fact, she'd assumed he was rotating among several single women in several offices and chatting them all up.

His address? No, he didn't have to tell her that; she was in charge of all their photographers' files and had easily found out where he lived in Tribeca.

Now the million-dollar question. Would she go? And if she did go, did she want to talk or "do a whole lot more"?

Gulp.

She laughed suddenly, and a guy exiting the subway shot her a "What have you been smoking?" look. This was so unreal! *Quinn* wanted *her?* She laughed again and started down the steps, the stale underground warmth competing with the chill above, blowing up dust and bits of paper that made her squint.

All the way to Brooklyn she sat rigid, cheeks hot, eyes bright, fighting bubbling energy urging her to get up and dance. Either she was over-the-moon excited or she was coming down with a high fever that would probably prove fatal.

Cathy and Quinn. It still didn't seem possible, no matter how many times she tried it out in her imagination. Thank goodness Melinda would be at work tonight, because Cathy wasn't even going to think about the silly horoscope. Quinn had issued an invitation to a one-night stand. Hers to accept or decline. Period.

On the one hand, what did she have to lose? She could go, model the underwear, spend the night with him as countless women no doubt had done, then say good-night and thanks for the memories. He'd be off to England for an entire year, and she'd be free to start a relationship with Jake.

On the other, she could stay safely at home and not feel like a sleazeball tramp in polyester lace with tacky marabou, and not risk being a major disappointment to him and not face any embarrassment or destruction of the fantasy. Then he'd be off to England for an entire year, and she'd be free to start a relationship with Jake.

And spend the rest of her life wondering what Quinn Alexander would have been like to…uh, be with.

The train reached her stop, and she trudged through the crowded car and station with the other exiting bodies, past a scary-looking musician butchering "Silent Night" on his saxophone. Day in and out she worked this routine. How often did a chance for something daring and different come her way? How often had she gotten to play the seductress? Tim, her only serious boyfriend since she graduated from Northwestern five years ago, had treated sex as a sacred act, so she'd never felt comfortable trying anything playful. And seducing Quinn would be a sure thing—the invitation lay in her bag. It wasn't as if she'd be showing up unannounced, way out of her league and risking rejection.

She climbed the steps out onto Fourth Avenue and sucked in a lungful of frigid air.

So did this mean she was going to do it? Put on sexy underwear, go to his apartment tonight and…do it?

Why not?

She practically ran home, and not because her toes had started to turn numb after half a block. She was going to do this. She, CathyAnnJohnson, was going to seduce Quinlan…Jussstin… Alexaaander.

An hour later she stood in front of her mirror, staring at her body in the red lace lingerie.

No way was she going to do this.

The lingerie was her size—Quinn undoubtedly had plenty of practice measuring women with his eyes—but while this kind of underwear always looked so alluring resting gracefully on the nonhips of catalog models, on her…well, the bright scarlet of the material made her skin look even whiter than it was. Her tummy wasn't exactly flat and toned, and the tiny elastic band on the panties dug in and made unappetizing bulges over and under. Her boobs might be happy and uplifted, but her arms looked soft since she still had a week and a half until her annual New Year's resolution to get in shape, which would last for two or three months of a gym membership until she got bored or busy and stopped going.

Aw, hell.

She took the lingerie off and tossed it disgustedly onto her bed. Forget it. Time spent with Quinn between the sheets would have to remain in her fantasies. Undoubtedly a much better place for it.

She pulled on plain white panties and a pair of gray sweats.

Melinda was working, so no company there tonight. And though Jake had politely said he hoped to see Cathy before tomorrow, it would be overeager overkill to knock on his door tonight when they had a date in the morning.

Whoopee. Instead of making wild, passionate love with the sexiest man alive, she'd spend the evening in an all too usual fashion—knitting, watching TV, wearing sweats.

Cathy crossed her arms over her breasts and gazed at the lingerie, scarlet and wanton, lying on her sweet flowery bedspread. She felt guilty for lusting after Quinn while she should be thinking about Jake in those terms. But a night with Quinn represented her chance to leave sweet and flowery behind, to try out scarlet and wanton just for tonight. Maybe the only chance she'd ever get.

If she and Jake became lovers, they'd do it the sensible way, which was her preference when starting a relationship. Dating a few times, becoming closer, eventually kissing—with all the trimmings—then finally, when each felt ready to make the commitment to an exclusive relationship, finding their way into the sack.

A night with Quinn could be fabulously unsensible. Forget eventually, forget finally. Now, tonight, immediately, what they both wanted. The kind of spontaneous go-for-it move Cathy never gave herself permission to make—with good reason. There lay the way to misunderstanding, heartbreak and possible serial killers.

But Quinn was leaving the country, so whatever happened tonight would soon be erased. She wouldn't have to face him in the office, worry about what would happen next, fret when he didn't call….

She screwed up her face, sucked in a long breath, then started tearing off the sweats and cotton.

Okay, Cathy Ann Johnson. This is it. Your big chance to be somebody you'll never be in real life.

Two hours later, standing in front of Quinn's building on North Moore Street in Tribeca, staring up at the third floor, shivering like crazy, Cathy Ann Johnson was starting to think trying to be someone else was a really stupid idea. She'd taken off the lingerie and put it back on twice more before she'd made it this far. She did have it on now but had worn a pink sweater and black stretch jeans over it, so if she lost her nerve, it would stay hidden.

After fifteen minutes waffling in the street, she was sure her nose and ears were as pink as the sweater…and what a sexy look that wasn't. Her choice had become going in, possibly embarrassing herself in front of someone she wouldn't see again for at least a year…or losing fingers or toes to frostbite.

Hmm.

She rolled her eyes and walked to his front door for the fifth try. This time she actually pressed the buzzer. Then, as adrenaline surged and took her shivering to a new and ridiculous level, she wished to God she hadn't. Could she run away? Or pretend to be a pizza delivery gone wild?

"Yeah?" His voice was deep and sexy, even distorted by the intercom system.

"Hi, Quinn. It's…Cathy. Johnson." Nearly an hour late.

"Cathy." He sounded surprised but pleasantly. He must have thought by now she'd decided not to come. "Wow, hey, come on up. Third floor."

"Thanks." The buzzer sounded. She pushed the heavy wood-and-glass door open and stepped into the lobby, small but immaculate, done in cream and olive-green, with about a dozen strategically placed pots of poinsettias and a huge wreath on the wall opposite, decorated with gold pine cones and a red velvet ribbon.

Most importantly it was blissfully warm. She waited a minute or two for her nose and fingers to regain full feeling, but her shivering barely subsided. How seductive was a quivering mess of a person?

She didn't want to answer that. Instead she forced herself into the tiny elevator, pressed three, then leaned against the back of the car. A small mirror hung to her left. She launched herself forward and peered into the glass.

Oh, thank goodness. She looked really nice. Her nose wasn't that pink, but her cheeks were, and her eyes were big and full of sparkling energy he didn't need to know was terror.

Maybe this would work.

The doors opened. She stepped off the elevator into a narrow hallway, and there he was, leaning against the jamb of his open door in jeans and a white T-shirt with a loose blue shirt open over it.

Oh, baby.

She sauntered toward him, managing what she hoped was a sultry smile. So help her God if she started stuttering and being Cathylike, she'd never forgive herself. This was it. Her shot. To prove she was worth red marabou-trimmed lace that begged, *Seduce me.*

The door on the left side of the hall burst open, and a white-haired woman in a bright red bathrobe emerged, holding a tiny plastic bag.

"Oh, hello, dear." She was undoubtedly speaking to Quinn, but she was eyeing Cathy speculatively, then glancing at Quinn, then giving Cathy another once-over, making Cathy completely flustered. For a change. "I'm just taking my trash out."

She held up the bag, which couldn't contain more than a couple of tissues.

Beside her, Cathy heard Quinn exhale in exasperation. "Hi, Mrs. Hoffman."

"Introduce me to your...*friend?*"

Quinn made the introductions, looking as if he'd rather tell her to go away permanently.

"Well." Mrs. Hoffman clapped her hands together, making the plastic bag swish loudly, and winked. "I'm sure you'll have a *wonderful evening.*"

Not only did she say *wonderful evening* as if she meant *kinky sex,* but then she stood there as if expecting she'd be invited in to watch.

Quinn thanked her, took Cathy's hand, propelled her through his door and closed it on Mrs. Hoffman, still standing hopefully outside.

"Busybody." He put his hands on his hips, shaking his head.

"Yeah, there's one in every building." Was there? She had no idea. It just sounded like the thing to say.

"True." He stood looking almost as expectant as Mrs. Hoffman had. "So...hi."

"Hi. Well. I'm…" She raised her arms out to the side. "Here."

"So you are." He spoke in that way he did, looking right into her eyes, and her heart gave a wild leap, then took off in an erratic rhythm that would probably break an EKG machine. "Come on in."

He gestured her into his living room, which looked exactly as she'd expected. Tasteful, not cluttered but hardly minimalist. Sophisticated, a few antiquey-looking pieces mixed with more modern. Photographs on the walls, some undoubtedly his own, some reproductions of the greats: Ansel Adams, Alfred Stieglitz, Man Ray… And on his coffee table, a tiny tree strung with small white lights, blue-and-red balls and tinsel.

"Nice place. Do you own or rent?" She turned her back on him, stomach sinking, pretending to examine a carved stone box on top of a small bookcase. *Good job, Cathy. Keep the hot sex talk coming.*

"I own it."

"Ah." She put the box down, slightly panicked. They both knew what she was here for, and she chose to discuss real estate? How did one casually segue into *Do me now, you hot love stud*? "And…so…are you renting when you leave for England?"

"My parents and brothers will use the place when they're in the city." He approached and stopped close behind her. She turned and smiled, so nervous her lip did a stupid quivery thing. Was she ever going to be able to look at him without falling apart?

"Would you like a drink?"

"Yes, thank you." She nearly gasped out her relief. Alcohol was a must to take the edge off this fear.

"Whiskey? Scotch? Brandy? Beer? Wine?"

"Oh. Well…" She tried to keep her voice low and sexy, praying she was remotely convincing. She didn't care what she drank as long as it was strong. "Brandy."

"Sounds good to me, too." He crossed to a dark wooden cabinet in the corner of the room and pulled out a brand that even Cathy knew was not cheap and two enormous snifters into which he poured generous amounts.

"Here you go." He handed her the glass, touched his to hers. "I'm glad you showed up tonight, Cathy."

"I am, too." She took a healthy sip and immediately started to relax as the powerful liquid burned down into her stomach, leaving a sweet, warm aftertaste. "I almost didn't."

"Why not?"

Aw, hell. She was supposed to be trying out the experienced-seductress role here. Now what? *Because I had so many men to choose from.*

Ew. She couldn't bring herself to shovel that much bull at him. "To tell you the truth, I wasn't sure I'd have the nerve."

He swirled his glass, inhaled over it and took a long, slow, practiced sip, the only person she'd ever seen indulge the ritual and not look like a pretentious idiot. "But you found it."

"Somehow." She drank more herself, not elegantly but with purpose—her nerve was becoming stronger by the second. "It's not like I do this a lot."

He put on her favorite half-amused look. "Which 'this' are you doing, exactly?"

Her hand tightened on her glass. He was asking, *Do you want to talk or do a whole lot more?*

This time she didn't have to think it over. "I have something to show you."

His eyebrow lifted. She took one more sip of brandy and put the glass on an end table beside his burgundy sofa. Then she stood straight and tall, trying to keep her legs from shaking, slowly reached down and took hold of the hem of her sweater. Slowly again, she pulled it up, up, until her breasts, barely covered by the red lace, felt the cooler air of his apartment. Up and up and...*ow.*

Her earring snagged the loose knit and pulled hard. *Ow.*

This could not be happening. She brought the material down an inch and tried again. Up and up and...*ow.*

Great. Just fabulous. She was standing there with her sweater covering her face, arms raised, boobs waving in the breeze... stuck.

She'd never actually wanted to have a heart attack before, but it would be a nice distraction. "Um…Quinn?"

"Yeah." His voice was close but—thank God—serious. If he'd been snorting and chortling, she would have died without the heart attack.

"My…earring caught on the sweater."

"No problem." He helped pull the material away from her face, which was undoubtedly pinker than the sweater, and started untangling wire from wool.

In the process, his fingers brushed her neck, which was the first time he'd touched her. And even though he'd done it to extricate her from a clumsy and mortifying situation, and even though she envied frogs hiding in the mud in the bottom of their ponds right now, she still felt a sharp thrill. Such was the power of Quinn Alexander.

The tug in her earlobe released; the sweater relaxed back where it had been when she'd walked in. "Thanks."

"You're welcome." He rested his hand briefly on her shoulder, then dropped it to his side.

Well. Here she was, with her fantasy man in his apartment, all her clothes on, feeling like a complete idiot. Worse, he was looking at her not with burning lust but with gentle sympathy, which at least beat scorn, but not by much.

She should have stayed home. She needed remedial lessons even for Seduction 101.

"You know, Quinn, this could probably be more embarrassing, but only if a flock of pigeons flew overhead right now and let me have it. Otherwise, I think I've reached the uppermost limit."

His grin came on quickly and faded slowly, while he gave her that intent Quinn look. "Maybe we should take this a little slower."

"That would probably be good." She hoped she didn't sound too miserable. Frankly she wasn't sure she was up to seduction part *deux*. Maybe he'd take the lead. Or maybe just talking was a better idea.

"Come on. Bring your drink."

She picked up her brandy. "Where are we going?"

"We can sit in bed and talk until we're comfortable enough to check out the underwear again. Okay?"

"Okay." She followed him through the living room down a short hallway to a door on the left, feeling a little warm and fuzzy, which wasn't at all what she'd expected. But Mr. International Playboy had just proposed something very sweet. Hanging out on his bed and talking sounded even better than sex. More…legit. More as though he cared about her as a person, not just a body in hot lingerie.

Right. *Paging Cathy Ann Johnson. Cathy Ann Johnson. Please return immediately from fantasyland.*

Honestly. Next she'd start believing in Melinda's true-love horoscope. Quinn had plenty of practice making women comfortable enough to get naked. He was a man on the job. She'd be a fool to start romanticizing him now.

His bedroom was done in the same tasteful manner as the rest of the place. Books and music crammed floor-to-ceiling shelves along one wall. No TV, and she didn't remember seeing one in the living room either. No sports memorabilia, no trophies. So he wasn't like her brother, consumed half the year by the Mets and the other half by the Giants or Knicks or Rangers.

"Here we are." He turned on a lamp on the oak desk at the back of the room and tipped the shade toward the wall. Then sat on the bed, swung his legs up, moved over and patted the dark blue comforter beside him. "All aboard."

She took off her shoes and sat next to him, less nervous than she had been in his living room. He arranged the pillows comfortably at their backs, then clinked her glass with his again and they both drank. The brandy burned less going down now and fortified her more. The seduction pressure was off. She was going to spend intimate time with her fantasy man.

This could be totally fun.

"Question-and-answer time." Her fantasy man settled himself against the pillow. "Tell me, Cathy…."

"Yes?"

"What's your favorite food when you're sad?"

She shot him a sideways look, equal parts surprised and charmed by the question. "You'll laugh."

"Try me."

"Okay." A deep, dramatic breath, as if she needed it for courage. "Oreos."

"That's funny?"

"Dipped in peanut butter."

"Still not funny."

"Then rainbow sprinkles."

"Hmm…"

"And mayonnaise."

He pressed his hand to his mouth as if to stop himself spewing brandy. "Please say you're kidding."

"I am." She giggled. "About the mayo."

"Good." He drained his glass and leaned over to put it on the floor. "Oreos with peanut butter and sprinkles is a perfect sad food. Why did you think I'd laugh?"

Cathy shrugged. "I don't know. Yours is probably loin of venison with juniper berry reduction."

"Ha! *Now* I'm laughing. Why would you think that?"

"Because…" She examined her glass, feeling foolish. "You're so…"

"Stuffy?"

"*No,* not at all." She turned toward him, and her heart lurched again when she met those deep, perfect eyes that turned down slightly at the corners and made her—

"Okay, not stuffy. Then what?"

She forced her gaze to her own feet so she could follow the conversation. "Experienced and…sophisticated and smooth and…"

"Macaroni and cheese. From a box. With a side of Ho Hos."

"Yeah?" She turned to him again, wondering what it was about being here on his bed that made him seem less intimidating, less fantasylike, in spite of the jolt she got from eye contact with him. Maybe it was the idea of him eating macaroni and cheese and Ho Hos to make himself feel better. Or even the idea that a man like Quinn had anything to be that upset about.

"Yeah. Now ask me one."

"Okay." She took another sip and moved to a more comfortable position, giddy at their unexpected camaraderie. "What's your favorite country to visit?"

"Since I'm going there next week, England."

"And if you weren't going there next week?"

"England."

"Why?"

"No language barriers, good restaurants in London, great pub culture. Short distances to Scotland, Wales, Ireland, the continent. I lived outside London as an exchange student when I was a boy and went back to spend a couple of summers after that. So it's a little like a second home."

"And what made you want to spend a year there now?"

"That's two questions, Cathy."

She grimaced, squashing a cheap thrill at the sound of his deep voice saying her name. "I cheated."

"Full pardon." He sent a contemplative stare out into the room. "I'm going because I've started feeling restless and dissatisfied, though I love my job at *Connoisseur*. Even though individual assignments still fascinate me, every year it feels like more of the same. I'm traveling to places only long enough to capture a surface portrait, then back home only long enough to reconnect with my life before I have to leave again. I want to delve more deeply into photography, academically speaking. And try my hand at some of my own artistic work. Not to mention just be in one place for a while."

"Wow." God, he had depth, too. More than that, she could relate to his feelings of restless dissatisfaction, only instead of traveling abroad and seeking new enriching challenges, she'd taken up knitting again.

She dared another glance at him. Who could resist? But just a glance or she'd start staring again like an adoring puppy. "That sounds incredible."

"It is what it is."

"I've never been anywhere."

"Nowhere?" He was clearly skeptical.

"Well, Canada. And summers in Vermont. And on a Caribbean cruise. And my family took a road trip out west. And—"

"That's not anywhere?"

"Well it's not...exotic and—"

"The Caribbean isn't exotic?"

"I mean it's..." She gestured impatiently toward the window with her glass. "Mostly I'm here."

"In the most culturally rich, dynamic, sophisticated city in the world. Yeah, I'd say you've barely lived."

"No, but..."

He reached over and—oh, heaven—laid his hand on her thigh. "Why are you putting yourself down? You do that at the office, too."

"I do?" She stared at the long, strong fingers spanning her leg, feeling his warmth seeping through to her skin, and she started to think that maybe talking wasn't going to be quite enough to see her through the evening.

"You told me you always eat boring food for lunch and—"

"I do eat boring food for lunch."

"—and you aren't as sexy as Gwyneth in editorial and—"

"She used to be a model! She's unbelievable."

"—Gerard Butler wouldn't look at you twice and—"

"He wouldn't."

"What makes you so sure?" He gestured, which meant he had to take his hand off her thigh, which she thought should be made illegal in all fifty states.

"Well, come on." She finished her brandy, happy and glowing, and put the glass on his bedside table. "He's...have you seen this man?"

"Yes. But he hasn't seen you, so you don't know."

"Oh, for—" She rolled her eyes in pretend exasperation. "I'm not the kind who turns heads. It's not a big deal, I'm not making myself out to be some gruesome Griselda, it's just the truth."

He turned toward her, head still resting against the wall. "You turned mine."

She caught her breath and gave up holding back the adoring-puppy stare, because there was nothing else she could do. "Oh...but..."

"But what? Would I have invited you into bed if I wasn't attracted to you?"

"That was the underwear." She was moving her mouth, words were coming out, but all she was aware of was blue, blue eyes that were looking at her with heat that reflected itself in some of her body's very favorite places.

"Even if you'd shown up without the underwear."

"Really?" She felt as if she were at the top of a high, very slippery slope, peering down and wondering how that first step would feel.

"*Especially* if you'd shown up without it." He gave a Groucho Marx waggle to his eyebrows and she burst out laughing. Saved from herself, thank goodness. Saved by this totally unexpected side of him that she was loving. At the office he was smooth, sexy, übermasculine, charming, sometimes flirty but not like this—casual and boyish and just...fun.

"My turn to ask you something, Cathy Ann Johnson."

She managed to stop laughing, but giggles stayed at the ready. "Okay."

"Where do you live?"

"In the ugliest building in Brooklyn, Fifth Avenue and Eighth Street."

"Eighth Street? I know that address. I love that building. It looks like some fabulous futuristic castle."

"Uh...it looks like someone ripped up the blueprints, taped them randomly back together and said, 'Okay, build this.'"

"When you get home, look again."

She made a face and shrugged. "If you say so."

"I promise it will be worth it." He nudged her gently with his shoulder.

She kept her eyes on her lap, suddenly nervous again and not sure why. "Okay. I'll look."

He nudged her again and a giggle worked its way up, seeking

escape. She turned to find him closer and the urge to giggle sprinted away.

"It's the kind of building you might not appreciate right away, even if you can't help noticing it. But once you see it in the right light and with the right attitude, you can't help being drawn to it. You should try to see that and understand."

"Okay." Her voice came out a whisper. He'd been talking about an ugly hunk of masonry, and somehow she was left feeling as if he'd been telling her she was the most wonderful, special person he'd ever met.

"Good." He smiled just enough to move his mouth and warm his eyes. Up this close, she could see the strong line of his jaw shadowed gold-brown with the evening's stubble, a tiny scar on the bridge of his nose and the shallow-lined texture of his lips. "Now you ask me something."

"Okay." She was caught again in his mesmerizing gaze, but this time her heart kept a steadier rhythm and her shyness began to recede. This was good. This was right. This was going to happen just the way it should. "What do you look like naked?"

"I'll show you." His voice dropped lower. "But later."

"Why later?"

"Because—" he leaned toward her "—right now I really want to kiss you."

"Oh." The syllable came out a soft, helpless invitation. *Yes, please.*

She moved to meet him, his lips touched hers…and huge cover-the-sky fireworks exploded.

3

KISSING QUINN WAS THE most…it was…oh, my… A sharp burn of lust traveled down a predictable path. Less predictable was the ache, part bliss, part longing, that started in her chest and began to spread.

Oh, no. *Oh, no.* To him, the kisses were simply a prelude to getting laid. This was foreplay, not romance, no matter what Madame Cassandra or Melinda or horoscopes said.

As if to prove her right, he drew back and looked at her—not dreamily, not burning with barely suppressed desire, but frowning, though with a hint of mischief.

She braced herself. "Is something wrong?"

"I'm worried. If just kissing you is this hot, I don't think I'll survive the night."

Wow. *Wow.* He felt it, too. Her confidence swelled. "And…do you care?"

"No." He grinned, looking so gorgeous in the dim light that it hurt. "But be prepared. You'll have to dispose of my body later."

"Okay." She sent him a look under her lashes. "Though there are a few other things I'd rather do with your body."

"I like the sound of that." He met her halfway for more kisses, and this time she managed to keep her heart quiet. Sort of. For the most part.

A minute later, however, the deep, fabulous kissing had turned urgent and a little desperate. Or maybe a lot desperate.

They broke apart again, breathing hard. Quinn smoothed back her hair. "I think I'd like to see that underwear now."

"I think I'd love to show it to you." Quite brilliantly, considering her brain was dissolving into hormonal mush, she remembered to take out her earrings before she slipped off the bed and stood—since her stomach would stretch tighter that way than sitting down—preparing for the unveiling. She wasn't going to think about all his other women and their supremely perfect bodies, beside which hers would pale in comparison. And speaking of pale...

Stop, Cathy.

She pulled the sweater off, wishing she had the nerve to do a bump-and-grind routine, to take this slowly and be outrageously seductive. But it took all she had to stand there and uncover her flaws.

"Oh, man." His words came out half-choked, and it occurred to her that he was a male, and she was a female about to get naked in front of him for the purpose of sex, and he probably didn't give a flying anything if she was too lumpy or too white.

She put her hands to the waistband of her pants, reminding herself that models were starved and scary-looking, and lowered the material, dragging her socks off as she stepped out of each leg so she wouldn't be left wearing sexy underwear with black wool-blend crawling up her ankles.

He gave an appreciative moan and started taking off his own clothes in a big hurry. Which she would take to mean he wasn't disappointed. At all. Not by a long shot. A tremendous sense of joy filled her. *Quinlan...Jussstin...Alexaaander* thought CathyAnnJohnson was hot, even stripped down to her lingerie-covered imperfections.

Which was a coincidence, because she felt the same about him, even fully clothed. And as he got closer to naked it became obvious, though not surprising, that his body was perfect, golden and muscled with dark hair in all the best places.

By trying very hard, she managed not to feel inferior. "So you like the underwear?"

"Um...yeah." He gestured to his bulging briefs. "You couldn't tell?"

She grinned like a fool. "I'm vain. I wanted to hear it."

"You're not vain, but you have good cause to be. You're beautiful." He pulled his briefs off and lay stretched on his side, naked and entirely unselfconscious, gazing at her. "Exactly as I pictured you when you opened the box at the office."

She beamed, feeling suddenly ten pounds lighter. "Well, Merry Christmas. And thank you."

"Merry Christmas, Cathy. And you're welcome." He pulled down the comforter, slid between the sheets and held out his arms. "Come on in."

She went. How could she not? Though she felt almost sorry they were progressing to sex so quickly. Because after he climbed on and they both climaxed—and please, God, let her manage that—it would be over. And she'd have to leave and return to reality.

He pulled her against him and covered them over with the comforter. She waited, tensing in spite of herself. She loved sex, but the first time with someone was usually less than great, and she wanted this to be so perfect, to explode into orgasm under him without him having to spend endless time on the appropriate amount of foreplay.

But then, one could only escape reality so far.

Instead of going for her breast, though, or reaching between her legs to get her going right away, he lay calmly and stroked her back—up to her neck, down to her waist, long, strong strokes, again and again.

"Mmm, that's nice."

"Yeah?" He kissed her forehead, drew his fingers lazily through her hair. "You feel really good."

"So do you." She sighed contentedly. This was so much more relaxing than worrying about her performance. She moved closer, wrapped her top leg over his, loving the feel of skin on skin, closing her eyes to take in every sensation, inhaling his scent, running her hands over the smooth, firm muscles of his back.

She could lie here forever.

Except then his hand reached past the small of her back and made a leisurely, warm exploration of her rear. She moaned involuntarily and felt his penis jump against her. He reached farther, taking advantage of the access her lifted leg offered. The feel of his fingers between her legs, stroking her through the red lace, made her desire to lie there forever vanish abruptly.

"Is that good?" he whispered.

"Yes." Oh, yes, yes, yes. It was good. It was beyond good.

He kissed her then, and the kiss went on and on and on, their tongues joining, their bodies straining against each other.

Arousal built in her to a crisis point. And still he made no move, went on kissing her and fingering her until she was shaking and desperate to come—and desperate not to, because it wasn't time, it was too soon. He'd want her coming with him later, and she couldn't manage more than one a night. She'd disappoint him.

She broke the kiss. "Quinn."

"Yeah." He was looking at her with hot, dark eyes that turned her on almost as much as his fingers.

"You're going too fast. I'll be done before we even—"

"You're close to coming?"

She closed her eyes and nodded. "Sorry."

"Sorry?" He pushed aside the panties and drove his fingers inside her. She cried out and arched her hips, taking him in deeper. His thumb found her clit; he circled, still pushing in and out. She found herself panting, thrusting her hips against his rhythm. "What are you sorry about?"

She could barely form a coherent thought. "I don't want to ruin it. I mean I—"

"Ruin it?" He stared at her incredulously. "For crying out loud, Cathy, what kind of idiots have you been with?"

"I…" She made a face, feeling naive and foolish. "Idiots who wanted me to come when they did, I guess."

"How could—" He shook his head in amazement. "Forget that. Come for me now."

She immediately tensed. Oh, no. Now he wanted her to come and she wasn't going to be able—

"Shhh." He kissed her again, slowly, thoroughly. "Whatever you're thinking, stop it."

"Okay." She squeezed her eyes shut, concentrated on the feel of him next to her, on his hand between her legs, but her arousal stubbornly receded, and the more it receded, the more her panic grew and the further it receded. This was horrible. She was screwing up the screwing.

"Quinn, make love to me." She looked up pleadingly. At least he'd get off that way, and maybe she could manage an orgasm later.

"You're sure?"

She nodded.

"Then it would be my extremely genuine pleasure."

Good. She wiggled out of the red lace bra and panties while he reached over her and opened his nightstand drawer, extracted a condom and put it on.

"You ready now or do you want me to touch you again?" He spoke softly, moving over her, arms straight, muscles bulging, looking at her almost tenderly.

"I'm ready." She swallowed against a tiny lump in her throat. She'd never been with anyone who seemed to care so much about her pleasure. Or at least with anyone who was so at ease talking about it.

He lowered his hips, keeping his torso lifted, then reached down to guide himself inside. She spread eagerly, felt the first nudge of his penis, then the slow, delicious slide of penetration that made her gasp and her body buzz. He watched her, and she forced herself to meet his gaze for a few long seconds, nearly overwhelmed by the intimacy.

"Is it good?" His muscles bunched and released, his rhythm was steady and unhurried. "Is that how you like it?"

"Yes. Very good." How did she like it? Any way he wanted to give it to her.

Her fingers drew careful designs on his buttocks. She lifted her hips to match each thrust, welcoming the low burn of her renewed arousal.

God, she hoped she could come.

Aw, hell. Why did she always start worrying about that? Why couldn't she just relax and enjoy herself?

"What is it, Cathy?" he asked gently. "Something's bugging you."

"Oh." She gave a stupid laugh. "Nothing, I…just…"

"Tell me." He waited, watching her closely, still moving.

She had to swallow again. This was like no sex she'd ever had. Being with Quinn made her other encounters seem furtive and secretive, almost guilty. She suddenly wanted to rise to the occasion, to be honest and open about her fears. More, she realized she trusted him to take them in stride.

"I'm…already worried I won't come." She laughed to show she knew she was being ridiculous.

"First afraid you would, now afraid you won't?"

"I know, it's stupid to worry so much."

"Then don't do it at all."

"I've tried not to, but—"

"No." He bent down to kiss her, then raised up, his arms steady and strong. "No, don't worry. Don't come."

"Don't—" She gaped at him. Every man she'd been with took it as a direct hit on his ego if she couldn't, so she'd taken climaxing during sex as her solemn responsibility every single time. "You don't care?"

"Are you enjoying this? Having a good time? Does it feel good?"

"Yes. Yes, it's incredible."

"That's all I care about and all you should. This isn't a judged event with required elements. It's you and me doing what feels right."

Her throat swelled and she had to blink rapidly. She knew he was amazing. You had only to look at him to see he was amazing. But she hadn't expected that deep down he'd be so…amazing. "Thank you."

He lowered his torso onto her, dug his hands under her rear, tilting her pelvis up. "Relax. You feel so good. Just have fun."

She did. She wrapped her arms around his back and concentrated on the push-pull feel of him inside her, the strength of his muscles, the masculine softness of his skin. Had she said before that she could lie there forever? Ditto that now and then some. She wanted this feeling, this beautiful closeness, this pleasure with him, to go on and on and on….

Except then Quinn rolled to one side and pulled out of her, leaving her slightly stunned. What was—

Before she could panic, he draped her leg closest to him over his side, trapped her other between his and pushed inside her again.

Mmm.

He moved slowly, lazily, watching himself go in and out of her, brushing his hand through her pubic curls. "Touch yourself if you want to. You know how best."

She hesitated, slightly taken aback. Touch herself? He wasn't threatened by that? He didn't expect her to be able to burst into orgasm merely by being penetrated?

Not a judged event. No required elements. Obviously she'd allowed previous partners to define lovemaking too narrowly.

Okay, then. She put her fingers between her legs and started to rub, self-consciously at first, then, as her body responded, in earnest.

His breath went in sharply. "Yesss. Like that. That is sexy as hell."

His words fueled her. She broke out in a sweat, felt her cheeks heating. He pushed harder, his breath coming harsher. The rough feel of him filling her made her crazy. Her fingers quickened and she felt herself building easily to a climax.

Oh, yes. Triumph rushed through her. Silly maybe, but he'd set her free to welcome this effortless wave of bliss, and she felt like cheering.

Instead she turned to look at him at the same time he turned to look at her, and her body gathered force for the approaching ecstasy.

"I'm…going to come," she whispered.

He groaned and clutched her hip, gazing steadily at her. Her climax hit, hot and powerful; she gasped and moaned, letting it wash over her. His fingers dug into her skin; he closed his eyes briefly, mouth half-open, muscles taut, and gave a low, sexy groan. Watching him come lifted her bliss higher, wave after wave, until it finally set her down, happy and sated, not as she usually was, relieved or ashamed or simply wrung out by the challenge.

He reached and touched her face, let his fingers glide down her cheek and come to rest under her chin. Her heart swelled.

Oh, my God. She was totally in love with him. Even if it was fantasy-fueled, even if it only lasted this second, this hour, this day, the emotion was so pure and intense and deep that she couldn't mistake it for anything else.

She smiled so she wouldn't cry, concentrated on what had just happened so she wouldn't think about the future, about leaving, about The End. He'd given her so much more than lingerie.

"Cathy."

"Yes."

He untangled their legs, gathered her to him, kissed her so sweetly her heart nearly split in half. "I am damn glad you showed up tonight."

"Me, too." She smiled over the ache in her throat. *Glad you showed up, babe. Great time, great lay...and goodbye.*

CATHY LEANED HER HEAD against the cold window of the taxi. So. She'd done it. Not quite the way she'd envisioned it, not showing up wild and sexual and bold, blowing his mind with a fabulous striptease, but she'd done it nonetheless. Worn the lingerie, made it to his apartment and slept with him.

The sex had been incredible, the first time and again a couple of hours later. In between they'd talked and talked and dozed together and woken to talk and make love again. She'd even come the second time, too. Major victory. Right now she should be feeling triumphant, victorious, elated, full of supreme confidence and sexual power.

She didn't. She felt lonely and empty and wanted to go back to his apartment and crawl into bed with him for every possible second until he had to leave. Wasn't that just like her? What made her think she could use his body and toss him aside? She'd even imagined herself in love with him after a few hours. She wasn't able to separate sex and emotion, never had been able to. Just because *he* could didn't mean it was contagious.

Though maybe if he'd been macho and swaggeringly sexual it would have been easier to leave. She hadn't expected his softer side, hadn't expected him to be so gentle and sweet. Her last boyfriend thought buying a greeting card was the ultimate in emotional communication. Quinn…well, he seemed to like her. Which he probably did. He probably liked all the women he slept with, at least to some degree.

But while finding out that he lusted after Cathy had made all kinds of sexual fantasies take hold of her, realizing he liked Cathy made even wilder fantasies take hold of her that had nothing to do with sex. And indulging any of those what-ifs was a complete waste of time and emotional energy.

He wanted sex with her. He got it, on an icy Friday night and into the wee hours of Saturday morning. He was leaving the country Tuesday. End of story.

She stared blankly at the storefronts and apartments rushing by as they headed for Brooklyn. Had he seemed regretful about the parting? He'd invited her to spend the night, but considering the temperature, he was probably being polite. And staying would have meant waking up together and facing each other in the cold light of day, and that had too many tempting aspects of "relationship" all over it.

Better to cut her losses, leave while the night was still perfect, while they both wanted more, while his memories were of her dimly lit and glowing from postorgasmic bliss, instead of pasty-mouthed and bed-headed and awkward the next morning.

And—oh, my Lord—she was having brunch with Jake in a few hours!

She closed her eyes, then guiltily pushed that thought out of her head. She'd deal with Jake after some sleep. Right now she wanted to relive every word, kiss and touch of her perfect night with a perfect man.

The cab pulled up in front of her building, which, to her disappointment, looked just as ugly as when she'd left, though it was too dark to see most of it. She paid the driver and hauled herself out of the cab into the frigid air, inside and up the elevator to her floor. She stood outside her doorway, fumbling with the keys, strangely reluctant to go in. Going in meant the adventure was over. That normal life was returning, that—

A noise behind her made her jump. Jake's door opening. Oh, no. Not him. Not now.

"Cathy?" He blinked at her, still dressed.

"Jake, what are you doing up?"

He was staring at her intently, and she wondered guiltily if Quinn had made some "I did her" mark that only males could see. Or maybe she looked thoroughly and blissfully laid all on her own. "I fell asleep waiting for you."

"*Waiting* for…me?" Whah? He'd worried about her being out so late? Or was he some scary possessive, controlling type who had to know where she was every hour of the day?

He pressed his hands over his eyes, then dropped them to his side. "Well, I mean, I was hoping you'd decide to come over. I guess you had other plans, though, huh?"

"I…we're having brunch later, right?" Was she entirely missing something here?

"I know, I know. I just thought…"

She stared at him blankly. "That I'd drop by?"

"Well, I mean, I invited you."

"You…did?" He thought *I hope to see you before tomorrow* muttered at the subway stop was an invitation?

He gestured between them. "I don't think we're communicating here, are we."

"Um…no." She laughed nervously. "I guess not."

"You got my present at the office yesterday."

"Huh?" She must be starring in some German surrealist movie. "At *my* office?"

"The red underwear. Glenda said you opened it."

The keys fell out of her hand and hit the floor with a sharp clank. She scooped them up and stood again, staring. Some response was necessary. She knew that. She was just unable to give one.

"O-kay." Jake scrubbed at his hair. "Look, I know it was out of line. Way too early in our friendship to go there. But I…well, I'm a guy, and I saw the underwear in a store window and thought of you and…I guess I got carried away. I thought you'd get a kick out of opening it at the office in front of everyone.

Melinda said you're always putting yourself down for appearing too dull, and...I guess I blew it. I'm really sorry, Cathy."

"The underwear..." She was trying very hard to process this. "Was from you..."

"Well, yeah." He was looking at her really strangely now. "I called your office and they put me through to Glenda, who agreed to help arrange it. I dropped the gift by Thursday night after you'd left. Didn't you get the card?"

"It was signed 'Guess Who.'" She was still barely getting the words out, gaping at him, aware that the enormity of this was going to hit her at some point and that it wasn't going to be pretty.

"Uh...my initials were on the envelope. In big black letters."

"I didn't see the envelope..." Her throat closed.

Surprised to get this at the office? You shouldn't be. Necessity is the mother of invention, and I need to get to know you a lot better—you've probably figured that out by the signals I've been sending lately. Come over tonight, eight o'clock—I don't have to tell you the address. Whether you wear the lace or not, whether you want to talk or do a whole lot more, I'll be waiting. Guess Who.

Oh, God. Oh, my God. Oh, my dear God.

He was looking suspicious now. "So who did you *think* it was from?"

"Someone...else."

What an idiot. What a complete idiot. Quinn hadn't spent the week at her desk chatting because he wanted her. He *was* just killing time. And last night while he'd been settling in for a quiet evening at home or planning to use the precious hours to get organized for his trip, some chick from his office he barely knew and hadn't encouraged showed up out of the blue and ripped off her clothes.

Oh, no. Oh, no.

She flashed back to Quinn's face after he'd rescued her from the earring disaster—which in this new perspective was ten times as mortifying. No, he hadn't been looking at her with lust—she'd registered that at the time—but with gentle sympathy.

Oh, my God. A pity fuck.

Her face turned fiery. Her stomach twisted into nausea. Tears of humiliation pricked her tired eyes. She couldn't stand it. The underwear was from Jake.

She'd seduced the wrong man.

4

QUINN WATCHED CATHY'S TAXI zoom down the nearly deserted street in front of his building. He shook his head, laughing a cloud of steam that glowed white-gray under the streetlight. Wow. He thought he'd be spending the evening packing, sorting through his things and deciding what to take to Europe, maybe wrapping presents for his family—expensive cigars and Philharmonic tickets for Dad; a silk scarf and a dessert cookbook for Mom; books, fancy scotch and personalized golf tees for his brothers. They all still lay in a pile in his closet.

He'd been too busy unwrapping a total surprise package.

Her taxi turned the corner and he spun around, aware suddenly of the cold penetrating his pants and shoes. Back in his building, he climbed the stairs to the third floor with muscles well aware they'd been used tonight.

Never in his wildest dreams would he have imagined Cathy Johnson taking a few conversations at her desk and a wink over a gift of underwear as an invitation to seduction. Yeah, he'd been attracted to her in abstract—who wouldn't be? She was pretty, funny, smart, did a fabulous job keeping the department running. But he never would have expected her to take that kind of initiative. Not in a million years.

She was a fascinating study in contrasts. At the office Secret Santa party after she'd unwrapped the lingerie, her mortification had been genuine. No one could act that well. Then she'd shown up out of the blue wanting sex—and admitted going after it wasn't something she did often. Her shyness early in the evening had given way to easy camaraderie and then…well, as he'd said earlier, wow.

In his living room, he shut and bolted the door behind him. He'd rarely had sex that good, that comfortable and fun, the first time with someone. Usually there was pressure to perform acrobatically well and to know intuitively what pleased his partner. Or the women he was with felt they needed to bolster his ego or cover their own nerves by overblown screeching and moaning as if they'd learned about sex from porn movies. Rarely had he experienced this natural a connection on a first…well, he couldn't really call it a date.

Keyed up, sure he wouldn't sleep, even at this hour, he went into his bedroom anyway. Busy days ahead. He should try to get some rest. Though, in spite of his fatigued muscles, he felt like working out, jogging, blowing off steam somehow. Maybe he'd call Cathy to see if she'd gotten home okay. Maybe invite her to breakfast later this morning or to dinner tonight.

He passed his hand over his eyes and rubbed his temple. What was the point? It was early Saturday. Tomorrow—Sunday, Christmas Eve—they both had family obligations. Tuesday he was gone. What the hell was the point?

He stood beside his bed, reached out and tweaked the rumpled covers, bent down and tried to capture her scent from the sheets. A glint of unfamiliar metal caught his eye on his nightstand, and he turned to see her earrings, small silver leaves with wire stems, dangling from delicate chains.

When she'd first showed up, he'd thought Cathy was there for a surprise friendly visit. Nothing had prepared him for the sight of her standing in his living room, face set rigidly against fear, lifting her sweater. He'd been stunned into silence, then frantically searched for words that would stop her and get him out of the awkward-as-hell situation without hurting her.

Plenty of women had tried to seduce him during his adult life. Mostly he turned them down. His reputation as a player was unfounded. What was the point collecting women for brief trysts? As far as he was concerned, the longer you knew someone, the deeper the affection and trust, the better the sex. But he found women on the whole more interesting to talk to than men and more satisfying as friends. So rumors flew that weren't worth his time and energy to argue against. People would think what they thought. Those people who mattered knew the truth.

He turned over the earring in his hand, noting the detail of veins etched into the metal. He'd been about to turn Cathy down, too, flatter her, invent some excuse to stay uninvolved and send her on her way after a drink and a brief chat. And then two things had happened.

One, her incredible breasts, barely encased in red lace, had emerged from under the sweater, exactly as he'd pictured them in the office when she'd held up her gift—maybe even better. Call him shallow, but, um, that caught his attention.

However, he'd like to think he was gentleman enough that he still would have told her to go home—if her sweater hadn't gotten stuck. If she hadn't gotten so sweetly and desperately flustered and hadn't handled it in such an honest and funny way.

The breasts were sensational, his reaction predictable. But her disarming self-deprecation brought out tender protectiveness that mixed with desire to form a much more powerful draw. He'd wanted her then, to make love to her and to make it really good—especially once he'd sensed she might not have had been with the most considerate partners.

More than that, he'd wanted to hang out with her and talk to her, listen to her wise, funny comments and try to figure out where she got the idea she was so average. While the sex was great and would undoubtedly get better if they were given the chance, the banter and conversation and sharing would make Cathy stand out in his memories.

He gave a dry chuckle and shook his head. Listen to him. He needed to focus on the future, give himself a little jolt out of his contemplative mood. Maybe he'd call John, an ex-*Connoisseur* colleague who'd emigrated to London to teach, and check if there were any last-minute arrangements that needed to be made regarding the studio they'd rented. Or just hear his friend's voice and remind himself what he was going to accomplish over the next year: hone his skills as a photographer, work on developing his own artistic style.

John picked up on the second ring. "What the hell are you doing up at this hour?"

"Couldn't sleep. How's our love nest?"

"Great. Just great. A bit of a dodgy neighborhood, but the studio's all right. Got painted last week. You're still coming Tuesday?"

"Yes." He found himself having to force enthusiasm into the word.

"Excellent."

They chatted briefly about the pubs they'd visit his first weeks there and the people he'd meet, until conversation ran dry and Quinn ended the call feeling slightly depressed.

Thinking about London hadn't helped erase Cathy the way it was supposed to. He not only still keenly felt her absence here, where he'd lived for eight years and where she'd been for mere hours, but his departure on Tuesday—long anticipated as the highlight of his new decade into his thirties, the trip that would quell this restless energy, this dissatisfaction with the rote feel of his everyday life in New York—had started to feel like a too-soon, fast-ticking alarm.

How had she done all that to him in such a short time? How much more could she do if he were able to spend every possible second with her before he had to leave? His surprisingly strong feelings could simply be the result of a one-shot fabulous night, where all the stars aligned and their chemistry and moods fell into place. If they met again, the spark between them could be gone, their meeting awkward and jumpy like the strangers they were at the office.

Or not.

Travel for his job made relationships difficult, though he'd tried. Three girlfriends in the last five years, relationships lasting a few months to a year. Nice women, good sex, fun times. But he'd always felt there should be something more, some special click of recognition, some organic connection they'd both feel immediately, and he'd never found that. Not quite. Sometimes he'd thought he was a hopeless romantic doomed to relationship failure by keeping the bar too high.

Tonight he thought there was a chance he'd simply been smart.

He held the silver leaves up, watched them turn and glint in the soft light of his desk lamp. He'd have to call Cathy and let her know her earrings were here, but he'd give her time to sleep for a few hours first. Not a bad idea for him to get some sleep, either. Maybe he'd wake up and find her presence had receded from his bedroom, that his trip abroad would again be the most powerful call to him, and he'd realize he was crazy wanting to pursue a relationship with Cathy for the next two days only to leave the country for a year.

One thing was sure: whoever had given her that lingerie, Quinn was sure as hell grateful. And sure as hell hoping she wasn't planning to wear it again for anyone else but him.

"So THEN WE RECOMMENDED firing seven management employees and zero lower-echelon people."

"Wow." Cathy put down her fork. She'd made little headway on an asparagus frittata at Sweetwater Restaurant with Jake. Not because the food wasn't excellent but because, in spite of her severe attempts to banish it, her brain was still filled with an odd combination of sparkling memories of Quinn, lingering mortification that she'd shown up without being invited and terror that Quinn had taken her to bed because he'd felt too sorry for her to kick her out.

Useless self-torture. What was done was done, as her mom loved to say. Quinn was leaving, he'd been very sweet, and in the end, he hadn't exactly suffered from her mistake. She needed to forgive herself and concentrate on poor Jake, who was giving this date his earnest best. "I bet management wasn't thrilled that you recommended firing a third of them."

"Nope." He grinned and took another sip of coffee, then gestured to the waitress for his fourth refill. "They weren't. But if you hire management consultants, you're going to get an opinion. We told them what we thought and we were right."

She wiped her mouth with her napkin, trying to appear fascinated, guilty that she wasn't. Jake was such a nice man, smart, fun, attractive, the most promising date she'd been on in months, and she wasn't even here. She was back in Quinn's apartment, feeling his warm body next to hers, on hers, in hers, behind hers, under hers…oh, my Lord, what they had accomplished in a few hours.

Okay. Enough. Quinn had probably forgotten already. Or, worse, was still chuckling over her initial abject failure at seduction. "So did they end up firing all those management people?"

"Oh, yeah. They followed our recommendations and their profitability soared, just as we predicted."

"That's fabulous." She tried to sound sincere. Quite honestly she didn't care. And that bothered her, because she was usually a really empathetic listener and managed to be excited for other people's triumphs even if they weren't triumphing over anything she could relate to. But talking to Jake was nothing like talking to—

Get over it, Cathy. Quinn was done, gone, finished. If she wanted to cling to the dream of him, fine, but she better prepare herself for a lot of lonely nights ahead.

She refocused on Jake, on his thick, wavy black hair, clear dark eyes and fair, faintly stubbled skin. On the way he used his hands to gesture when he spoke, on the way he exuded energy and confidence and sex appeal.

"So, anyway, enough of boring work talk. Melinda was telling me a little more about you last night."

"Oh?" She sent him a jokingly suspicious look. "She didn't mention the bodies in the basement, did she?"

"Um…no." He grinned. "She didn't get that far. But I asked what you did in your free time and she said you read a lot? And you like to knit?"

Oh, and didn't that make her sound like the world's most fascinating human. The kind of woman men like Quinn would kill themselves to be near. But it was exactly the truth, and could she *please* stop thinking about Quinn. "Yeah. I used to knit when I was a girl and took it up again a few months ago."

"What are you making?"

"A sweater. Pretty complicated pattern, so it's going slowly. But I get too antsy watching TV or listening to music without having something else to do." She groaned silently. He was being so polite and sweet making himself ask about her knitting, but it couldn't possibly interest him.

"What kind of music do you listen to? I'm into alternative jazz, some fairly esoteric classical, some hip-hop, some indie rock."

Of course he was. And she listened to soft rock, like every other average Cathy on the planet. "My tastes are pretty ordinary. Soft rock, oldies…"

"Hey, nothing wrong with ordinary when it's good."

"True." She tried to smile back at him, but it fell flat. Ordinary. Right.

"Have you heard of the Arctic Monkeys? You might like them. They have a pretty appealing sound."

"Melinda loves them. She plays them all the time." While Cathy resisted the urge to cover her ears. She took another sip of lukewarm coffee, suddenly exhausted and ready to go home. She'd probably gotten a total of three hours of sleep, and even those hours had been restless and disturbed.

Jake launched into a catalog of favorite songs and performers, then TV shows, movies, all good, fun topics. She managed to chat and laugh for another half hour until she felt she could end the date. It wasn't Jake's fault. This wasn't a good day to try to get to know him. She was too tired, too much in turmoil over what had happened.

By the time they got back to the hall between their apartments, she was forcing energy into a body that was out. Worse, along with the weariness had come depression. A crash after the high of the night before. Of course, her time with Quinn had only been a fantasy. But a wonderful one. Now life would go back to its same old pointless routines….

She sighed. Gee, nothing like exhaustion to give one a healthy perspective.

"Hey, I'll get that CD I was talking about. I don't think Melinda has this one."

"Oh, okay." She nodded, lifting her eyebrows because she couldn't even summon the energy to smile. "I'll leave the door open."

Inside, she glanced at the machine in spite of herself. Zero messages. Of course. He wouldn't call. She didn't expect him to. He wouldn't know that she desperately needed him to say, "Hey, just wanted to let you know last night wasn't a horrible mistake I regret with every fiber of my being."

She needed to push him out of her mind. A good night's sleep and a merry Christmas would do it.

She hoped.

Jake's tap-tap-boom knock came at the open door and he pushed his way in, holding out a CD. "Here you go. Hot off the shelves."

She took the CD and thanked him, willing to give the Arctic Monkeys a try. It would be nice if she and Jake could like the same type of music. A small thing, of course, but…

A particularly pregnant silence fell between them, the kind that falls when one person has something uncomfortable to say. Since Cathy had nothing uncomfortable to say except maybe *Please go away, I'm really tired and will have to try to fall in love with you another day,* she looked expectantly at Jake.

Who was coming toward her. Saying her name. Thanking her for the date, reaching for her shoulders and kissing her.

Kissing Jake felt as wrong as being with Quinn had felt right.

Darn it. How was that possible? She didn't belong with Quinn, no matter how she thought she felt about him. Even Melinda's stupid horoscope would have to predict true love with Jake now. But last night she sure as hell hadn't been thinking about Jake while Quinn was kissing her. She hadn't been thinking about anything, only feeling. And here she was kissing Jake—or rather being kissed by him—while conducting an impromptu analysis of her romantic situation.

She drew back, and that most horrible of horrible moments resulted—when there's nothing to say after a first kiss.

Cathy gave a nervous giggle and instantly hated herself. Jake leaned in again. *Oh, no. I don't want to deal with this. Not now.*

The phone rang.

"I…better get that." She moved to answer, thinking that if Quinn had been about to kiss her and the phone interrupted, she'd let it ring until it couldn't anymore.

The number was unfamiliar, so it wasn't Mom calling with a change of plans or her brother, Brad, calling with last-minute present questions. She should let the machine pick up. But she needed this break to figure out what to do with Jake.

"Hello?"

"Cathy." The voice was deep and rich and instantly recognizable. Blood rushed into her cheeks and her head started feeling dizzy and light.

"Hi…hi." *Oh, my God. Oh, how incredible. Oh…crap.*

There was no way she could sound or act remotely normal on the phone with Quinn if poor Jake was standing behind her listening. "Can I call you back?"

"Soon?"

"Does it need to be soon?"

"It does, yeah." His low, sexy voice started her heating up. Her tiredness vanished. She could run a marathon. Twice. He sounded as if everything was as intimate between them this morning as it had been last night. As if he hadn't been appalled by her showing up with no invite and really wanted to—

Okay, she couldn't let her fantasies run away with her.

"I'll call in a few minutes." She hung up and took a deep breath before she turned and smiled apologetically at Jake, sure her face was still flaming. "Sorry about that."

His eyes narrowed slightly. "I guess you need to call back?"

"Um…yeah." She kept the smile going, feeling like the world's biggest jerk. She owed him some explanation, but what the hell could she say? "I'm sorry. It's… I—"

He held up a hand. "Not a problem."

"It was just…someone I—"

"It's okay, Cathy. You don't have to tell me." He smiled, but his eyes remained wary. "I really enjoyed our date."

Her breath came out in a rush. "Oh, I did, too, thank you."

"Sure." He backed toward her door, his normally exuberant face still stiff. "We'll do it again sometime?"

"I'd like that. I'm sorry about this…call, but I would like to see you again." She would. Quinn was her best ever fantasy, but Jake was real. And with Christmas Eve tomorrow, she'd have a break from both of them, be with her wonderful, loving family, get spoiled by her parents and teased by her older brother, and get her head back down from the clouds. Then she could come to a date with Jake and really be there, instead of being back in Quinn's arms as she was now, mentally speaking, with even his scent still fresh in her memory.

The door closed behind Jake; she tried not to feel relieved and failed. His footsteps receded and his door thunked closed, leaving her apartment eerily silent.

Time to call Quinn back.

Her heels thudded too loudly on the hardwood floor as she crossed back to the phone and stood staring at it. She cleared her throat and the sound seemed to explode into the room.

She shouldn't—*couldn't*—get her hopes up. He was undoubtedly calling for an entirely unromantic reason. Maybe she'd left something at his apartment, in which case she'd matter-of-factly provide her address so he could mail it back. Maybe he wanted to warn her not to tell anyone at the office what had happened, in which case she'd swear earnestly to keep the icky truth untold. Maybe he had a message for someone at work he wanted her to pass along before he left, in which case she'd jot it down cheerfully and wish him happy trails.

Maybe he just wanted to know, the morning after, what had put it in her head to show up at his house expecting sex?

In which case she'd tell him, of course, and get to be embarrassed all over again.

Heart hammering alarmingly in her chest, she picked up the

phone, bobbled it, recovered, then nearly dropped it a second time. This was crazy. She'd barely been nervous for her first face-to-face date with Jake, and here she was nearly losing it trying to call Quinn back after they'd been intimate for hours the previous night. Good thing there was no chance of long-term dating or she'd probably develop an ulcer.

Summoning courage she shouldn't have needed, she dialed his number. Quinn answered on the first ring. "Cathy, hi. Thanks for calling back."

Sigh. Even him saying that much was sexy to her. She closed her eyes and let the thrills have their way with her. "Hi, Quinn. You're welcome. It sounded urgent?"

"It is."

The thrills took on a panicky flavor. "Did something happen?"

"Yeah." He chuckled. "I've got this crazy need to see you again."

Cathy's eyelids shot up; her jaw dropped. She caught herself starting to ask why and managed to spare herself that humiliation. "Wow. I'd…wow. When? I mean, you're leaving and—"

"Right now. And this afternoon. And tonight, all night. And tomorrow until we have to go see our families."

"Quinn…" She started laughing. She couldn't help it. He wanted to see her! How the hell had this happened?

Who knew red underwear could give a girl this kind of power?

"Meet me at Hotel Peninsula at Fifth Avenue and Fifty-fifth Street in an hour for some champagne?"

Yes went from her brain to her lungs, which cycled breath up toward her vocal chords…which clenched and refused to let it out.

What did he hope to accomplish by spending twenty-four more hours in bed with her and then saying goodbye?

Well, okay, beyond orgasms. It wasn't as if she was his last chance ever to have sex. He could find someone else by walking out of his apartment and announcing his need. The problem would be whittling down his choices.

"Cathy?"

"I'm here. I'm…" She was what?

"You don't want to? You have other plans?"

"No. I…" *Come on, Cathy, you have to say something.* In desperation, she tried the truth. "I'm just surprised. I…wasn't expecting to see you again."

Silence. Her stomach sank.

"Wow. Okay. My mistake. I thought there was more than sex going on last night."

Cathy turned abruptly around, as if someone had sneaked up behind her and tapped her on the shoulder. "You did?"

"Look, never mind. You showed up in the underwear—I had no reason to think it was anything but one night. I just thought we connected. Anyway, have a great Christmas, Cathy. Maybe I'll—"

"No. Wait. I thought we connected, too. I just didn't think you did."

"Why?"

"Because…you…have all those other women."

"What other women?"

"Sandra said—"

He let out a groan of exasperation. "She's not worth my time. When she makes comments about me having a girl in every city, what am I supposed to say? 'Actually, Sandra, I believe sexual relations should take place in a committed relationship supported by a strong emotional foundation'."

Cathy giggled and stupid hope rose in her chest, even knowing she and Quinn had no time to lay down such a foundation. "I'd love to see her face if you did."

"Me too, actually. So is that it? Your only worry?"

"Uh…"

"What else?"

"You're…who you are, and I'm…Cathy." She cringed. Even to her ears, she sounded utterly pathetic.

"Well, just call yourself Catlaina or Catriona, or Ekatarina." He rolled the *r*'s and made each name sound more lovely and exotic than the last one. "You'll be fascinating to me either way."

"Oh," she said in a thrilled, breathy whisper.

"However, I will warn you, if you put yourself down one more time, I'm going to introduce spanking into our next session."

"And…is that a threat or a promise?"

He laughed, and she felt herself soaring into the outer space of happiness. Making Quinn laugh made her feel…there was no other word for it…special. Which was so deliciously dangerous she needed immediately to make sure he understood about last night—and who she wasn't.

"Quinn, I have to confess something."

"Uh-oh. You're seriously into S and M?"

"No. God, no. It's about the underwear."

"Aah, the underwear." He sounded so wistful she giggled again.

"When I opened the present at the office, you were the only person not laughing. And then you winked at me, and so…I thought you gave it to me."

"Wow."

Silence. She cringed. "I never would have shown up if I didn't think you wanted me there."

He chuckled, low and deep. "I did want you there, Cathy. I just didn't know it yet."

She closed her eyes blissfully, a sappy smile firmly in place. She'd offered another confession, and gotten another vote of absolute acceptance in return. "Thank you."

"I also want to see you at Hotel Peninsula in an hour."

And she wanted to see him. Maybe for once she wouldn't overanalyze and overthink but just go with her heart, even if it was doomed to be pulverized.

She took a deep breath made unsteady by her giddiness. "Yes. I'll be there."

"HEY THERE, GIRLFRIEND, you have some explaining to do."

"I do?" Cell phone to her ear, Cathy hailed a taxi to take her to the Hotel Peninsula. Usually she took the subway, but on her second and final date with Quinn, she'd spare no expense. "About what?"

Melinda groaned in exasperation. "C'mon, I'm on break, I don't have all day. Where were you last night? Jake was over looking for you, and we hung out for a while waiting till he gave up and went to bed. I didn't even hear what time you came in, and you were still asleep when I left this morning."

"I know." Cathy raised her eyes to the heavens and said a silent thanks. Last night, after the encounter with Quinn and then Jake, she hadn't been in the mood to come up with a version of events for Melinda before she'd sorted through the turbulent feelings herself. Of course, she *still* hadn't been able to. As soon as she thought she'd reached a place of solid understanding, the emotional ground shifted again.

"All I can say is you better have been out with girlfriends, because Jake is one fabulous piece of man flesh, and I will hate you if you hurt him. Or hurt you if you hate him. Or both."

Cathy sighed. She'd answered the call from her roommate without expecting to have to defend herself. "I was with Quinn."

"*Quinn?* Quinn from the office? Mr. International Playboy?"

"Yeah." Her giggle sounded hideously foolish—she couldn't help it. "Believe it or not."

"I can't believe it. You had a date with Jake today and you spent last night with someone else?"

Cathy's mouth opened, but nothing came out. Her roommate

sounded furious. Not the reaction Cathy had expected at all, and she found herself instantly prickly. "I'm not married to Jake. I don't owe him undying faithfulness over one brunch. I even tried to tell him about Quinn and he cut me off. If I'm being horrible, it's to Quinn, rolling out of his bed to go on a date with someone else."

Melinda snorted. "Like his type would care?"

"You'd be surprised." A cab pulled over and Cathy clambered in. Until Quinn's phone call today she would have thought the same thing. "Anyway, the whole thing started as a misunderstanding. I wasn't supposed to be at Quinn's last night."

"So, what, you went to his place completely by accident?"

"Melinda…" Cathy carefully covered the mouthpiece of her cell and told the driver where she wanted to go. "Sarcasm helps nothing."

"Okay, okay. Where are you, by the way? The signal's terrible."

"In a taxi."

"Going…*where?*" Melinda's tone reminded Cathy of her sixth-grade teacher, Mr. Bonaparte, just before Henry Ross got in his next nasty heap of trouble.

She rolled her eyes. "To meet Quinn."

"You don't deserve Jake."

"Jake is a wonderful guy. I would like to get to know him better and I intend to in the coming weeks. Quinn is leaving the country. Today is my last chance to see him. He's… It's like…" She searched for an analogy Melinda could relate to passionately. "It's like if Ashton Kutcher showed up and told you he wanted you. Wouldn't you want that experience at least once?"

"Not if I had someone like Jake."

"Aw, c'mon, Ashton Kutcher?"

"He's a movie star. He's fantasy material. We're talking real life here and the real feelings of a guy who likes you."

"Fine. I'm a shallow jerk." She bounced back against the seat in frustration. "But I only went to Quinn's Friday night because I thought my Secret Santa present came from him. I didn't know Jake sent it."

A small gasp. Then silence. Uh-oh. Melinda didn't know about the underwear?

"Melinda?"

"Jake gave you a gift? Yesterday? *Jake* did?"

Cathy let her head drop into her hand, guessing what was coming. "Yes."

"But that means…your horoscope…" Melinda sounded as if she were about to start crying. "All the good stuff happens to you."

Cathy lifted her head at her roommate's wail. "Come again?"

"You're beautiful, built, totally together, you have a glamorous job, you have this incredible guy after you…." She sniffled. "*Two* incredible guys after you."

"Uh, hello? Melinda? Are we talking about the same me?"

"And now, on top of it, Jake turns out to be your true love. While I'm a plain old waitress and can't get a date to save my life, even when my horoscope says good things are going to happen. Like this month, I'm supposed to find great happiness. Right. I'll probably not step in dog poo for the whole of December and that will be it for me."

"Jeez, Melinda." Cathy put a hand to her forehead, not sure where to start reacting to this unreasonable outburst. "First of all, deep down you have to know that astrology stuff is a load of—"

"Be right there," Melinda called distantly. "I gotta go, Cathy. I'll be home at four."

Cathy sighed. This was going to go over like a lead balloon. "Uh…Melinda?"

"Yeees?"

"I won't be home until tomorrow afternoon."

Long silence, then the loud click of Melinda hanging up.

Aw, hell. Cathy stuffed her phone in her black shoulder bag, into which she'd packed the bare essentials for an overnight at Quinn's. Her glow of happiness at the prospect of seeing him again had been invaded, both by the rare fight with Melinda, whom Cathy was starting to suspect had much stronger feelings for Jake than lust, and by Melinda's accusations, which made Cathy feel like the dog poo Melinda wasn't going to step in this month.

Maybe it was wrong of her to rush off into Quinn's arms when Jake had every reason to think she was starting a relationship with him. But she'd thought Quinn was out of the picture when she went on the brunch date today, and he'd caught her totally by surprise with his phone call. She'd been so flustered with Jake in the room she hadn't known what to say to either of them.

So she'd make a bargain with herself. One more day with Quinn, another brief taste of feeling every inch the woman-who-had-it-all Melinda described, then she'd come down from Planet Fantasy, become Jake's love puppy and follow him, panting, all around New York.

Done.

The rest of the way into Manhattan, through the usual bumper-to-bumper traffic of midtown, she replayed Melinda's other comments. Beautiful? Built? Totally together? Glamorous job? Who was that?

Every day Cathy got up and took her neatly packed lunch to work, came straight home and watched TV or knitted listening to music. That's all she did, aside from dinner or a movie with friends, drinks with people from the office, occasional visits to museums, even more occasional plays, concerts, operas, ball games. Weekends at home with Mom and Dad or with friends at the Jersey shore. Family ski trips in the winter. Summer vacations in Vermont. Reunions with college friends as excuses to take Caribbean cruises…

She shifted uneasily and adjusted her seat belt, which had become too loose.

Her life didn't sound all that dull. Did it.

The cab pulled up at the hotel on Fifth and Fifty-fifth Street and stopped with a jerk. Adrenaline poured through her at the thought of Quinn, the one and only wild oat Cathy had ever sown. Never mind that she'd stupidly become infatuated with this particular oat. Feelings that came on this strong this fast couldn't be real. Inevitably they'd die as quickly as they'd sprung to life.

She fumbled for her purse, passed too much money to the driver and jumped out into the chilly sunlit day, tugging down the clingy black slitted skirt she'd bought a year ago at Melinda's urging and had never worn, in spite of it being flattering and sexy, because she'd never felt it suited her.

She squared her shoulders and walked into the magnificent lobby. Today it suited her. Today she was Catlaina or Catriona or Ekatarina, woman with a thrilling life. Tomorrow she'd come down again and behave, acknowledge Jake and what she owed him, treat him with the honesty he deserved.

Until then, it was going to be all about her and Quinn.

QUINN WATCHED CATHY emerge through the gold-and-glass revolving door of the Peninsula Hotel and walk toward the lobby seating area where he waited. Was it his imagination or had she grown more beautiful in the few hours they'd been apart?

Her features hadn't knocked him smitten immediately. Thick, straight medium-brown hair fell in a blunt sweep to her chin; hazel eyes shone dark-lashed and deep over high cheekbones covered by perfect skin. Her nose was average, lips slightly full. She had the type of neutral-palette face with excellent bone structure that photographers itched to paint and then capture. Beyond that, she exuded an air of freshness and joy irresistible in this city of hard-edged neurotics.

The circumstances that had brought them together still amused and amazed him. The evening and her reactions made a lot more sense now that he understood why she'd come over. Only one question remained, and he'd waited to ask until they were together so he could see her face while she answered.

He greeted her with the return of her earrings and a brief kiss on the lips—brief because if he started kissing her for real, he wouldn't want to stop, and the hotel probably wouldn't enjoy two people going at it on one of their beige Queen Anne sofas.

Though he undoubtedly would.

However, he had no problem tightening his arms around her, pressing her against him and not wanting to let go. "Get any sleep?"

"Not much." She was beaming, looking refreshed and happy. "You?"

"Not much." He kissed her again, longer this time. "I thought we could have a drink here...."

"That sounds nice." She turned her head to examine the double staircases that swept down nearly to the front door. "This hotel is incredible, I've never been in here."

"But I just realized there's no way I can sit across from you at a table and keep my hands to myself."

"Ooh." She turned back, expression mischievous. "That *is* a problem."

"I know. Big one."

"So?" She gripped the lapels of his favorite bomber jacket, her eyes glowing, undoubtedly to match his. "What instead?"

"I was thinking we should walk for a while on Fifth Avenue."

"I'd love that. It's so pretty this time of year."

"And then..."

"Yes?" She gave a short laugh that sounded like pure happiness. "Then?"

"Grab an early dinner somewhere."

"Mmm, good plan."

"And then..."

She raised her eyebrows. "I think I'm going to like this part."

"Go back to my place."

"I *know* I'm going to like this part."

"And try to wear each other out."

"Perfect." She smiled up at him and his heart started to hurt. Even making plans with Cathy was an emotional experience? He was in trouble.

"But first..."

Her smile dimmed at the change in his tone, and he squeezed her reassuringly. "I want to ask you something you don't have to answer if you don't want to."

"Okay." She spoke warily, eyes cautious.

"Who did give you that underwear?" He watched her carefully, hating the jealous fear that had been eating at him since she'd told him about the mix-up, praying she'd burst out laughing and name one of the female employees at *Connoisseur.*

Her expression did change but not into laughter. "Uh…a guy who lives across the hall from me. It was unexpected, to say the least."

He was gripping her too tightly. He forced his hold looser and made sure his next question came out playfully. "So you planning to model it for him, too?"

"No. God, no." She was genuinely horrified, and he had the grace to feel sheepish. He should have known better. The green-eyed monster didn't generally twist his brain this badly.

Did he say he was in trouble? Serious trouble.

"Okay." He kept his tone light. "Thank you for answering. I know I'm leaving soon and I have no right to—"

"Quinn, believe me." Her eyes were so earnest he had no choice but to believe her, no matter what came out of her mouth. "I'll never wear that underwear again. I couldn't. Not for anyone but you."

And if he thought he was in serious trouble before, he'd now proceeded to crisis. Emotion barreled up his chest. He doubted he could speak, so he kissed her instead, trying to keep calm so he wouldn't scare her.

He wanted to ask more questions, demand guarantees he didn't deserve. Why did this guy think underwear was an appropriate gift? How did she feel about him? If she'd known the lace was from him, would she have gone to his house last night instead? Was she planning to see him after Quinn left?

But where Cathy was concerned, he had no rights after tomorrow. What's more, today was still before them, sunny and mild, and he had the choice either to let questions and jealousy continue to feast on his mood and his outlook or to take the look in her eyes right now as his answer and drop it.

He took her hand and they left the sumptuous hotel for the holiday bustle of Fifth Avenue, turning south to join last-minute shoppers and tourists crowding the sidewalks. Fate had given him only a short time with Cathy, so he'd make the most of it. And if this extra day together made leaving her tomorrow and going to England harder than it would have been if they'd left well enough alone in the wee hours of the morning, so be it. He didn't see any point spending the rest of his short time in Manhattan wishing she were with him.

They passed Gucci, Fortunoff, Brooks Brothers, Ferragamo….

"Look." He lifted his chin toward a tiny blue-haired woman swathed in a thick brown fur coat toting several shopping bags toward a waiting limo. "Bet she has a different rock for each finger."

Cathy giggled. "And gloves made to accommodate them."

"Penthouse apartment overlooking Central Park…"

"With a special refrigerator for champagne and caviar."

"Bingo. Your turn." He bumped her gently with his shoulder, tickled at how immediately she'd understood the game. "Another Manhattan snapshot."

"Oh. Okay." She sent him a look of smiling bemusement and started scanning the crowd. "There. There's one."

She'd chosen a tall arrogant-looking young man with perfect dark hair, wearing a long wool coat, talking on his cell and clutching a Starbucks cup in his other hand, from which dangled a Brooks Brothers bag. "He makes six figures and hosts perfect parties that his perfect wife does all the work for."

"And to thank her for her perfection, he cheats on her."

"With their nanny." She eyed the man warily as he brushed past, giving a mock shudder. "Your turn again."

He gestured to a middle-aged woman in a faded red jacket gazing wistfully into the window of Versace. "Works hard but will never get ahead."

"Tried to be an actress, now works as administrative assistant to the VP of a struggling Web design company."

"Who harasses her daily."

She nodded toward a teenage girl coming out of the same store, loaded with bags, yapping on her cell in a shrill voice about giving "that jerk Steven" what he had coming to him. "*Doesn't* work hard but will always stay ahead."

"Will marry Steven in spite of hating him, have his babies, then leave him."

"For another woman."

He laughed and pulled at her hand so she bumped against him. "You're good."

"I try."

They crossed Fifty-second Street, where the Cartier building was, as usual, decked out for the holidays in a huge red ribbon and sparkling light bow, with two tiaras of lights over each entrance. He turned to grin mischievously at Cathy, not able to remember when he'd enjoyed someone's company more. "I'd like to compose a picture of you wearing only diamond jewelry and a Santa hat, planted in the middle of that bow."

She shivered. "Sounds chilly."

"No, no. Very hot." He stared at the building, imagining her there naked, wishing he'd brought his camera, wishing he had the time to come back and get the background shot. "I don't think I'll ever look at Cartier the same way."

She put gentle pressure on his fingers. "Me neither."

Her wistful tone squeezed his heart much harder than she'd squeezed his hand. He had a flash of the long year ahead in London, the city he loved so much, which wouldn't have memories of Cathy to color its streets.

They stopped at the soaring Gothic spires of St. Patrick's Cathedral, then backed toward the curb to avoid being mown down by passersby.

He turned with a question, then paused. The breeze was lifting her hair and dropping the heavy strands back down in place; her eyes were bright, cheeks and nose tip pink. He studied her carefully so he could call her back to his memory whenever he wanted, kicking himself again for not bringing a camera.

"Yes?"

Obviously he'd been staring too long. "When did you come back from the Midwest?"

"Five years ago."

"Ah, so you missed the scandal."

"What scandal?"

"In 2002, a local radio shock jock encouraged New Yorkers to have sex in public places around the city. He broadcast a program here from St. Patrick's, where he claimed to be watching two people going at it in the vestibule."

She screwed up her face in disgust. "That is really offensive."

"What is, sex in public?"

"In a church!" She waved her hand at St. Patrick's.

"Agreed." His brain immediately came up with a picture of he and Cathy going at it somewhere less sacrilegious. Like in Central Park at dusk. Or on a deserted subway car. Or…

Why torture himself? They'd have no time to try.

"Maybe somewhere *else* it would be fun…." Her brown eyes shot him a teasing look.

He pulled her forward until they joined from the waist down and kissed her, his body responding instantly to the eagerness of her mouth. "You read my mind."

"If it was warmer out…"

Her face fell, and he knew what she was thinking because he was thinking the same. When it got warmer out, they wouldn't be together.

He kissed her again and pulled her around to keep walking until they joined the crowds lingering outside Saks Fifth Avenue's Christmas windows, this year showing characters from a children's book Quinn wasn't familiar with. Tiny black mice scampered over a huge green dragon out of whose nose gold and red streamers flickered to represent flame. His paws lifted one by one in a vain attempt to brush off the mice, who avoided his every move.

Cathy laughed and leaned in for a better look. "These are great. I don't know the story, do you?"

He shook his head. "Been a while since I read a kids' book. Even my nieces and nephews are too old for this level now."

"How much older are your brothers?"

"Fifteen and eighteen years. I was a surprise."

"So you essentially grew up an only child."

"Yeah. With three fathers." The bitterness in his voice surprised him. He'd meant to sound amused. "You have one brother?"

"Brad. Older by three years. Horrible tease. He still calls me the Catheter. But we're good friends now. He married and moved to Arizona, so I don't see him as often as I'd like. He'll be home for Christmas, though."

"You're close to your family." He didn't need to make it a question.

"Yes. I moved back east to be nearer. I take it you're not close to yours." She turned to him with sympathy. "I'm sorry. It must leave a hole in your life."

"No, not really." His response was automatic, but her words stayed with him as they came to another window, in which a little boy hugged an animal that looked like a friendly, furry dog-eagle hybrid. A hole in his life? He had a great job, good friends he spent time with when he was in town, some of whom he'd known since he was a boy. Unlucky in love so far, but that could change at any second. Maybe it was already changing.

If only…

"Look at that." She was laughing at the pink tongue that incongruously emerged from the eagle's beak, lapping at the boy's face, which turned cheerfully side to side in a vain effort to avoid the bath. "I'll have to find this book. Looks like one I would have loved as a kid."

He let go of her hand and put his arm around her waist, drawing her close so they walked as a unit, and to hell with people around them who got pushed aside. One second she was talking about sex in public, the next she was enthralled with a children's story. The short time he had to explore her seemed only crueler as the minutes ticked by. As did the idea that Underwear Boy would have all the leisure in the world as soon as Quinn was out of the picture.

He couldn't bear to think about it.

They reached the last window, and crossed Forty-ninth Street to wander around Rockefeller Center, admiring the huge Christmas tree, watching the skaters on the below-street-level rink, stopping for a very late lunch/very early dinner at the Rock Center Café, where even at that odd hour they had to wait at the bar for a table. He didn't care. As long as he was with Cathy, he'd happily sit at the bottom of a sewage tank.

The longer he spent with her, the more time he wanted. Three days from now he'd be starting his last assignment for *Connoisseur,* then settling in to register at Sotheby's, setting up his own studio in the city....

A strong sense of suffocation nearly took away his breath.

What the hell? He forced himself calm, pretending to search the room for the waiter to pay their bill.

That feeling had hit him once before, suddenly like this, and it had changed his life.

He'd done some impetuous things in his time—okay, quite a few as a teenager and college student, though he'd stayed out of jail. Then he'd settled down to take life seriously, much to the combined delight and relief of his parents and older brothers.

Life had gone smoothly until he'd woken up one morning, the day before his second year of medical school, with this same sense of panic and impending suffocation at the thought of the coming year.

He hadn't thought twice. He'd walked to the dean's office and given notice that he was dropping out. After that he'd pursued photography—to his parents' unrelenting dismay, even though he'd made nothing but a success of it so far. They had their own definition of success, about as narrow as their views on everything else.

That decision to leave had been made at the spur of the moment, on no more than a feeling—granted, a strong one. And that decision had turned out to be absolutely the right one. Had he simply gotten lucky? Or did he have a good instinct that he needed to trust when it spoke to him?

He didn't know. But he'd have to pay attention and give it some serious thought. Because right now his instinct was telling him Cathy was The One and he'd be a fool to risk leaving her.

6

CATHY STEPPED INTO QUINN'S living room—after another narrow escape from Mrs. Hoffman—a little more than twelve hours after she'd left, though it felt like days longer than that. Suitcases stood next to the door and she looked away determinedly. They still had until tomorrow afternoon; she wasn't going to allow herself to get morbid already. Their day together so far had been perfect and the night would be, too. She'd deal with goodbye when it was time.

Then go home feeling like death would be a fun vacation.

"Can I get you a nightcap?"

"No, thanks." Wine was still singing through her veins from dinner. "I'm fine as is."

"Okay." He crossed to a cabinet next to where he'd gotten the brandy the night before, opened a door and revealed a fancy-looking sound system. He pushed buttons, adjusted knobs, and she waited, curious what he'd choose.

A slow swing number played by full orchestra filled the room with a dreamy old-fashioned sound, which could not have been more perfect.

"Dance with me?" He held out his arms and she gave a laugh of pure delight. A man who danced! If he turned out to be any more wonderful, she'd have to start checking for mechanical parts.

"Love to." She took his hand and put hers on his shoulder, moved close and found—of course—that he was a really good dancer. "Are you bad at anything?"

"Sure." He rested his chin against her temple. "Bowling, football, baking, jigsaw puzzles...and saying goodbye."

"I'm…" her voice broke "…about to get really bad at that, too."

"In that case…" He kissed her forehead and pulled her closer. "We'll pretend we have forever."

"Good plan." She slid her arms all the way around his shoulders, laid her head in the curve of his neck, closed her eyes and swayed to the music, humming along with the familiar parts, drinking in the pleasure of his body being so close, his arms strong and secure around her.

The song flowed on and ended with a slow improvised flourish; the last chord held, died away. Cathy lifted her head and found Quinn looking down at her with an expression of such tenderness her heart bounded, and that piercing, sweet emotion swelled in her again.

I love you. She knew it wasn't true—it couldn't be yet, not real love—but she felt the power of it so fiercely she nearly said the words out loud, which would ruin everything.

"Ekatarina…"

Her heart sped again and launched her into fantasy. He was going to say he loved her, too. Or he was going to say he'd stay in New York. Or he was going to invite her to—

The next song came on abruptly, a jazzy, crashing version of "Take The A Train" that jolted them both. Quinn took a step back and held out his hand.

Whew. Saved by the New York City transit system.

A minute later, thankfully, she'd regained emotional balance and was successfully having the time of her life all over again. The man could even Jitterbug. Who knew those painful dance lessons her mother had made her take would actually be useful one day? Cathy would have to tell Mom, to give her the pleasure of a teasing I-told-you-so.

Tomorrow at this time she'd be on her way to see her family. For the first time, packing for the familiar trip at Christmas would be bittersweet instead of joyful.

Quinn spun her out, then back, his dark blue eyes flashing, his face slightly flushed, leading her so expertly through the steps that her body seemed to know what he wanted before he even asked for it. The way she responded to him in bed. And when they played silly games or talked together. This was her fantasy man? Being with him felt more real to her than any of her time with Jake.

The song ended. They broke apart, breathing hard, waiting for the next one, smiling expectantly. A new piece started, a raucous, brassy number she didn't recognize, suitable for a strutting chorus line...or a striptease.

Hmm...

She made her decision instantly. Her attempt the previous night might have been laughable, but everything had changed between them now. She was here legitimately because he wanted her to be. She was here without fear.

And he was going to get it.

She planted her hand in the center of his chest and pushed, walking him backward toward the couch in time with the music, gazing wickedly from under her lashes. He went willingly, one eyebrow arched, until the couch hit the back of his knees and he sat abruptly.

Cathy—no, Catriona, Catlaina, Ekatarina—sauntered to the opposite side of the room, turned around so her back was to him and rotated her hips slowly, hands raised, feeling her cheeks flush. But not with embarrassment this time.

She worked her tight pale yellow sweater up slowly, then off, not caring that her bra wasn't red or black, wildly revealing or cleavage-enhancing, but plain ivory. The black slit skirt came down, too, inch by gradual inch, her panties a matching ivory with only a touch of lace at the sides.

The coy glance over her shoulder was purely for effect. She wasn't even worried he'd think she was ridiculous. Because if he did, he'd just laugh and scoop her up and kiss her and they'd make love all night anyway.

But, um, judging by the look of blue-eyed rapture on his face, he didn't find her ridiculous.

The brass section blared. She turned to face him, confidence rising even higher, and tossed her hips to one side, arms over her head, then slid her hands down her stomach and back up to unhook her bra and slide it off her shoulders.

He closed his eyes briefly, moved his hips up, pants straining to cope with his arousal.

Oh, baby. She was hot. She was fabulous. She was on top of the world, and Quinn had put her there.

Arms open wide, she did a slow shimmy toward him, her nipples hardening even in the warmth of the room. A foot away she stopped and, without questioning her actions or her daring, she slid her hands slowly down into her panties.

Even with the music thundering, she heard him groan. He unfastened his pants, lowered his briefs and...*mmm, yes.* He was ready, and the sight of him so hard increased her own excitement. She continued to touch herself, drawing a hand up now and then to caress her breast or circle its tip with her thumb.

Another groan and he stroked his erection a few times, then wrenched his hands away, clasped them on top of his head and watched her, jaw set, eyes narrowed.

He was suffering deeply. She loved it. She'd never felt this wild, euphoric freedom before. Not with anyone. Not even close.

Her panties came off, dragged down with her thigh-highs. She stepped out of her shoes and flung the clothes off to the side with an elegant flick of her wrist.

Naked. And proud.

In an amazing coincidence, the music stopped just as her stockings and panties hit the floor. The silence in the room was electric. She held his eyes, waiting, preparing to take her cue from the mood of the next piece.

The tropical rhythms of "Begin the Beguine" poured out of the speakers. She crouched between his legs, drew her hands up his chest and helped him off with his shirt, then the rest of his clothes. He only touched her twice—as if he knew this was her show but couldn't bear not to—once brushing his palms over her breasts, sending a jolt of desire through her, once sliding warm hands up her back as she lowered his pants. The rest of the time he let her undress him, helping when necessary, watching her as if he was intent on memorizing her every move.

Now… She pushed him back on the couch after his pants had been flung to join her underwear, knelt slowly, swaying to the music, put her hands on his muscular thighs and took him into her mouth, reveling in his gasp of pleasure.

He was a perfect size, not small but not too large to take in comfortably. She started slowly, exploring, tasting with lips and tongue, intent on giving him pleasure, wildly turned on where she usually felt oral sex was something of a duty. Sensing him watching her turned her on more. She closed her eyes and tried to imagine herself into his mind, imagining what he'd want her to do, then doing it. Sucking the tip, then deep-throating his entire length, pushing down on the base of his penis with her fingers to increase the tension.

"Catriona." He sounded a little weak, and she tried not to smile.

"Mmm?"

"Do you want to go into the bedroom?"

She shook her head and went down on him again.

"Catlaina." He reached and dragged her up next to him. "If you want to do anything but this, you need to give me a break."

"Oh?" She smiled teasingly. "Okay."

"I'll get a condom." He left the room briefly and returned, tall and athletic and totally unselfconscious, walking naked, fully erect, in front of a woman he'd barely known a day. Her chest constricted painfully and she pushed the sadness away. He was hers tonight and she was crazy about him. That was something to celebrate.

Quinn sat back on the couch, rolled on the condom and opened his arms wide. "I'm all yours. Do what you will."

"What a good idea." She straddled him, then began rotating her hips in a tiny circle to the music, lowering until the lips of her sex brushed the tip of his penis, and he gave a soft moan.

"I am not sure I'm going to survive this."

She lowered another careful inch, trapping the head of his erection at her opening, the promise of penetration making her breath unsteady. "You said that last night."

"I did, didn't I?" His eyes closed; he took hold of her waist to hurry her the rest of the way onto him.

She resisted. "And you're still here."

Another inch. He drew in breath, a sharp hiss. "This time the pleasure is going to be fatal. I'm sure."

She paused, watching his face, knowing she was putting her heart in danger again. She should take him in to the hilt right now and keep the mood raunchy and fun. But she waited until he opened his eyes into hers, then slowly sank the rest of the way onto him, maintaining their powerful connection, her emotional shield all but gone.

I love you.

He wrapped his arms around her and moved her carefully sideways on the couch, then settled himself between her legs and resumed his rhythm, gazing into her eyes.

She gazed back, utterly at ease. *I love you.*

"I can't bear to leave you tomorrow, Ekaterina."

Her heart jolted. *Then don't.*

She left the thought unsaid. What good would it do? He wasn't going to change his plans and career choices after knowing her twenty-four hours.

"It will be…" She should say something sensible like, *difficult, but time will fly, and before you know it you'll be back again.* Instead she said, "Really horrible."

He nodded and then he stopped moving, stared down at her with a look of intense absorption, and she felt herself stiffen, crazy fear and excitement rising in equal amounts.

"I'm…"

"Yes?"

"I'm going to London on Tuesday."

She rolled her eyes, almost angry in her disappointment. "Trust me, Quinn, I know that."

He began to move again, as if whatever trouble had been gripping him was released. Then he lowered his head so his lips were right next to her ear.

"Come with me."

CATHY WALKED UP FIFTH Avenue in Brooklyn, toward Eighth Street and home. The sun was out, temperatures in the mid-thirties, fairly mild for that time of year. It was Christmas Eve…and she was miserable.

Quinn's invitation last night had broadsided her. He liked and desired her enough to want her with him for as much vacation time as she could take from *Connoisseur* while he completed his last assignment for the magazine, before he started his year of study.

Immediately every part of her had prepared to scream an eager yes.

And then…her natural caution had kicked in, and she'd started to analyze.

If she thought past the bliss of a week—or more, if her boss let her—in London with Quinn, helping him on his assignment, traveling, exploring, then spending lots of time in their hotel room doing even more exploring, she'd face another separation, this one made even more painful by the inevitably stronger feelings she would develop.

Or…what if their week wasn't blissful? What if she got to London and found their wild weekend here was simply a combination of opportunity and chemistry and fantasy which should have stayed in Manhattan? What if their habits didn't mesh, their attraction staled and the whole love affair turned sour? She'd be stuck in London with a man she barely knew who would no longer want her there and have to come home ten times more miserable than she was now.

So she'd said no. No to adventure, no to love, no, no, no and goodbye. Maybe a year from now, when he came back, they could pick up where they'd left off. That would be nice, though it didn't help the lead in her stomach feel any lighter. The year ahead stretched on forever—three hundred and sixty-five days; eight thousand seven hundred and sixty hours; five hundred twenty-five thousand six hundred minutes. And without Quinn or Catriona, Catlaina or Ekatarina, Cathy Ann Johnson would be left alone, undoubtedly second-guessing her decision even more strongly than she was now, to count them all.

Well not entirely alone. She still had Jake....

Cathy stopped stock-still. She didn't want Jake. Deep down she'd known that for a while, probably from the first moment Quinn had kissed her, maybe before. Around Jake she felt as dull and ordinary as she felt sexy and fascinating around Quinn. Having tasted that thrill and connection, she couldn't go back to lukewarm, comfortable interest.

A woman edged around her, giving her a questioning smile for standing in the middle of the sidewalk. Cathy lurched back into motion. She couldn't turn to Jake now. Especially since she suspected Melinda felt about him the way Cathy did about Quinn, and maybe the two of them deserved a shot.

She rounded the last corner and stopped abruptly again, staring at her building. The early setting sun made the windows glitter and slanted across the masonry so it glowed a rich, ruddy sand color. The stone protuberances on the roof threw regular shadows that looked nearly like battlements. The bizarre asymmetrical entrance flanked by narrow trees decorated for the holidays could be about to lower a drawbridge across the sidewalk moat.

Cathy took in a long breath. Melinda's horoscope had been exactly right. Cathy *had* gotten a gift from her true love. Not underwear from Jake. But a new, finer, clearer vision of her city...and her home...and herself. From Quinn.

She ran the rest of the way to her fabulous futuristic castle and charged up the stairs, too impatient to wait for the elevator. This was going to be the best Christmas she'd ever had.

Inside her apartment, she was halfway to the phone to call Quinn when Melinda's door opened and out came...Jake. Naked.

"I'm getting water, babe. You want a—"

He froze, staring at Cathy, who clamped down on a giggle and managed a placid smile. "Hello, Jake."

"Uh..." He covered his manly parts with his hands and started backing into Melinda's room. "Hi...*Cathy*."

Melinda's gasp could be heard from inside her bedroom.

"Merry Christmas, Melinda," Cathy called. "I guess you found something that made you happier than dog poo?"

Melinda sidled out of her bedroom, cheeks flushed brilliant red, curls a tangled mess, still tying her robe. "Cathy. I'm— It was— I mean we just happened. He was— Well, it was like we couldn't help it."

Cathy's eyebrow rose slowly. "Different when the moral shoe is on the other foot?"

"Oh, um, yeah." Melinda examined her toes. "I'm sorry I came down on you so hard. I guess I was jealous."

"It's really okay." She lowered her voice. "Jake and I weren't destined for true love after all."

Melinda frowned. "Yeah, your horoscope must have meant some other gift."

"It did." Cathy laughed. "Believe it or not, it was absolutely right."

"Well, duh. Why would I believe in something that wasn't legit?"

Jake reappeared wearing a T-shirt and jeans, and both women turned, Melinda gazing adoringly. He cleared his throat. "Cathy, I'm really sorry about—"

"Don't be." Cathy held up her hand to stop him. "I wasn't totally honest with you. I met someone else. I didn't think it was going to be serious, but…it got that way really fast."

"Yeah." He reached to touch Melinda's hair. "I know what you mean."

The three of them stood smiling enormous smiles, equal parts relief and happiness, until it became painfully obvious none of them wanted to be standing there smiling enormous smiles anymore.

"Well. So. Good." Cathy beamed at them both. "And now I have a phone call to make and some packing to do."

"That's right—you're going to your parents' house!" Melinda winked at Jake, who leered back, obviously thrilled at the idea of Cathy's imminent departure.

"Yup." Cathy turned and hightailed it into her bedroom, shouting back over her shoulder just for the thrill of hearing the words out loud. "And then…I'm going to London."

QUINN UNLOCKED THE DOOR to his apartment, totally exhausted, then barreled in and slammed it behind him when he heard Mrs. Hoffman's door opening across the hall.

Christmas had been the usual toxic affair, with forced cheer and goodwill between Quinn, his brothers and his parents. Even his nieces and nephews were grumping in teenage hell, though they provided him with the only good conversation and genuine affection of the two days. Expensive presents, excellent food, exquisite wine and the annual walk on the Griggstown canal, though it was gray, damp and bitterly cold. Merry Christmas. Ho, ho, ho boy was he glad that was over.

Except now there was nothing between him and the trip he'd started thinking of as London Without Cathy.

He wearily carted his overnight bag into his room, unpacked it and took out the items he'd also be taking to Europe, to add to the cases already packed and waiting.

Three steps toward his living room, his fatigue increased, his chest tightened, his breathing passages narrowed to panic. Again.

He sank onto his bed and forced himself to face what he was feeling. This was ludicrous. He couldn't make a major decision based on a whim, not at his age. He was no longer a kid and had long ago given up trying to understand or please his parents. There was no one to rebel against anymore except…himself.

Three steps to the window, and he threw it open, breathing in the New York air tinged with the damp coming of snow. In an hour and a half he'd be leaving for the airport. Going to his second home city, embarking on all the new, fresh and invigorating enrichment he thought his life here lacked…

He was full of it.

Five strides to his bedside table, and he picked up the phone, dialed the international code for England, London, then his friend John's number. When John's answering machine picked up, he left a message for his friend to call back.

Energy flooded him. And relief. He practically ran to the table in his living room where he'd scrawled Cathy's number on a business card. He punched in half the digits, then screwed up and had to start over, impatient fingers clumsy.

The call connected. Rang once. Twice. *Come on, be home.* Her machine answered; he hung up, cursing. Leaving a message didn't cut it. He wanted her *now.* But he didn't even know her cell number. Or what time she'd planned to be home from her parents' house.

God, this was crazy. After breaking up with three women in the past five years whom he'd dated for months but hadn't been willing to stick with, he was changing his entire life for a woman he knew next to nothing about, whom he'd dated for a little over thirty-six hours.

It felt damn good.

Where the hell was she? His euphoria began dissolving into frustration. He had to be on that plane tonight. He couldn't cancel his assignment for the magazine. But if he didn't reach Cathy before he left to let her know he'd be coming back to her…well, he could call her tonight from London, but it wasn't the same. If he reached her now, she might even be able to spend a little time with him at the airport before his flight.

A knock on his door had his hopes rising even though he knew he was being ridiculous. But he couldn't help hurrying, throwing the door open, preparing himself for disappointment.

"Hello, Quinn, dear." His neighbor, holding out a package.

"Hi, Mrs. Hoffman." The disappointment he was supposed to be prepared for nearly crushed him. "Hope you had a nice Christmas."

"Very nice. This came for you while you were gone. Too big to fit in your box downstairs, so I picked it up for you."

And undoubtedly all but had it X-rayed to see what it was and who had sent it.

"Thanks." He started to close the door, then thought better of his rudeness. "Uh, Happy New Year."

"You going somewhere?" She peered around him, obviously catching sight of his suitcases.

"Yes. But I'll be back in two weeks." He couldn't help grinning. Hot damn. Two weeks.

"Are you seeing more of that lovely girl?" she asked slyly.

His grin turned into a chuckle. "I hope to be seeing that lovely girl for the rest of my life."

"Oh!" To his utter amazement, her eyes filled with tears. "How wonderful. I'm so happy for you. And frankly, it's about time."

"Thanks, Mrs. Hoffman." He wished her a Happy New Year again, thanked her for her offer to keep an eye on the place while he was away—as if she didn't while he was here—and finally got the door closed. Inside, he eyed the package curiously. No postage; it must have been hand-delivered. He tore off the wrapping, lifted the lid of the box and gaped.

A male thong, with the head of an elephant strategically placed. Immediately Cathy's voice came back to him from the office less than a week ago—*It's your job to provide the trunk.* And written in silver marker across the broad gray forehead: *Seduce me.*

His turn to feel tears pricking at his eyes. God, if only he *could* seduce her right now. But even he could stand waiting two weeks if it meant he could seduce her anytime he wanted after he got back.

Another knock. He rolled his eyes and went to answer, wondering if Mrs. Hoffman had stood outside counting seconds until he must have opened the package so she could barge in and see. He opened the door and froze.

Cathy. Holding a suitcase. And waving…a passport.

He stared at her, unable to take in what she was doing there. "Cathy."

The door behind her opened again, and Mrs. Hoffman's beaming face poked out. Quinn grabbed Cathy through the door and shut it, shaking his head.

"Busybody." He chuckled at the déjà vu.

"Yeah, there's one in every building."

"True." He remembered their exact exchange last Friday night and probably every word they'd exchanged since then. "So…hi."

"Hi. Well. I'm…" She raised her arms out to the side. "Here."

"So you are. Come on in."

She stepped past him into his living room, rolling her suitcase behind her. "Nice place. You own this or rent?"

He grinned. "Are you by any chance wearing really exciting underwear?"

"Actually, yes."

His cock jumped predictably, but for this woman, so did his heart. "And would you by any chance be willing to show it to me in a London hotel tonight?"

She dropped the suitcase handle and stepped up to him, beautiful hazel eyes full of tears. "I'd love to."

"And…" His voice dropped to a husky murmur. "Would you like to spend two weeks there, then come back home to Manhattan with me and fall the rest of the way in love?"

Her mouth opened to speak. Then what he said must have hit her, because she closed it, looking as stunned as he'd felt opening the door to her.

"I'm not going, Cathy. Not for the year."

"But…why?"

He put his arms around her, drew her close, where he wanted to feel her for the rest of his life. "Remember when you asked me if not being close to my family had left a hole in my life?"

"Yes," she whispered, eyes shining with hope, and he knew that if they both lived to be a hundred, they'd still be together and that he'd never forget a single detail of how she looked right now.

"It did, though I didn't realize. I've been trying to fit a yearlong trip to London into a hole with your exact size and shape."

"Quinn." She was crying now, and he gathered her close, kissed her and kissed her again, tasting her tears and his future.

"Catriona—"

"No, no. Ordinary Cathy is fine." She was shaking her head, laughing unsteadily. "Because everything else will always be extraordinary with you."

MISTLETOE MADNESS
Jennifer LaBrecque

To all the romance readers who love the genre and the stories. Thank you.

1

MERRY CHRISTMAS AND ho, ho, ho. And just who was the bright bunny who'd come up with the whole Secret Santa schmiel? Oh, yeah, boss's daughter. Tatiana Allen rolled her eyes. Yep. It was brilliant. Double brilliant that now, in addition to everything else, with less than two weeks left until Christmas, she had to buy a Secret Santa gift…and for Cole Mitchell no less. Ugh. Cole, Where's-My-Silver-Spoon, Mitchell.

Of course, truth be told, it wasn't exactly as if her Christmas activity cup runneth over. For the second year in a row, after both retiring from the local power company in Yurgash, Indiana, her parents were taking a Christmas cruise. Late-December snow and ice in Yurgash or a float trip through the sunny Caribbean? That was a no-brainer. And after working hard all their lives, they'd informed her, they were learning to play before it was too late. In fact, her mother had been on something of a crusade for Tatiana to break what she called the curse of the legendary Rumasky work ethic. Crazy talk. Mom definitely needed a break.

Last year Tatiana had joined Grandma Rumasky for Christmas. This year Grandma and Ivan Chertoff were headed to Vegas for a Chapel of Love holiday hookup and a honeymoon parked in front of the slots. Grandma Rumasky didn't have the best of luck with husbands—they tended to die on her—but she and Ivan were both determined to seize the day. More power to them.

And Tatiana was a big girl. At twenty-eight, there was no reason she couldn't spend Christmas alone. In her co-op. In the city. Not a big deal.

Tatiana crumpled the piece of paper bearing her fellow food

critic and archnemesis's name and tossed it into the garbage can beneath her desk. Okay, so maybe she did have time to shop for a gift. Maybe, in fact, she had time in spades. But for Cole? As long as no one expected her to be filled with the spirit of goodwill when she shopped for *him*.

"Have you checked your e-mail?" Elle said, sticking her head in the door of Tatiana's office.

When Elle, administrative assistant to their department head, made inquiries like that... Foreboding reared its ugly head. "No. Why?"

"Melvin's had a brain fart." Elle massaged her temple. "I swear, I think his therapist is screwing around with his Prozac dosage."

Melvin, their esteemed department head, functioned optimally when medicated. And Elle, unlike her boss, was emotionally stable and a straight shooter without chemical enhancement. She called it the way she saw it. This must be bad.

Tatiana planted her forearms on her desk. "I'm braced. What is it?"

"Melvin has decreed, via e-mail, that in keeping with the spirit of the holiday, we'll be celebrating the 'Eight Days of the Season.'"

"Oh, boy. This sounds like a real winner. How'd he come up with this?"

"In order to be politically correct, he took the twelve days of Christmas, the eight days of Hanukah and the seven days of Kwanzaa. He averaged them to come up with the Eight Days of the Season. That means eight Secret Santa gifts and a biggie on the last day."

Color her a whiner, but this holiday season was going from bad to worse. She did a quick calculation. And Melvin's math skills sucked. It should be nine days, but she wasn't saying squat.

"Do you know why the windows don't open here on the twenty-seventh floor?" Tatiana jammed a thumb over her shoulder in the direction of the window. "Because we'd be too damn tempted to jump."

It was a good thing Melvin was brilliant at his job, because the other stuff that went along with him... Eight Secret Santa gifts—for Cole. Not only did she have to endure him at work, now she had to spend her hard-earned money on him, too. "Please tell me this is Melvin's idea of a joke."

"Uh…no." Elle shoved her straight blond hair behind one ear. Tall, model-thin, sophisticated, it'd be so easy to hate Elle, except she was too genuinely nice to hate. Unlike Cole Mitchell, who was easy fodder.

Connoisseur had a long-standing reputation as *the* premier travel/food magazine. And Tatiana had known she wanted the high-profile spot of *Connoisseur* restaurant critic since she'd waitressed her way through college. Traveling to foreign, exotic locales to taste, test and review eateries for discerning travelers was her dream job. She'd worked long and hard, with unwavering determination, to earn one of the two coveted positions at the magazine. And then Cole had waltzed into the same job through family connections. She might've managed to overlook it if they hadn't struck sparks off one another from day one. No, Cole Mitchell was easy to dislike. And his good looks and easy charm were simply another strike against him in her book.

"That's Melvin, spreading love and peace, eighteen people at a time," Elle continued. She stepped closer to the desk and lowered her voice. "So who'd you get?"

"Oh, no. I'm not telling." Elle was fun and a great source of departmental information, but she was also an inveterate gossip. And the animosity simmering between Tatiana and Cole was something the whole department had been avidly watching. There was no way Elle wouldn't spill the beans. "You'll slip up and I'll be outed to Melvin. Then he'll come up with something totally horrible because I screwed up the surprise element of his Eight Days of Secret Santa Season. No can do."

"I would *not* slip up."

Uh-huh. Just like a fat man and eight reindeer were gonna be making rounds on Christmas Eve. "Not deliberately."

"Well, go ahead and pull up the e-mail. Read it and weep. Ta." Elle left as suddenly as she'd appeared.

Tatiana clicked on her e-mail icon and skimmed Melvin's

missive. Eight gifts for Cole Mitchell? Maybe she could start out with a personality to go along with his ego. Unfortunately she didn't know where to purchase a personality for Mr. Arrogant Imbecile, but she knew just what she could order for his first gift. She clicked on the search and typed in her request. An evil smile played about her mouth. She loved online shopping.

TATIANA ALLEN. COLE Mitchell rolled his neck, to no avail. Tatiana pain was mental, not physical. And anyway, she was a pain much farther south than his neck.

Eighteen people in the department and he got stuck playing Secret Santa to Ms. Acid-Tongued Shrew. Oh, joy. Maybe he could buy her a one-way ticket to some far and distant place. Trouble was, she went to far and distant places, but she always returned—like his recurring pain. Perversely he'd begun to anticipate matching wits and trading barbs with her on the occasions when they were both in the office.

He reconsidered. Maybe this wouldn't be so bad after all when her Santa gave her just what she deserved. And he got to make that decision. It would definitely be something that would leave the group laughing and her squirming. Hey, this Secret Santa could be heady stuff.

His phone extension buzzed. "Cole?" Elle's disembodied voice came over the intercom.

"Yeah?"

"Melvin needs to see you in his office. ASAP."

"Sure thing." Cole pushed back from his desk and picked up his day planner.

Melvin was a bona fide nut job. One of those guys you looked at and wondered how he'd made it as far as he had with his numerous quirks. Lucky for him, he had a damn fine eye for critique and editorial. Professional schizophrenia.

Of course, quite a number of people considered Cole's success questionable. He knew that accounted for much of Tatiana's attitude. She only saw what he had seemingly stepped into. She had no clue what he'd walked away from. It had taken about five whole minutes for word to spread of Cole's father's meeting with *Connoisseur*'s publisher. Of course, no one other than Cole knew his father had been there to try and thwart his son's career move. But if that's what people wanted to believe, screw 'em. He'd quit playing the if-you'd-give-me-a-chance-you-might-like-me game when he was a kid.

Cole strolled down the hall, bypassing the cubicles. He paused outside of Melvin's corner office. Elle, on the phone, waved Cole in.

He walked in, closing the door behind him. Great. The Evil Fairy Queen was already planted in one of the two guest chairs facing Melvin's desk. Red unruly curls and piercing green eyes. A prominent nose reminiscent of Streisand. A generous mouth that deceptively led to thoughts of hot kisses…until one encountered her rapier tongue. More striking than pretty.

Melvin, thin, angular and prematurely balding, motioned Cole into the chair next to Tatiana. Cole slid into the seat, noticing, not for the first time, her legs. Nice legs. Very nice legs…especially for a virago. She smiled at him and he didn't trust it for a second. She was either sick or up to something. "Not feeling well today?"

"I'm just fine." Her smile, even though it was faux sweet, sent a jolt through him. "Thanks for asking."

Melvin spoke up. "You're probably wondering why I wanted to see the two of you."

Cole slanted a sidelong glance at Tatiana. He could all but see her bite back a scathing comment. He had to admit, things were never dull with Madame Snark around.

She swallowed and said, "You wanted to tell us firsthand that the Eight Days of the Season was a practical joke?"

Melvin recoiled. "Absolutely not. It's a wonderful opportunity for us all to grow closer."

Oops. Someone had been adjusting Melvin's feel-good pills again.

"I really want you and everyone else to think about what

their person might want or need. As I mentioned in my e-mail, the gifts should speak to both the giver and the recipient."

Cole couldn't contain a grin. He planned to speak to Tatiana with his gifts, for sure.

"See, Cole's excited about it. You've just got to enter into the spirit of the season, Tatiana."

She skewered Cole with a look that suggested he nosh on something vile.

Okay, there was no holding it back. His grin gave way to a full-blown smirk. Thank you, Melvin. Score one for him.

"Now on to the matter at hand. As you both know, the magazine market is getting tighter and tighter, and it's increasingly important for us to evaluate on an ongoing basis…"

Cole's eyes began to glaze over. He'd heard this about a freaking million times. Melvin pulled out the same state-of-the-industry preparatory speech and meandered through it for ten minutes before actually making a point. Cole's attention wandered to Tatiana's legs. Shapely. Curvy, like the rest of her, with nice muscle tone in her calf. Slender, sexy ankles. Just the kind of legs a man could imagine wrapped around his waist or thrown over his shoulders.

What would Tatiana Allen be like in bed? Would she always be jockeying to be on top? He'd bet the family farm she wasn't a quiet, gentle lover. No way. She'd moan and scream his name and sink her red nails into his shoulders, nipping and biting. Climbing into bed with her would be like going to war. And damn it if the thought didn't leave him squirming in his chair and more than a little turned on.

What would she taste like? It'd been his experience that no two women tasted the same, whether you were lazily licking along her neck, kissing her mouth or something more intimate.

Wasabi. Tatiana would taste like wasabi. Not hot to the initial bite, but then it set your senses on fire. That's what she'd be— exotic, spicy, hot, with an incendiary afterburn….

"So, Cole…" Hearing his name snapped him out of his sexual contemplation and back to the present, "What do *you* think?" Melvin asked.

A quick glance at Tatiana made up his mind. She looked disgusted and thoroughly pissed off. Anything that elicited that kind of response in her, he was all for it.

"I think it's a great idea." Did she actually grind her teeth? "I think you've got a real winner." Yes. He was sure he just heard enamel on enamel. He laid it on thicker. "Best I've heard in a while."

Melvin preened. "See, Tatiana, Cole likes it."

If looks could kill… "That's because Cole is an imbecile with a mouth. He doesn't have a clue as to what he just endorsed. He was drifting along in la-la land. And besides, he wouldn't know a good idea if it came up and bit him in the butt."

Oh, shit. She was far more observant and sharper than Melvin. Well, except for that bit about a good idea biting him in the butt. Still, he knew the best defense was a good offense. "Just because you don't like the idea…" What the hell was the idea? "Well, darling, you really shouldn't sulk, because it's not very becoming." He tossed her a flirtatious smile. "And I'm flattered you've noticed my rear."

Her look turned docile, almost sweet, and the hair on the back of his neck stood up. He'd pushed too far. "Maybe you're right. Maybe it is a great idea and I just need to see it the same way you do. Why don't you recap it for me but with your spin on it? You know, a different perspective."

Damn her. Melvin jumped in, saving his proverbial butt.

"Perfect. This is just the kind of thing we want to play up. Siskel and Ebert. Hepburn and Tracy. Michael Jackson and Bubbles?"

Mother of God. What the hell was Melvin babbling about? Siskel, Hepburn and Tracy were dead. And Jackson and Bubbles?

"Melvin, be reasonable." Tatiana adopted a conciliatory tone. "It's the holidays. I have obligations and a full schedule. I'm sure Cole does, too."

Melvin templed his fingers in front of his mouth. "I appreciate that and I also appreciate that this takes precedence over anything else you're working on for *Connoisseur* at the moment. You and Cole will just have to figure out when you can get together and take it from there. I'm not worried because I know I have two consummate professionals in front of me."

Well, Melvin had just neatly backed Madame Snark into a corner. Any further protest would mark her as unprofessional. Nice job, Melvin.

And what the hell had he agreed to?

2

"ABOUT THIS PROJECT..." Cole said, his voice a deep rumble behind her as they left Melvin's office.

She'd prefer to ignore him, but then she'd be labeled noncooperative, which would translate to unprofessional. It wasn't the assignment itself she objected to as much as the methodology.

"My office," she said without turning around. She strolled down the hall practicing deep breathing. Damage control. It was a done deal and she'd simply make the best of it. She waited until Cole trailed in behind her and then closed the door. She turned to face him.

Her already small office shrank considerably with six feet of broad-shouldered male sucking up space. It seemed patently unfair that someone so utterly loathsome should have such startling blue eyes, somewhere between blue and silver. And equally unfair that her pulse leaped every time she was around him—it had from day one.

Of course, that was part of what made him so loathsome—he traded on his dark-haired good looks and what seemed to pass for charm with some people. Sexy with no substance. But, then again, what would you expect from someone who bought their way into a job rather than got there through hard work?

She assured herself that the rapid-fire beat of her heart was a product of Melvin's latest dictate and had nothing to do with being in closed-door proximity with Sir Superficial.

"You don't have a clue as to what you agreed to, do you?"

"Nope." He grinned, and she once again assured herself it

was irritation that set her heart thudding against her ribs. "Guilty as charged."

She skirted him, rounded her desk and sat in her chair. With a flick of her wrist, she invited him to sit in the guest chair. "Why waste everyone's time? Was it too much to ask for you to actually pay attention?"

Instead of taking the seat, he followed her and propped against the rear corner of her glass-topped desk, which felt too close and too intimate with his hip and thigh inches away and a faint whiff of his aftershave scenting the air. But she'd be damned if she'd ask him to move.

"Oh, come on, Tatiana. Give me a break. You know Melvin goes into that same soliloquy every time and it takes him forever to get to the point. Besides, it was your fault I missed the point anyway."

Oh, no. At least he could take ownership of his own ineptness. "Hardly."

"Most assuredly. Your legs distracted me. They're extraordinary, really. And I started thinking about—"

"Stop right there," she interrupted him, her pulse racing like a fully stoked steam engine. "I don't need to be privy to the vagaries of your mind. Did you catch *any* of what he said?"

His gaze roved the length of her legs, clearly visible through the translucent glass, and lingered on her ankles, leaving her tingling as if he'd blazed that trail with his fingers…or mouth. "Nary a word."

Better to get this over with and him out of the confines of her office. "Douglas Creighton wants *Connoisseur* to have more of a Web presence."

"Smart. Subscriptions have been flat for the last year and a half."

"Exactly. He wants to launch a pilot Web piece January first, along the lines of a she said/he said article where we each give our take on the same restaurant. He thinks it'll generate interest because we each have such distinctly different styles and taste."

"Okay. I stand by my original assertion. It's a damn good idea." He crossed his arms over his chest, and since she was neither blind nor dead, she did, in fact, notice he had a nice broad chest. But she wasn't about to be distracted by Cole Mitchell's chest.

"Except they want us there together. Same time. Same table." Maybe he did have a brain rattling around somewhere up there, because he appeared suitably appalled. Up to this point, they'd each had separate assignments. Their contact had been limited to the odd interoffice skirmish. "Budgetary constraints. If we're at the same table, we can sample each other's food. Twice the bang for their buck. Plus, we're evaluating the same wait staff at the same time."

"And this starts when?" he said.

"Rollout is January first. They want our pieces in before Christmas so Andi and Tory have a chance to verify and proof-read. The pilot features one local restaurant each week, alternating from high-end to moderate-priced so they appeal to every reader. They want four weeks' copy in to begin, which means four restaurant visits."

"That means we'll have to do dinner almost every day from now until Christmas," he said in a sick tone.

She'd delight in the fact that he looked as if he'd just tasted something bad, except she was dining from the same dish. "Yep. Of course, half an hour ago it was the best idea you'd heard in a long time."

"I've got a life."

What? And she didn't? Well, technically it was arguable, especially according to her mother lately, but he didn't need to know that. "News flash—so do I. Bring your girlfriend along if you want." Wouldn't that make for a fine dining experience? Tatiana, Cole and his ho *de jour*.

"I'm in between."

Well, at least they could skip that acid-reflux-inducing three-some. "Depriving the women of New York?"

"Hiatus. What about you? Are you towing along a boyfriend?"

"There's no one in the picture at the moment." Uh, make that several moments that culminated into several months, but, once again, he didn't need to know that.

His teeth flashed in a grin. "Ah, giving the unsuspecting men of New York a break, are you?"

"Except you, as of now. Let's divvy up the list for reservations."

"Okay. I'll take the last two on the list. We may as well line them up so we can knock them out and get it over with."

She'd second that. This was turning into the holiday from hell.

THE NEXT DAY COLE laughed at Misha Siebowitz's joke and positioned himself in Melvin's Seasonal Circle of Love across from Tatiana. He wanted an unencumbered view of her expression when she opened her first Secret Santa gift. He'd made sure it was something "tasteful."

Melvin had declared the break room the official gift-exchange center. The bistro tables had been pushed to the walls and he'd instructed Elle to arrange the chairs in a circle around one of the tables with the Secret Santa gifts. The break room wasn't that big, and they were packed in as tight as the cliché sardines in a can.

A rosemary bush trimmed to resemble a tree sat in the middle of the table. Someone—most likely Elle—had strung red chili-pepper lights around the table's edge. Mambo holiday tunes played on a CD player—a campy blend and actually sort of fun. Or maybe it was just the anticipation of the she-devil's face when she opened her elegantly wrapped gift.

Melvin clapped his hands. "Well, it looks as if we've had some very busy Secret Santas, so why don't we get started? Now, remember, it's *secret,* so don't give it away when your gift is opened. We'll start with Elle and work our way around the circle. Elle, if you'll go and find the gift with your name on it."

Tatiana sat next to Andi, one half of the androgynous proofreading duo of Andi and Tory, who was next to Elle. Perfect.

Everyone oohed and aahed over a set of cocktail napkins with a Santa hat topping a martini glass. Andi's package contained Jordan almonds. Nice gifts but rather boring. Cole realized this wouldn't be nearly as much fun if he hadn't gotten Tatiana's name.

He bit back a smirk when she stood and crossed to the table

to find her gift. Had she deliberately worn those stiletto-heeled black boots so he couldn't look at her legs today? If so, he hated to break it to her, but those boots paired with that short plaid skirt and black sweater…well, it was hot.

She sat back down and tore into the wrapping paper—he knew she wouldn't be one of those that took forever and opened carefully. She peeled back the tissue, and color washed her face. Ho, ho, ho and ha, ha, ha.

"What is it?" Andi asked, peering over Tatiana's shoulder.

"Hello? You have to show, you know," Elle said.

Tatiana held it aloft, and Melvin's Seasonal Circle of Love erupted into hoots and raucous laughter. *The Complete Idiot's Guide to Good Food.*

Elle looked at Cole questioningly and he shrugged, raising his hands, palms upward. "Don't look at me." He paused for effect. "But I do think it's a brilliant gift." Okay, he hadn't technically denied giving it.

"If it's brilliant, that *would* knock you out of the running," Tatiana murmured and everyone laughed again.

Damn. When was the last time he'd enjoyed himself this much? Nothing like having a shrew insult you in front of your contemporaries because you'd just bested her, even if you couldn't take credit for it.

He paid scant attention as the other presents were opened. He was too busy gloating inside. Misha elbowed him. "Your turn."

With so few gifts still on the table, he quickly spotted his. He carried the gold gift bag embossed with silver evergreens back to his seat. He pushed aside the tissue. What the…? Laughter welled up inside him and erupted.

He pulled out a huge oversize bib, and the department laughed along with him.

"I'm sure it was someone who wished they got Tatiana's name and was hoping I'd loan this to her," he said.

The rest of the department opened their gifts—more of the same tasteful, boring stuff. Soon enough the group dispersed and Cole stopped by Tatiana's office.

"I wanted to stop by and offer you the bib." He held the gift bag in the air.

She acknowledged his salute by arching her eyebrows over her cat-green eyes. "How thoughtful, but no, thank you."

"Just trying to be helpful. What time is dinner tonight?"

"I made reservations for seven-thirty." She pushed the *Idiot's Guide* to the edge of her desk, toward him. "Feel free to borrow it. You've got enough time to read a couple of chapters. Every little bit should help." She treated him to another pretense of a smile.

"Generous, as always."

She had the absolutely sexiest mouth on the planet. A hunger that had nothing to do with food and everything to do with her full lower lip gnawed at him. Just once. Just a taste. He didn't need to eat an entire crème brûlée to appreciate the mastery—or lack thereof—behind it.

Cole found it amusingly paradoxical that of all the millions of women inhabiting the greater island of Manhattan and the areas immediately beyond, the viper-tongued Tatiana was the one who revved his engine. Or maybe it was simply getting to be a tendency to want what was deemed off-limits. First the job. Now the woman?

He planted his hands on her desk and leaned over the sleek expanse of glass that showcased her legs in those boots. Any other woman would have shrunk back as he blatantly invaded her space. Tatiana didn't budge. Dammit, she brought out the absolute worst in him. He leaned closer still until her breath, warm and minty, mingled with his own. He glanced down through her glass desk. "Are you going to wear those boots?"

"Do you want me to?" Jesus, the way she'd said it left him aching. Her voice was low, husky, seductive…and he wasn't fooled for a minute.

"Hmm. I suspect you don't play fair."

"And you do?" She looked pointedly at his hands braced on her desk, his blatant encroachment of her personal space.

Well, there was that. He straightened, leaving behind the tempting proximity of her full mouth and her scent. "If I say I want you to wear them, you'll be sure to leave them at home. If I say no, you'll be sure to wear them. Surprise me."

Genuine amusement lit her eyes.

"Always. Close my door on the way out, would you?"

Let the battle commence.

3

TATIANA GAVE THE CAB driver the address and pulled out her compact to check her makeup. This was work. Not a dinner date. Not an assignation. Work, plain and simple. But, really, she didn't show up for dinner looking like a hag, regardless of whether it was work or play. And she was not "prettying up" for Cole Mitchell.

She took care of a mascara smear beneath her right eye and refreshed her lipstick even though it looked pretty good, all things considered. Long-wearing lipsticks were a woman's best friend.

Her hair? Well it was just there. She'd hated the tight corkscrew curls and the dark red color that had plagued her during adolescence. She'd longed for a fall of straight honey-blond hair like that of Rena Pitman who'd sat ahead of her in freshman algebra. Rena's mane had taunted her relentlessly through complex equations. The same way Rena's pert little nose had taunted her. Rena'd pretty much embodied every physical trait opposite of Tatiana's—which was, of course, exactly how Tatiana longed to look.

That was many moons ago, and while she knew she was no great beauty, she'd learned to embrace the traits that were hers alone and set her apart. Or, in the words of Grandma Rumasky, making the most of what God gave her, crazy hair and big nose included. She'd finally stopped being intimidated by the Rena Pitmans and Elles of the world.

She snapped the compact closed and slipped it into her purse. She was within a block and a half of the restaurant.

"Hey, let me off at this corner," she instructed the cabbie and gathered her shopping bags. She'd walk the rest of the way. It wasn't hip to admit, but she adored Christmas in New York—all of it. The rampant commercialism, the crowds of shoppers, Santa wannabes clogging the corners, the bell-ringers seeking donations for those less fortunate, the decorations. She simply got too caught up in her obligations sometimes and forgot to enjoy the season.

She paid the driver, pocketed her receipt and turned west toward the restaurant. She shivered into her wool coat and skirted an icy patch on the sidewalk. It was a little colder than she'd thought, but she'd warm up in a minute.

Half a block down, a big yellow school bus sat at the opposite curb loading what must've been at least thirty Santas milling about on the sidewalk. It struck her as an only-in-New-York moment. Where were they going, night school for St. Nicks?

She was still smiling when she spotted Cole outside the restaurant. A tremor ran through her. There was something about a man in a black winter coat, even if it was Cole Mitchell. He looked up, and for a split second an unguarded moment shimmered between them, devoid of hostility.

"Hi." His breath hung like smoke in the cold air.

"Hello," she said, her breath mingling with his. "Why aren't you inside where it's warm?"

"I didn't want to miss you and I didn't want you to get here and wait outside, thinking that I hadn't arrived yet."

No. This was wrong—and dangerous. She didn't want to discover any underlying gallantry in Cole. He could save it for someone else. She didn't like him. She wasn't going to like him. End of story. "Whatever. Before we go in, I'm Tempest Altman." Some food critics didn't use pseudonyms when dining out, but she felt she couldn't do her best job without anonymity. Once she'd written a less-than-flattering piece when a chef refused to take back an overcooked fish. After the piece came out, the chef remarked he'd have taken it back had he known who she was. Case in point. How could she write an honest piece if restaurants afforded her preferential treatment?

"Tempest suits you."

"It's my middle name."

"Your parents must have been psychic."

Ha. She was one of the least tempestuous people she knew, except when it came to him. "Apparently I kicked a lot when my mom was pregnant. And I was breach."

"Why doesn't this surprise me?" He snapped his fingers. "Maybe because you're the most contrary woman I ever met."

Tatiana had a mental image of vacant-minded beauties parading through his past. "From you, I'll consider that a compliment. I'm sure your ideal woman is a twit."

"Twit? You wound me, Tempest. Truly." He clutched at his chest, and it was so ridiculous that had it been anyone else, she would've laughed at his melodrama. But he wasn't anyone else. He was Cole, whose dad had wrangled his esteemed position at *Connoisseur,* the same position she'd worked her ass off for. "And for your dining pleasure tonight, I'm Mitch Coleman." He grinned and added under his breath, "It's easy enough for my simple mind to keep up with."

"Well, that is a consideration. If you're done with the theatrics, I'd like to go in before my feet turn to ice."

He bowed mockingly from his waist and opened the door for her. "After you."

Did he tack a "Your Highness" on there under his breath?

They were punctual, and the maître d' promptly seated them at a table midway the room and to the right. Tatiana mentally made a note that none of the wait staff seemed harried despite all the tables being full, and the customers appeared content except for a couple across the restaurant, and that just appeared to be a personal disagreement.

So far, so good.

A few minutes later they'd gone with the sommelier's wine recommendations for appetizers and dinner. She was glad he'd steered them to midrange choices on the list rather than pushing the higher-end vintages. Another point in the restaurant's favor if the wine played out as he'd suggested.

She looked across the table into Cole's silver-blue eyes, and an awkward silence fraught with awareness settled between them. She shifted her silverware a few inches over on the white linen tablecloth. It had been one thing to study the menu and spend time considering and ordering...but now what? They couldn't exactly discuss work because their cover would be blown if anyone overheard them.

Cole shifted and his knee brushed hers beneath the table. Adrenaline rushed through her, and she made a mental note that the tables were too small and too intimate for a business affair. *Affair.* Poor choice of word. Make that a meal.

A slow, lazy smile, doubtless intended to disarm, curved his lips. Despite herself, she couldn't help the instinctive flash of attraction that ricocheted through her.

"I see you wore your boots after all. Very nice choice." The look in his eyes sent heat spiraling through her.

She shrugged. "Not particularly a choice. I'm too far out to go home and change before dinner." Not when she was schlepping out to Brooklyn on the train. Manhattan rental prices were definitely out of her league on her salary. And it wasn't exactly that she was cheap, but she liked to hold on to her money. "Besides, I had some shopping to do." Secret Santa day two was tomorrow.

The wine steward arrived and served them, immediately followed by the waiter bearing her calamari and Cole's bruschetta. Calamari wasn't one of her favorites, but it was a standard in so many restaurants she always ordered it because she knew so many other diners would and it was her job to evaluate the establishment with the diner in mind. She forked up a bite. Nice light batter and a hint of ginger lent an interesting note, but disappointingly the squid itself wasn't as fresh as it should be given the price attached. The suggested pinot grigio, however, was a perfect companion wine, crisp and delicate. She was about to sample Cole's bruschetta when a man sporting brushed-back, slightly long blond hair stopped at their table.

"Mitchell? Is that you?" He clapped Cole on the back. "Long time no see. What's it been? Five years?" After four years of living in New York, Tatiana had gotten pretty good at pegging people. This Matthew McConaughey wannabe exuded Wall Street with his white button-down shirt, top button undone and his loosened tie.

"Something like that." Cole's manner, usually annoyingly outgoing and engaging, shifted subtly. He was still smiling, but he'd erected a wall of reserve.

"Aren't you going to introduce us?" The man looked pointedly at Tatiana and her flesh crawled. When Cole had looked at her earlier, he'd been sexy and flirtatious. This man's look made her feel slimy.

Cole turned his attention to her, "Tempest, this is Parker Longrehn. Parker, Tempest Altman."

"Hello," she said, pleasant but distant.

"The pleasure's mine." The words were innocuous enough, yet his tone left her feeling as if he'd pinched her on the butt.

Cole looked at her as if they'd just rolled out of bed an hour ago, his glance unmistakably possessive. "Tempest is a…very good friend."

What? Tatiana barely managed to keep her jaw from dropping. She thought about refuting that status, but she decided to go along with him instead, just to see where he was taking this. And particularly because she didn't want to take anything any further with Parker.

Parker looked pointedly at her naked left finger. "Well, old man, I don't see any No Trespassing signs posted."

She and Cole might strike sparks off one another and she might not respect how he got his job, but Parker Longrehn was slick. And presumptuous. And rude as hell, to boot.

Tatiana reached across the tablecloth and twined her fingers with Cole's. She could swear energy passed between them. "Consider them posted," she said, casting Cole a smoldering look to reinforce the claim. His return glance sent heat cascading through her, even if it was for Parker Longrehn's benefit.

"You win some and you lose some." Parker flashed white teeth, bleached to the near-blue degree, at Tatiana. "But if you decide to trade up…"

This guy, a class-A jerk, deserved to be served. "I already have." She decided to lay it on thick. "Anyone other than Cole would be trading down."

Parker's smile wasn't quite as nice this time around. Fine. If he thought she was just going to sit here while he insulted Mr. Heated Glance, he had another thing coming. It was one thing for her to insult Cole, but Mr. Blue Teeth needed to rethink his position.

Parker shoved his hand in his pocket. It took Tatiana a second or so to realize he was rolling his change between his fingers. Congratulations. Parker had just won the Cheesy and Annoying Award.

"So." He turned his attention back to Cole. "I heard your father got married again. Is this four or five?" Parker said.

Cole shrugged. "I'm too busy these days to keep track." His smile didn't reach his eyes. "Let me know when you figure it out."

Parker paused and assumed an expression of rueful sympathy that fooled no one. "Maybe this wife will be happier to have you around."

"We'll see, won't we?" Nothing, absolutely nothing about the cavalier smile on Cole's face or the droll amusement in his eyes indicated that Parker Longrehn had scored a direct hit, but she felt Cole's inner wince with some sixth sense she'd never known she possessed. Either that or maybe it was simply the wine on a near-empty stomach.

She piped up in Cole's defense. This Parker guy was grating on her last holiday nerve. "It's definitely their loss. My parents adore him almost as much as I do." She hoped her look approximated fawning adoration, something outside of her usual Cole Mitchell repertoire.

Parker looked down his nose at her, as if *that* might intimidate her. "Do I know your parents?"

"Not unless you've recently visited Yurgash, Indiana." There you go. She'd just painted herself with the scarlet H to this Manhattanite—Hick.

"I don't think so. Listen, got to run. Say hi to Connie for me. Stay in touch."

"Later."

Parker left, trailing slime behind him. Good freaking riddance. What the hell had that just been all about? And who was Connie?

"Yurgash, Indiana?" Cole raised an eyebrow. "Really?"

"Really. Heartland, USA." And if he thought he was going to gloss over the weirdness of the last five minutes... She stared at him. Waiting. She reached across the table for a bite of his appetizer.

He speared a piece of her calamari. "We were fraternity brothers." He paused to eat.

Fraternity brothers fit. And Parker was such an absolute... "ARU? And he was the president?"

Cole sipped his wine. "ARU?"

"Assholes R Us."

He laughed and adopted a hurt expression. "Anyone ever mentioned you're fickle? A few minutes ago, you and your parents adored me, and now you're signing me up for ARU."

Albeit unwillingly, she was amused and intrigued. "Okay, so it wasn't ARU, but you just publicly claimed me as your girl-friend. Let's hear what's behind that, because there's either a story here or some mental illness floating around. And you're a lot of things—" annoying, sexy, nepotistic, to name a few right off the top of her head "—but you don't strike me as mental. I'm putting my dollar on the story."

She bit into the crusty Italian bread topped with fresh tomatoes, garlic, herbs and slivers of Parmesan cheese. Delicious. The perfect ratio of basil to oregano.

"Parker and I were fraternity brothers. He came home with me one weekend. My sister Connie is three years younger than me." Ah, so that explained Connie. His sister. Not some former lover. "Parker seduced Connie's best friend, Bethany. When Bethany turned up pregnant, Parker turned his back on her." Anger darkened his eyes. "I know it happens, but it broke Bethany's heart. Her parents had to take the bastard to court to prove, thanks to DNA testing, he was the father. So Bethany has a seven-year-old and Parker has his day-trader career. He's trouble you don't need."

There was something so…well, sweet and downright gallant about him trying to protect her from Parker that she found herself at a loss for words. And God knows *that* didn't happen often. "Uh, well, I can take care of myself, but thanks anyway. He was easy to spot with that trail of slime he left behind him."

"I wasn't taking any chances. I was responsible for what happened to Bethany because I brought him home with me."

It was a disconcerting glimpse into his character. Parker was a creep and Bethany'd made a mistake, but even Tatiana couldn't fault Cole. And she never had any problem faulting Cole. "Did you encourage her to sleep with him? Did you throw a wild party and invite her? Did you ply her with alcohol?"

He shook his head, but the look in his eyes didn't change. "No. But he showed up with me. I was the reason he crossed her path. So now I don't take any chances."

This just sucked. Why couldn't it have been some maligned ex-girlfriend who'd recognized him and dropped by to vilify him? But no. Now not only did she know he wasn't vacuous but she had to discover he possessed a damn conscience.

"Why not just tell him to drop dead and get lost?"

Cole offered his familiar grin. "Why give him the satisfaction of knowing he has any impact on my life?"

Hmm. She'd never thought of it from that angle. Yet another insight into Cole Mitchell's gray matter. "Well, thanks for protecting me from the big, bad…slug."

Cole laughed and it did funny things to her insides. "Parker wouldn't mind being called a big, bad wolf. I think he likes to think of himself that way. But a big, bad *slug?* You know how to wound a man, Tempest." Now why in the world would that make her feel all fluttery and flushed? "And thanks for jumping in there and backing me up."

Rather an odd position to find herself in, having his back as opposed to stabbing it. "Don't get used to it."

"Certainly not," he drawled. "It must have been almost painful for you to look at me as if you—" he adopted a horrified expression "—*liked* me."

"It was a stretch, but I managed." She pretended to preen. "Rather well, if I do say so myself."

"You were brilliant, darling. You almost had me convinced you—what was it?—oh, yeah, *adored* me. I could get used to being adored."

"I wouldn't if I were you. I'm sure it would be all too short-lived." God help her, but she was enjoying herself. "Maybe if this job doesn't work out for me I might consider a career in acting. That wasn't a bad stab at improv considering I didn't get what was going on. Especially at the end."

The waiter appeared and cleared their appetizers and refilled the water glasses. Mediocre calamari, excellent bruschetta and flawless service so far.

She looked pointedly at Cole. "So what was that all about at the end?"

"Let's just say holidays were awkward when we were kids. The new steps weren't thrilled to have the leftovers from the first marriage show up on the doorstep. Once we were old enough to make our own choices, Connie and I started doing our own holiday thing, just the two of us. Now she has a husband and a munchkin and I get together with them."

That knocked her notion of him as a pampered daddy's boy for a loop. She might not be spending Christmas Day in the house she grew up in Yurgash, but it'd still be there whenever she was ready for a trip home. A hint of vulnerability lurked beneath Cole's droll pronouncement, which he'd probably deny with his last breath.

The waiter served their entrées. Pork medallions for Cole and roasted chicken for her.

"What about you?" he asked. "Are you gearing up for a big holiday?"

"It'll be quiet." She gave him the brief overview of her parents' trip and Grandma Rumasky's impending nuptials.

"They sound like nice people."

"They are." Dammit. Now she felt guilty because he'd obviously been shortchanged in the parental department while she'd grown up with great parents.

"No brothers or sisters?"

"Nope. I'm a lonely only," she quipped.

"It's just as well. I don't think the world could handle another you running around." His smile crinkled the corners of his eyes.

Without thinking, she stuck her tongue out at him. Like the dimming of theater lights signaling the beginning of the next act, the mood shifted, intensified. The look in his eyes sent a shiver through her. "So are you?"

Breathing? Yes. A woman? Definitely. Capable of standing with him looking at her that way? Not so sure. This was different from his earlier flirtatiousness in her office. This was quiet and intense…and all the more powerful. "Am I what?"

"Lonely?"

She could easily blow him off, but considering he'd just had one of his own vulnerabilities exposed by Parker the Slug, she answered him truthfully. "Sometimes I wish I'd had a sister. But then I see how many siblings despise one another and I think it's just a crapshoot."

"I wasn't talking about a brother or sister."

Oh. Her parents had given her a firm foundation. She knew the value of a dollar, hard work and herself. Even though sometimes she longed for something more, it wasn't loneliness. "No. I'm not. I'm content with my own company."

Her mind shouted for her to leave it there, but her mouth didn't seem inclined to cooperate. She plowed forward even though she really shouldn't ask. She knew too much already. "What about you? Are you lonely?"

"I've known a moment or two." A quiet truth underscored his offhandedness.

This was turning into a true disaster. Not only was she horribly aware of how devastatingly sexy Cole Mitchell was, but now she'd discovered he was a nice guy, as well.

4

"HOLA." ELLE POPPED HER blond head around the door frame. "Ten minutes. Break room. Time to spread more holiday cheer."

"Thanks. I'll be there," Cole said.

"And Melvin wanted me to check with you on how dinner went last night," she said.

Translation: when was he going to have his preliminary notes together on the first restaurant? "It went well. I'm working on it now."

"I won't hold you up, then. See you in ten."

"Sure."

Elle wasn't holding him up, he was holding himself up. He couldn't seem to focus...well, at least not on what he was supposed to focus on.

He looked from the blinking cursor on his computer screen to outside his window. The odd snowflake drifted past on the other side of the glass. He'd always thought that was the strangest thing. Where were all the other snowflakes when one lone flake journeyed down? Even though no two in the universe were alike, weren't they supposed to stick together?

He shook his head. Last night had totally messed with his head. Parker Longrehn could drop off the face of the Earth and Cole would consider it good riddance. No, what was screwing with his mind about Parker wasn't so much encountering him, although he would've gladly skipped that happy experience. No, it was Cole's reaction to the way Parker had looked at Tatiana. True, he would warn Parker off any decent human being, but when Parker had looked at Tatiana as if she was his for the picking, possessiveness had gripped Cole and squeezed. He, who never felt possessive about anyone, except maybe his sister, because possessiveness required some degree of attachment. And Cole didn't do attachments.

Nope, that had been one of those early childhood lessons learned the hard way that had stuck with him. You let people know something mattered and they held it against you. If you sought approval, it hurt like the devil when it was deliberately withheld. If you became attached to someone and the person wasn't attached in return, that pretty much sucked, as well.

He'd adopted a life policy of getting along with everyone and caring about nobody, not giving a crap what they thought of him one way or another. It had worked out well for the most part.

His claim to Tatiana had been as responsive and instinctive as an involuntary muscle. Next thing, he'd be looking for a bush to pee on. But Parker had given her that look, and a single word had blazed through Cole's brain: *mine.*

There was no need to wig out about it. Tatiana was amusing, interesting. He enjoyed matching wits and trading barbs. And there was an undeniable attraction that simmered between the two of them. He wasn't being egotistical or weird—a sexual energy pulsed between the two of them whether she was ready to admit it or not.

Not that it was anything to worry about. His life policy was still strictly in place. Things were simply more interesting with Madame Snark on the scene.

"ADMIT IT. THE SECRET Santa thing was fun today, wasn't it?" Elle said from the adjacent treadmill in the workout room on the third floor of the Jackman Butler Building that housed *Connoisseur* on three of its fifty-six floors.

Sweat dampened Tatiana's T-shirt and trickled down her neck. "It was definitely more fun than this," Tatiana said. Some people loved to exercise for the sake of exercising. Uh…she wasn't one of them. She dutifully showed up at the workout center five days a week because otherwise she'd blimp up even more. Yep, it was the horror of her butt taking on the proportions of Staten Island rather than a love of the treadmill that brought her here.

"Exercise is your friend." So sayeth the sylph in size-two spandex running like the Energizer bunny stuck in "fast" mode.

"I wouldn't go that far. How about it keeps food from becoming my mortal enemy," Tatiana said with a grin. "And, yes, I was a scrooge at first, but the gift-exchange thing is fun." She'd been irritated to get Cole Mitchell, but now she was kind of getting into it. "I don't know how things are at your house, there haven't been many Christmas surprises at our place the last few years. We exchange a list and then pick something on that list. So this is kind of cool."

"Cole definitely had the best gift yesterday," Elle said and Tatiana managed not to preen. "But you won the Best Present award today." Elle laughed, which always came out as something of a snort. It was a little shocking, considering Elle appeared so elegant and her laugh was anything but an elegant noise. "You should've seen your face when you opened the strawberry-and-champagne massage oil."

Tatiana grabbed her water bottle from the holder and took a swig without breaking stride. Two miles on the treadmill and she was sweating like a pig. She'd never managed that glistening business. She sweated and it wasn't pretty. She plonked the water bottle back in the space above the treadmill's digital readout.

"It certainly wasn't what I was expecting." And the massage oil had definitely captured her imagination. Along with the tongue-in-cheek typed note attached to the bottle. *To ensure your good taste.*

"Hey, it's the unexpected stuff that's the best," Elle said. "You'll have to let me know when you've tried it. I might pick some up for me and Teddy."

Elle and her fiancé hadn't already been there and done that? Surprising. Elle spilled all kinds of details about herself and Teddy, the wonder hottie in an accountant's guise. "It won't be anytime soon. Flavored oil strikes me as a two-party event, and right now there's no one on my invitation list."

The frequent travel that came with her job had been the death of her last relationship. Hel-lo. What had Max expected? *Connoisseur* was a *travel* magazine that catered to food aficionados, *travel* being a definitive word. She'd marked Max off the list several months ago and she'd had neither the time nor the inclination to replace him.

And just because Cole Broad-Shoulders Mitchell came to mind now didn't mean she wanted to taste-test with him. Maybe she'd had the brief, passing thought of his square, very masculine hands—so shoot her that she'd noticed he had rather sexy hands—smoothing the fragranced oil over her shoulders, along her back and to various and sundry points of interest. Heat flashed through her that had nothing to do with her treadmill workout.

She most definitely didn't have a thing for him. It was just one of those situations where he was front and center, unfortunately, in her world, since she had to buy gifts for him and meet him for dinner and work on those stinking articles with him. And maybe he had a way of looking at her that made her think of…well, things best not thought of. Nope, it was simply a case of him being the most prominent male in her life right now that had her playing him into the love-me-lick-me scenario in her head. And how sad was that?

"Want to trade gifts?" Elle offered.

Tatiana's treadmill slowed down and then stopped. Two and a half miles. "Your box of biscotti for my flavored massage oil?" She pretended to consider it. "Uh…no. The massage oil should keep for a while until I find someone willing to slather it on and nibble it off."

Elle laughed. She'd hardly broken a sweat. "That's what I thought you'd say, but it was worth a try. Aren't you dying to know who your Secret Santa is and what they have in mind next? Massage oil today…what about tomorrow?"

Tatiana spritzed the treadmill with disinfectant and wiped it off for the next victim. She blotted sweat from her face and neck.

"I don't know. I'm curious, but it could be anyone. Except Melvin, of course. I don't think—jiggy meds or not—he'd give me flavored massage oil. Maybe somebody meant it as a joke."

"Maybe. Maybe not. What if it wasn't? What if your Secret Santa is actually a secret admirer?" Elle possessed a dramatic streak.

"I think my Secret Santa is someone with a sense of humor," Tatiana said.

"There were definitely more funny gifts today. Melvin's was a riot, but I thought Cole's was a little mean."

"I thought they were both funny and apropos." She kept her voice and expression nonchalant. Elle was fishing. Someone had given Melvin a weekly pill organizer with three daily slots, like the one Grandma Rumasky used to organize her meds. Given that Melvin's medications were public fodder, everyone, including Melvin, had found it hilarious.

She'd found the silver-plated spoon at the second store she'd checked. Once again the group, Cole included, had laughed. She didn't feel a bit guilty. Well, maybe just a hair. But it had been funny and it was a much-needed reminder to herself that no matter how charming and entertaining a dinner companion he was, he'd still slid into his job without paying his dues. If he wanted to play the family-influence card to get his job, then he'd have to play with the whole deck.

5

HALF A WEEK LATER, ON Wednesday evening, they had two meals down and two to go. Cole watched candlelight flicker across the porcelain planes of Tatiana's face. Tonight it was a seafood restaurant that served the theater district. Last night had been a new barbecue eatery in Harlem, around the corner from Clinton's One Hundred and Twenty-Fifth Street law offices.

"At least Melvin gave us a variety," Tatiana said.

"Definitely. Last night barbecue, blues and rousing fun. Tonight seafood, saxophone and sultry romance." Although it had limited the number of tables the restaurant could accommodate, each table was practically an island unto itself with the placement of potted palms, ferns and privacy screens. The decor and the music created a nostalgic *Casablanca*-esque mood.

Cole put down his fork. Sweet mango married with a hint of red pepper and delicate sea bass melted against his tongue. Interesting without being fussy.

"Good choice," he remarked to Tatiana, offering his opinion on her entrée. He'd eaten countless meals. He loved sharing good food. Of course, the downside to reviewing restaurants was that he'd likewise shared some mediocre to outright lousy food or service or, worst-case scenario, a combination thereof.

Good food and the enjoyment of good food held an inherent sensuality, but tonight, with Tatiana, it took on a new level of intimacy. What was it about this woman that sparked such an awareness in him?

"Want to try mine?" he asked.

"Just a bite."

Normally he'd place a bit of the cedar-plank-smoked trout on a butter plate and pass it to her. Instead something drove him to offer her the taste on the tip of his fork. She had the most exquisite mouth. Not too full and pouty and not too thin-lipped and small, but the perfect blend of the two, with a slightly full lower lip. Her mouth sent his mind wandering into the dangerous territory of long, hot, lingering kisses and the even more dangerous terrain of Madame Snark plying her gorgeous mouth over his chest, down his belly, trailing tendrils of her red hair against his skin as she sucked and kissed her way down to his waiting— No. He did not need to go there in his mind in the middle of a working dinner. Sitting across from her and fantasizing his way to a hard-on wasn't the brightest idea.

She hesitated for just a second and then leaned forward and wrapped her lips around the tines. She held the sample in her mouth for a moment, her eyelids lowered to half-mast, as if she was totally focused on assimilating the flavors, the texture. Then she began to chew slowly. Lust gripped him, and with each slow, deliberate chew, it wound a little tighter inside him. Finally, thank goodness, she swallowed.

"I wasn't sure if the fennel would work with the trout or if it would overpower it, but it works nicely," Tatiana said.

"Uh-huh." He'd nearly had a moment watching her chew a piece of fish.

Briefly awareness shimmered in her eyes and then vanished. "What's your favorite place you've traveled in the last year?" she asked. Was that a hint of desperation in her husky tone?

He decided to take advantage of the change in subject. "No doubt about it. It's Corfu, with its sun-drenched days and fresh, simple fare. There's a taverna that sits at the edge of the white-pebbled bay, and they serve prawn saganaki—fresh prawns in garlic, olive oil, tomatoes, feta and cream."

"Stop. You're making my mouth water!"

He grinned. "It's incredible. I stayed in a whitewashed villa set in the middle of olive trees. My bedroom overlooked the Ionian Sea, and during the day the sun slanted in onto the bed.

I could lie there and watch the occasional cloud sift through all of that blue sky. They hung the sheets to dry in the sun. I was thirty years old before I'd ever experienced sun-dried sheets."

She laughed, a softer, gentler sound that caught him off guard. "There's nothing else quite like it, is there? Grandma Rumasky and my mother both hang their sheets outside to dry. It's one of my favorite things about going home." She sipped from her wineglass and regarded him over the rim. "You paint an alluring picture of Corfu. It makes me want to go there. And, of course, I'd have to eat at your taverna and room at the villa with the sun-dried linens." Her spontaneous smile stole his breath.

"You'd like it." Oddly enough, after spending three evenings with her, he thought he had a fair enough idea of what she would and wouldn't like. The thought flashed through not just his mind but his entire being that he wanted to be there with her. He'd like to stretch out naked on the simple cotton coverlet of that bed warmed by the afternoon sun and make slow, leisurely love to her until they were both sated and drowsy from good food and even better sex.

"It sounds great."

He started and then realized she was talking about Corfu, not his fantasy. He had a gut feeling it would be great between them. "What about you? Your favorite place?"

"Hands down, Prague. Have you ever been there?"

He shook his head and she continued. "There's an old-world elegance to it that seems to have been lost in some of the other more well-known European cities. The River Vltava flows through the city. The stone Charles Bridge is lined by Baroque statues and it's possibly one of the most romantic spots on earth when you take a walk at dusk with the city's spires as a backdrop. Not only is it beautiful but it probably also appeals to me because it's not so very far from my roots. My great-grandparents left Russia in 1916, before the Bolsheviks took power."

Tatiana had intrigued him before. Now he was outright fascinated. "How did they leave?"

"How much Russian history do you know?"

"Very little."

"Bottom line, there were lots and lots of have-nots. The majority of the country were peasants. My great-grandfather was a printer."

"Ah. A family history of publishing," Cole said.

"I never thought of it that way." She picked back up with her story. "Dyda, as we called him, was smart and had access to books. He'd heard the Socialists and he knew what was coming. It had the makings of the French revolution when the blood of the aristocracy flowed like water through the streets of Paris. If you were a peasant, socialism was a step up. If you were an aristocrat, it was a death sentence. And for anyone in between, like him and his family, well, their fate could hinge on the whim of whomever was standing armed in front of them. He and my great-grandmother secretly made plans. One night they left. They and their five children packed one bag each—I think it was more along the lines of a sack, actually—and they walked away from everything else. They bribed their way out of the country. They arrived in Yurgash, which had the largest population of Russian immigrants, with twenty dollars in their pockets."

"Twenty dollars and five kids. What'd they do?"

"They worked hard—it's the Rumasky way. My *dydushka* delivered newspapers. My babushka baked. And the children shined shoes, picked up sticks, whatever they could do to earn a nickel. Within ten years, Dyda had his own printing operation again."

"That's an amazing story." He'd enjoyed it all the more because she'd forgotten to be on guard with him. It was like sitting in on a session of *Tatiana Unplugged.*

"I've always thought so. I used to love to hear the stories about their journey to their new country. I'd sit in the kitchen while Grandma Rumasky and Babi Tatiana baked *koliadki* and *baba romovaya* and they'd tell about the old country. Dyda actually caught a glimpse of Rasputin, just in passing once. Pretty amazing. He was an everyday man who brushed shoulders with a figure pivotal in world history. Sort of a Forrest Gump moment."

She stopped and looked a bit self-conscious. "Sorry. I got carried away."

"Are you kidding? It's incredibly interesting. I could sit and listen all night. Your family history is like a rich, wholesome broth. My family's cornered the market on dysfunctional, but there's no interesting history behind it like that. Not that I know of, anyway." There'd been no family history passed down, just money and the apparent inability to stick with a life mate. He laughed. "Let me take a wild guess. I bet no one in your family's ever gotten a divorce."

She shook her head. "You'd lose that bet. Cousin Katrina's husband Barney worked the night shift. She decided to surprise him one day at home by coming in early. Except she was the one surprised when she walked in and found Barney decked out in her underwear. Apparently Barney looked better in her merry widow than she did, so she dumped him." She winked. "Cross-dressing is not that well-received in Yurgash."

Cole laughed aloud at her droll delivery.

Her green eyes glittered with wicked merriment and she shoved a red curl behind one ear. "And Grandma Rumasky's husbands keep dying on her, but that falls under good old-fashioned 'till death do we part,' not divorce."

"Is her tongue as sharp as yours? Maybe that's the problem."

"Very funny." She adopted a sanctimonious expression. "All of the women in my family are charming and sweet."

Cole snorted. "You do an excellent job of hiding it."

"Careful. All that flattery might go to my head," she responded.

Cole realized he was having one of the best times he'd had in…well, he couldn't quite remember when. Conversation with Tatiana was unpredictable and kept him slightly off-kilter. And an undercurrent hummed between them, as if she was as aware of him as he was of her. They were a dessert and after-dinner drink away from being through, and he wasn't ready for the evening to end.

As if he'd picked up a mental cue, their waiter appeared and cleared their dinner plates. "Shall I bring over the dessert menu?"

"Give us a few minutes," Cole said, preempting Tatiana. The waiter nodded and faded away, dirty plates in hand.

Tatiana arched an inquiring eyebrow.

"We should dance first," Cole said.

Surprise widened her green eyes. "Why?"

"Because it's part of the total experience, the atmosphere." A sax-and-string quartet played in one corner. A small parquet floor accommodated couples. In his book, the restaurant got top marks.

"I suppose." She didn't look particularly convinced.

The music enhanced the dining experience. Some establishments screwed it up by playing too loud for conversation. Some chose the wrong music and it clashed with the ambience. This was right on the money.

"So shall we?" Two days ago, her reluctance would've delighted him.

He stood, unsure for the moment whether she'd leave him standing there alone.

"I promise not to bite," he said.

"I'm not sure whether I'm disappointed or relieved."

He drew her into his arms and a jolt of sexual awareness hit him. Who would've suspected she'd feel so soft, so right? That her curves would fit his angles so completely, as if she'd been custom-made for him?

Her hand was warm in his and he pulled her closer. Her scent drifted around him. In her heels, her head grazed the line of his jaw, bringing her temple tantalizingly close to his lips. They turned at the edge of the dance floor and her hip shifted against his for a brief incendiary moment. Tatiana filled his senses.

He bent his head, bringing his mouth to the tempting curve of her ear. Her hair teased against his cheek and his nose. "You're a good dancer," he murmured into her ear, her translucent skin just a fraction of an inch away from his lips. He gave way to an instinct as natural as breathing and nuzzled the tender lobe.

She tilted her head, and for a moment it struck him as an entreaty rather than a rejection, but then she turned, moving her ear and neck out of range but bringing her lips achingly closer to his, her cheek brushing against his jaw.

"Don't." Her breath feathered over his skin and desire flowed through his veins.

He'd never in his life been at a loss for a glib response. But right now, the comeback king couldn't think of a damn thing to say. He was too mesmerized by her.

With a startling clarity, he suddenly realized exactly what he wanted for Christmas.

He inhaled her scent one more time and smiled.

Now all he had to do was convince her.

6

THE FOLLOWING AFTERNOON, Tatiana finished editing her notes and saved the file. She rubbed at her temple. She didn't have a headache, but by all rights she should.

No doubt about it. This had morphed into the worst holiday season in her personal history. She'd done the unthinkable. The unconscionable. She'd had a brain lapse and slipped into some silly infatuation with—dear God, just shoot her now—Cole Mitchell.

She wasn't even sure how or when it had happened. All she knew was one second he was talking about Corfu and looking at her with those slumberous blue eyes and all of a sudden, she wanted to swim naked with him in the Ionian Sea and then share those sun-laundered sheets.

Or maybe it had started when Parker Longrehn had slimed by their table? What the heck, it could've even been the very first time she met him and felt the impact of his silver-blue eyes and his smile tingling through her all the way from the top of her head to her toes, when she'd been happy to latch on to his dad landing him his job so she didn't tumble head over heels and land at his feet.

She thought about the brief fling she'd had in Prague with a philosophy student she'd met at a small café. They'd both considered it an intense cultural exchange. It would be different with Cole, who wasn't part of the culture but would be there to savor and share it from a perspective similar to her own.

But the true moment of her wits' capitulation had been that dance. Had anything ever been more perfectly romantic? She must've lost her mind, because it now topped her most-romantic chart, bumping her adventure in Prague down to numero two.

Her entire body had felt more alive, more perfectly attuned to the world with his hand at her waist, with the play of his muscles beneath her left hand, the tease of his warm breath against her skin, that brief brush of his mouth against her ear that had set her on fire. She'd longed for him to keep going. Thank goodness she'd rallied her remaining sense before she'd done something totally stupid like kiss him on the dance floor.

She just needed to keep her distance. Get through the holidays, wrap up this slate of Web assignments. Then he'd go his merry way, she'd go hers and things would be back to normal. Holiday depression was quite common this time of year, and Tatiana was sure she'd simply developed some weird fixated form of the malaise. At least that explanation sat better with her than having developed a terrible case of lust for Tall, Dark and— at this juncture—Dangerous to her peace of mind.

"Ready?" Speak of the devil… Cole poked his dark head around her door.

They were doing an early seating tonight and they'd both had late work, so they were cabbing it together to the restaurant. She shook her head. What was the point in trying to deny the way her breath caught in her throat or the way her heart raced at the sound of his voice?

"I'm almost ready," she said. "I just need to close this program and get my things."

An hour and a half later Tatiana was proud of herself. So what that she had some ridiculous infatuation with Cole? Maybe she'd been terribly aware of his body heat in the cab next to hers, but she'd handled it. And dinner tonight was a far cry from last night's romantic ambience, with its low lighting and sultry notes of the saxophone.

She glanced around. Café Tatu was bright and noisy with the feel and look of a Japanese high-tech sushi bar. Conversation was limited, and the longer they sat there with limited contact, the more in control Tatiana felt. She finished the last of the restaurant's signature drink, a sake martini. In an effort not to gain too much weight, she never ate all the food on her plate—and she noticed Cole had the same approach—or drank all the wine in her glass. Tonight, however, she polished off her drink. So was it considered a sakini or a marsake?

Heck if she knew, but it was tasty, and she was feeling fully in control of herself. Downright jubilant, in fact. She was no longer suffering from some delusional state of infatuation over Cole Mitchell brought on by holiday depression. True enough, she might feel a touch of lust blooming low in her belly over the way the bright light brought out a hint of brown in his dark hair, but that really didn't mean anything. Half the women in the room had shot inquiring looks his way, some bolder than others. Grudgingly Tatiana had to give him credit. This was business, not pleasure, and he could've easily collected half a dozen phone numbers, but he had been seemingly oblivious to the looks.

They stepped out of the warm, overly bright restaurant on the trendy Upper East Side into the bracing, cold night. It had begun to snow when they'd first entered the restaurant and it continued to fall steadily now.

"Amazing, isn't it?" Cole said with a grin, snowflakes catching in his dark lashes.

"What?"

"It's as if the city gets a new coat of paint. All the dirty snow is hidden by the new stuff and for a while, everything is fresh again."

At the corner stood one of the numerous horse-drawn carriages found around Central Park's periphery. The horse, a dappled gray, snorted, and its breath rose like a smoke signal among the falling snow.

"Are you in a big hurry to get home?" Cole asked.

The quiet of her co-op's eight-hundred square feet, complete with tabletop tree and her stocking hung by the microwave in the kitchen—hey, as close to a fireplace as she was likely to come—seemed more bleak than appealing after Café Tatu's noise and bright lights.

"No. I'm not particularly in a hurry. Why?"

He nodded toward the carriage. "How about a ride through Central Park?"

"Why? This isn't like dancing last night. It's not part of the dining experience."

"Maybe because it's there and we're here and Central Park at Christmastime with the snow is beautiful." He peered closer at her. "You have taken a carriage ride through Central Park before, haven't you?"

Tatiana crossed her arms over her chest. "You don't need to make it sound as if I've committed a sin."

"But you have." Cole grinned at her and she wanted to grin back like an idiot. "It's a cardinal sin of omission, but I can help you with that right now." He took her elbow and steered her toward the horse and buggy.

"With you?"

"That was the general intent." His smile, with a slight edge of sarcasm, didn't waver, but Tatiana thought she saw a flash of hurt in his eyes. "I don't see anyone else forming a line."

The word *no* hovered on the tip of her tongue until she heard her mother admonishing her to learn to have fun. She had an empty apartment waiting, and Central Park would be beautiful in the snowy onslaught.

"Why not?"

"Gracious, as usual," he said.

"I wouldn't want you to think aliens had taken over my body." She figured if she could just keep things on the same footing they'd been on since she met him, she'd be okay. Holidays or not, she wasn't expected to be nice to him.

Cole strode over to the driver, his shoulders impossibly wide in his wool winter coat, snow dusting his hair. He exchanged a few words with the man, some folded cash and something else she couldn't make out at this distance. In less than a minute the driver handed her up into the vehicle. She settled on the worn velvet upholstery and Cole climbed in behind her. Suddenly it was all too close and too tight and he was too large to share such an enclosed space. Her heart thudded against her ribs. But she could hardly leap up and jump out of the carriage simply because they were now sitting shoulder to shoulder, hip to hip, even though that minimal contact sent heat surging through her.

She gritted her teeth and looked in the other direction. Their guide spread a blanket over their laps. A half roof, similar to that of a convertible, with "windows" cut into each side, sheltered them from the wet stuff.

Then the driver climbed onto his seat and took up the reins and with a quiet "Heyya," they were off.

It was like being transported someplace magical where green boughs hung low beneath the weight of white powder and the lights of the city were a far and distant place in the future. A quixotic blend of lassitude and longing stole through her.

Cole turned his head, which brought his mouth a mere inch or so from hers. "Cozy? Warm enough?"

She shifted slightly, enough to put a gap between them. "Toasty. Thanks."

"You know, I think I've finally figured you out," Cole said.

"Really? Please enlighten me."

"You want to kiss me."

She tried not to sputter. "You're delusional."

"You can't add that to your long list of my sins." The look in his blue eyes filled her with a delicious heat. "Why else would you sit under mistletoe?"

"I didn't, Mr. Half-Baked Brain." She glanced up. Sure enough, a sprig of mistletoe hung suspended from the carriage top above them. "Let me remind you, this was your idea." Precisely. That was the other thing she'd seen him hand the driver.

"Are you implying I want to kiss you?" he said.

"I'm not implying anything." A woman could drown in the depths of his eyes. "I'm saying it outright. I'm stating it so your simple mind can grasp it. You planned this." She wasn't sure whether she was annoyed at his manipulation or flattered.

"Just because I dream about your mouth at night, how it would feel…" He skimmed his fingertip along the bow of her upper lip and she nearly forgot to breathe. His voice was low and seductive in the cocoon of their carriage. "How it would taste…" He traced the seam of her mouth and she felt his touch all the way to her toes. "Is not proof that I would deliberately manipulate you under a sprig of mistletoe. I'm not that kind of guy."

She nipped the tip of his finger between her teeth. "You're exactly that kind of guy."

"Then I might as well live down to your expectations." He reached beneath her hair and cupped her neck in his hand. She could easily pull away, protest, but—God help her—she just wanted to kiss him. Once.

The air was cold and his mouth was warm and she kissed him back.

"Tatiana," he murmured her name against her mouth and fisted his hand in her hair. Then he kissed her again and she realized she'd been wrong. She wanted—no, desperately needed—more than one of his kisses. She pressed closer to him, hungry for his warmth. Her tongue met his in a languorous sweep, and she was drowning in the sensation of cold air bracing her skin and the heat of his mouth.

Kissing Cole was like a stiff measure of brandy that warmed her from within and made her nearly drunk from the pleasure. Sweet, hot desire pooled between her thighs and left her breasts feeling full and aching for his touch. Instinctively she shifted and he pulled her nearer beneath the blanket.

They might have gone on kissing for…well, who knew for how long if the carriage hadn't rocked to a stop, and Tatiana realized she was half sitting on his lap. Her body hummed like a finely tuned instrument ready to be played. If she was a Stradivarius, there was no mistaking the hard press of his bow next to her hip.

Tatiana blinked her eyes open. She scooted off his lap. Ostensibly they were back where they'd started, except she knew with a surety they'd never be back where they'd started.

The air's chill seeped into her. If they hadn't been in a public place, she wouldn't have stopped. Desire and promise simmered in his gaze. He wouldn't have stopped either. She felt it and she knew he did, too. It was there in his eyes. The next time was inevitable and they'd finish what they'd started tonight. This had satisfied nothing. Instead it had aroused a ravening hunger in her for the touch of his hands, the taste of his skin, the exquisite slide of him inside her.

Cole appeared all too satisfied with himself. "I told you you wanted to kiss me."

She reached above them, tweaked down the mistletoe and dropped it in his lap.

"Well, darling, if you insist... You certainly won't get any resistance from me." His grin was sheer arrogant wickedness.

She offered him the sweetest smile she could muster. "*If* I wanted to kiss you, I wouldn't need a piece of greenery to do it."

She stepped past him and the driver handed her down.

It might not have been the truth, the whole truth and nothing but the truth, but it was a damn good exit line.

7

COLE PLOPPED INTO HIS seat in the Circle of Love. Friday afternoon. The final gift exchange. And he'd damn near missed it. He'd ditched work this morning because he'd decided on a new final Secret Santa gift for Tatiana after their carriage ride last night. He'd been ready to toss in the towel when he'd finally found what he was looking for. Whew! He'd barely made it back in time.

He bit back a smirk. She'd know without a doubt who had given her this gift. And without a doubt, she wouldn't reveal him as her Secret Santa. He looked around. Everyone was here except her.

Melvin beamed at the crowd. "Well, it's time to open the final gifts—"

Cole interrupted. "Hold on. Aren't we going to wait for Tatiana?"

"She's already left for the day," Elle said.

But he'd caught a glimpse of her early this morning. "What?"

"Yeah. She thought she was coming down with something so she left," Elle explained.

Melvin rubbed at his balding spot. "Yeah. I meant to tell you earlier, but I got hung up on something else. You only have that final restaurant visit tonight. She asked if you could do it separately and e-mail the reviews in. That's the new plan."

"What's wrong with her?" He felt a foreign sense of panic that she was ill.

"She thought it might be the flu and didn't want to make everyone sick for the holiday weekend."

Andi spoke up. "I'm sorry she's sick, but thank God she didn't stay and spread germs. I've got twenty people coming for dinner on Sunday. Getting the flu would be a disaster at this point."

The gift exchange wasn't nearly as much fun without Tatiana there. He'd so looked forward to throwing her off balance with his gift. And he hated to think of her at home, all alone and sick.

He retrieved his gift and opened it. He'd begun to think his Secret Santa might just be Ms. Snippy herself, but this blew that theory to hell. Someone had baked him homemade cookies. He'd had cookies from a bakery any number of times, but his mother or any of the subsequent steps had never been of the cookie-baking variety. He pulled off the plastic cling film and inhaled deeply. Ah, a hint of almond. Slightly brown around the edges. It was quite possibly the nicest gift anyone had ever given him.

He knew a moment of intense possessiveness. No one had ever done this for him before, and he wanted to save them, hoard them as his own. But it was Christmas and he was thirty, not three, so he offered the plate around and everyone except Misha, who struggled to control his diabetes, took one. Finally he took one for himself. He bit into it. Perfect. And he still had about half a dozen left.

After the exchange, everyone began to pack up to go home. The day'd been pretty much a blow-off anyway. Melvin had dismissed the department with holiday wishes. Tatiana's gift sat pathetically alone on the now-empty table next to the rosemary topiary.

Elle began moving the chairs back to where they belonged. Cole pitched in to help.

"Thanks," she said. "I'm trying to get out of here as soon as possible."

"No problem." She was gorgeous, but he'd never been interested in asking her out, even before her engagement. She bore a faint resemblance to Connie. "Heading out of the city?"

"Teddy and I are going to D.C. to see his parents tomorrow. I have one more gift to buy and then I have to pack." She rolled her eyes. "First holiday with the almost in-laws. Teddy's mother considers me the whore who seduced her son. His neurotic sister is also coming with her shih-tzu who has potty issues. It should be delightful."

Cole laughed. "Sounds like fun."

"So what're you up to?"

The same vague holiday restlessness he experienced every year around this time seized him. Everyone seemed to have a long list of last-minute preparations except for him. "I'd planned to spend Christmas Eve and Christmas Day with my sister and her family in Connecticut. But she called this morning and my niece has the chicken pox. I've never had them, and since, according to Connie, it can cause impotence in adult males, I'm opting to stay home alone."

"Yeah. Sounds like a good choice to me. What about your parents?"

"They've got other plans." He didn't have a clue what they were, but they'd had other plans for the last fifteen years.

They finished placing the last of the chairs around the smaller tables that had been pushed to the wall. Elle picked up Tatiana's gift. "I suppose I'll leave it on her desk for her. If my schedule wasn't so crazy, I'd run it by and check on her, but I suppose she's okay or she would've called me."

Quite frankly he couldn't imagine Tatiana picking up the phone and calling anyone for help unless it was a dire emergency. She could be home alone, running a fever, sick....

He had nothing but time on his hands. "I'll take it by and check on her."

"That's nice, but I'm sure you have other things to do."

"The only thing on tonight's schedule was dinner with her, and now that's not happening. It's no problem."

Elle handed him the gift he'd bought earlier that morning.

It wasn't as if he was disappointed that she couldn't make dinner tonight. It wasn't as if he was worried about her. It wasn't as if that carriage kiss had tormented him since last night. No, he simply had time on his hands to kill.

TATIANA PULLED HER tattered pink chenille bathrobe closer around her. This was her special robe. Guaranteed to make her feel better. Its healing powers had been attested to for the last twelve years, ever since Grandma Rumasky had given it to her and told her it was guaranteed to cure whatever ailed her—even if redheads shouldn't wear pink. Today she was in major need of a cure.

Jimmy Stewart flickered on the screen in black and white as the townspeople rushed his family's bank for their money. This was her least favorite part of *It's a Wonderful Life.*

She shoved off the couch and wandered into the kitchen. Cole would've opened his cookies by now. She was almost sorry she'd been too much of a chicken to stay and watch. She'd come home last night in such a state, longing to do something for him…well, yeah, she'd like to do *that,* but she also wanted to do something special that went beyond sex. The anonymity of Secret Santa afforded her the opportunity. Home-baked Christmas cookies. She knew what it would mean to the man who'd grown up without any holiday traditions other than making the most out of being exiled with his sister. She'd felt the longing she wasn't even sure he knew he possessed when she'd talked about her family. For the span of one present, she could give him the gift of caring enough to prepare something special for him.

She opened the canister on the counter and counted out four almond cookies. Four should do her. Forget it. She put two more on her plate. She was going for six. People, on average, gained one and a half pounds over the holidays. She could at least do her part to uphold one holiday tradition considering everything else was a lost cause.

She poured herself a glass of organic skim milk and settled back down on the sofa. She dipped a cookie in the milk and then nibbled at the sodden edge. She'd spend her holiday stuffing herself like a turkey. And, who knows, maybe she'd actually get sick after telling that whopper of a lie earlier. Still, it had gotten her out of dinner with Cole. She'd been at an all-time low today when she'd skipped out of work—

A knock interrupted her cookiefest. Who was this? Maybe it was Mrs. Abramonoff's Harry & David fruit delivery. Ostensibly Edgar should have snagged the delivery guy in the lobby, but Edgar was the worst doorman in New York. Mrs. Abramonoff spent each December in Miami with family, and it seemed her December pears usually came after Christmas, but maybe this year… Tatiana would like to ignore it and pretend not to be home, but she hated to think of those pears in some frigid warehouse. "Just a minute," she called out.

She left her cookies and milk on the coffee table. It was a testimony to her Indiana upbringing that she had already thrown the dead bolt by the time she looked through the peephole. No brown-shirted delivery person bearing fruit stood on the other side. Nope. All six feet and some inches of broad-shouldered, blue-eyed, set-her-on-fire-with-his-kisses Cole Mitchell stood there.

She looked down at the chenille robe with its bald spots and the thick socks on her feet. Yep, she was pretty much hideous.

He knocked on the door again and she nearly jumped out of her skin. "Tatiana? Are you okay? I heard the lock. Are you too weak to open the door? Do I need to call 911?"

Although it might serve her right for lying, she didn't need him to call 911. She did the only thing she knew to do under the circumstances. She opened the door…and hoped she didn't live to regret it.

8

"WHAT ARE YOU DOING here?" she asked.

"You know, you could give a guy a complex. I told Elle I'd drop off your Secret Santa gift," Cole admitted stepping into her apartment. At work she was the cool snark. At dinner she was engaging. And more than once he'd imagined her naked or nearly naked. But this was a version of Tatiana Allen he'd never imagined. In her boxers and tank top with thick socks and a pink robe, her hair pinned up with a giant clip, she looked cute. Adorably sexy.

"You really shouldn't have."

"Well, it's a lousy time to be sick." Except she didn't look very sick to him. In fact, right now he'd peg her for looking extremely guilty. He hefted the bag in his right hand. "I stopped by Lemwitz Deli and picked you up some chicken soup. Mrs. Lemwitz makes it fresh every day, including her own noodles. Nothing's better than chicken soup when you're sick."

"Thanks. Thanks a lot. I'll just take these and you can be on your way. I don't want to tie up your time."

Hmm. She looked a little flushed, but he didn't see any watery eyes, red nose or signs of a cough. And her voice didn't sound scratchy. Not to mention that she was trying to hustle him out of there faster than a two-bit pimp.

"I've got plenty of time. Remember, I was planning to spend my evening with you anyway. So I'll just put these in the kitchen. I'm not going anywhere until I'm sure you're okay." More like until he was sure she'd faked being sick, which seemed increasingly likely. "You sit down and I'll warm up a bowl of chicken soup."

He stepped around her and into what was obviously the

kitchen. She followed behind him. "You don't listen very well. I don't need to be taken care of."

"You obviously don't listen well either since you're not sitting on the couch like a good girl waiting on me to nurse you back to health."

"I don't need to be nursed. I'm feeling better. Do you ever listen?"

"Huh?" He laughed at her flash of irritation. "I do listen, but sometimes my other senses distract me. Like my sense of sight, which happens frequently when I'm around you. By the way, you look adorably sexy in that outfit and not nearly as intimidating as you do at the office."

"There's nothing adorable about me in general. And as for sexy in this outfit, you obviously think I've developed a brain flu if I'm buying that."

Cole laughed and shrugged. "It really doesn't matter whether you buy it or not as long as it's what I think."

"You're infuriating."

"Am I?" He brushed the back of his hand down the length of her neck. "Hmm. No fever." He bent his head and breathed in the scent of her skin, her heat. "Well, you're enchanting even when you're at your snarkiest."

"You're sick."

"Very possibly. I'm feeling rather lightheaded now." He nuzzled the length of her neck.

"I might be contagious," Tatiana protested but didn't pull away. Instead she wrapped her arms around his neck.

"I'm sure you are and I'm sure I've already got a pretty bad case. I've got a theory."

"I can tell by your voice it's going to be something gnat-brained."

"Maybe I have a masochistic streak, because I love it when you talk like that." Her fingers in his hair, against his neck, caused heat to sizzle through him. "I think you bagged work today because you've got the same thing I've got."

"Mere supposition on your part." She leaned back and looked at him, but didn't let him go. Desire rolled off her in waves. They were so right together. Her eyes sparkled with wickedness, but he didn't miss the caution lurking in them as well. "What do you have?"

He knew what he had. What he wanted. Caution be damned. "I'm besotted, infatuated, tied up in knots over you. It's as if I've walked by the same bakery every day for almost a year wanting the pastry in the window, but the shop's always closed. And the more I pass it, the more I want it. It whets my appetite until nothing else appeals and all I can think about is sampling that pastry that I can't have."

"That sounds obsessive."

"Hmm. It is. Obsessive. Disquieting."

"You don't need me to tell you that chances are the pastry won't live up to expectation."

"I beg to differ. I've just had a sample of the pastry and found it even more addictive than I thought."

"This doesn't make any sense," she said.

She wouldn't be Tatiana if she didn't argue with him.

"It makes perfect sense. Are you really sick?"

She quirked that sexy mouth and pretended to consider his question. "I believe I am. I believe I've come down with a bad case of infatuation." She smoothed her hands over his chest. "I thought if I stayed home today I'd get over it soon enough."

He slid his hands beneath her T-shirt and cupped the fullness of her breasts. They fit perfectly in his hands, but then, that was no surprise because he now knew she was the perfect woman for him. "I've got just the cure." He brushed his thumbs over her nipples and they sprang to attention, which in turn brought him to full attention.

She pressed her breasts against him and pressed her thighs against his erection. She licked a path from his neck to his ear and nipped the lobe, the sensation arrowing straight to his arousal.

"I'm thinking it's more of a vaccination," she murmured into his ear while she pulled his shirt out of his pants.

"Look at it this way—either way we'll be cured. But the first thing we need to do is get you to bed."

TATIANA FELL ONTO the bed and Cole followed. They'd lost their clothes on the short trip from her den to her bedroom and a rush of sexual energy shot through her at the slide of his bare skin and heat against hers.

He drove her into the mattress, the comforter cool against the back of her while she was burning up from the inside out.

He scattered kisses down her neck, wreaking havoc to her central nervous system. "That day in Melvin's office—"

Her laugh came out breathless. "When you were in la-la land—"

"No la-la land. I was thinking about this." He flicked his tongue against her nipple and she arched up off the bed at the jolt that ran through her.

"Really? You were thinking about licking my nipples until I couldn't stand it any longer and had my evil way with you?"

"Technically, I was thinking about how you'd taste…" He slid down her body, trailing kisses down her belly followed by an occasional lick. Oh, she liked where she thought this was heading. She opened her legs farther and he obligingly ventured farther, his cheek, with its faint stubble, scraping against her thigh. "Everywhere." He dipped his tongue into her slick channel. Sensation rocked her and she fisted her hand in the coverlet and moaned aloud.

"Delicious appetizer."

On a bad day, when Cole grinned it was spine-tingling wicked, but this was a good day and he'd never been sexier than now when he flashed her an I'm-going-to-eat-you-up hot look from between her thighs.

"Far be it from me to interrupt your dining pleasure but it seems unfair that my plate's empty."

She slid to the edge of the bed and pulled a flavored condom from her night stand. Changing direction, careful not to kick him, she brought his masculine thighs, flat belly and hard cock into mouth-watering proximity. She sheathed him, then nibbled her way along his thigh, inhaling his heady scent. Surprise flashed in his eyes only to be replaced by the glitter of hot sexual arousal.

He rolled to his side to face her and wrapped his big masculine hand around her thigh, continuing his nuzzling between her legs.

Tatiana had never been so intimate so quickly with anyone, but she and Cole had been engaged in a pas de deux for nearly a year and after denying the attraction, resisting it, there was an inevitability to being here with him akin to the sun rising every morning.

"Appetizer for two," she murmured and licked the length of his impressive erection. He groaned against her wet folds and pleasure radiated through her.

She'd thought she was hot before, now she was gripped by a fever of want. He lapped at her while she took him in her mouth and lavished attention on his cock.

"Baby, if we don't stop now I'm never going to make it to the main course."

She was nearly mindless with want. She rolled onto her back and Cole rolled off the bed. He stood by the edge of the mattress. He was big and aroused and looked at her with a mixture of pure lust, adoration and possessiveness that intensified the ache between her thighs. She quivered with the need to feel his hard length inside her.

She eyed his jutting penis with a reciprocal measure of admiring lust. "I know exactly what I want for a main course."

Cole laughed, low and wicked. He grasped her behind her knees and dragged her across the bed until her bottom was even with the edge of the mattress. Oh, baby. He hooked his arms beneath her knees and entered her in one smooth, long stroke. She cried out and rose up to take him as deep and hard as possible.

Buried to the hilt, he paused, "You don't know how many times I've fantasized about you. You're even hotter than I thought."

Talk about the right thing to say. She clenched her muscles around him, lifting her bottom, nudging him even deeper. "I've had a few fantasies of my own about you, but they never felt this good."

He set a pace of hard and fast then slow and gentle, bringing her close to an orgasm and then backing off until she was writhing frantically. His jaw was clenched with the effort not to come too quickly.

"Please…" She sank her nails into the bulge of his biceps. "Dessert…together."

Tremors started at her core, from somewhere deep inside her soul, something she'd never offered to any other man, and rolled through her until she was too much for herself. She screamed her release as Cole exploded inside her.

"THANK YOU FOR THE COOKIES." Cole's warm breath stirred the hair at her temple.

Tatiana didn't move. Couldn't move. Cole had returned from a quick bathroom trip and had stretched out on the bed, pulling her on top of him…was it two minutes ago? Five? A lifetime? She was still sprawled on top of him, boneless with satisfaction. She smiled against his warm, naked, just-the-right-amount-of-hair-on-it chest and murmured, "What cookies?"

"The almond cookies that I smelled when I came into your house earlier. The ones sitting in the canister on your counter."

"Oh, those." She rolled off him with a grin and pulled the sheet up over them both. "I didn't think you noticed."

"You're cute in that pink robe, but I didn't miss the food."

She smiled. She was so not cute—especially in that robe, but apparently cute was in the eye of the blinded-by-lust beholder. "Did you know when you opened them?"

"No. With the bib and the spoon I had sort of pegged you. But the cookies were too nice. I thought it must be someone else." She threw a pillow and hit him in the head. He laughed and pinned her to the bed. "You're never nice to me."

She bit him on the shoulder. "Because I don't like you." She loved him. For better or for worse. For whatever he was or wasn't, she loved him.

"You liked me well enough a few minutes ago."

"I wouldn't say actively liked. More along the lines of tolerated."

"If you screamed that loud when you were merely tolerating me, I'm not sure my ears could stand it if you actually liked me."

"Just imagine how deaf you'd be if I was idiot-brained enough to fancy that I loved you."

He traced the line of her bare shoulder, his touch sending tingles through her. "Umm. Terrifying. All these years I thought I could make the decision not to care about people, not to let them close to my heart. And then you came along and I found out free choice doesn't exist when it comes to love. The only control we have over it is what we decide to do about it."

"Excuse me, but did you just bumble your way around a declaration of love?"

"Ladies first. Did you just snark your way through an admission of being idiot-brained?"

"I think I may have."

"Coward."

"I am not a coward. Ducking out of work and ditching dinner wasn't cowardice, it was an inept attempt at self-preservation. Okay, I have a feeling you're going to shamelessly use this against me, but, yes, I do love you. Satisfied?"

"I'm getting there." She suddenly saw what made much more sense than where she'd been going all along. Cole obviously wasn't on the best terms with this family. He spent Christmas with his sister but not his father or his mother. He'd worked at *Connoisseur* for almost a year, and never in that time had she heard of his father revisiting Mr. Creighton. "Your father didn't get you the job at *Connoisseur,* did he?"

He shifted to his back, one arm beneath his head, seemingly at ease except for his wary eyes. "What makes you say that? And what difference does it make?"

"All this time I thought you'd just waltzed into a job the rest of us had to work our butts off to get."

"Yours came back. And very nicely, if I do say so."

"Oh, no, you're not going to sidetrack me. Your father didn't get you the job, but he was there and he did meet with Mr. Creighton." She considered the type of man who would let his new wife—or, as was apparently the case, wives—allow his children to feel unwanted. "He didn't want you to have this job, did he? That's why he met with Mr. Creighton—to try to keep you from getting the job—isn't it?"

He sighed. "No, he didn't want me to have the job. And, yes, he'd told me if I insisted on working in publishing, it could at least be for a publication that he thought worthy. He had connections and he'd make sure I had a position with the *Wall Street Journal* or a job as a foreign correspondent if I wanted the travel aspect. I didn't want to work for the *Journal.* So he paid Douglas Creighton a visit to try to dissuade him from hiring me. Luckily Creighton thinks every man succeeds or fails on his own merit."

"You let us all think…"

"No. You thought what you wanted to think."

"But you could've told us…."

"No. I learned a long time ago, people either know me and like me for who I am or they don't."

"Your stepmothers?"

"Yep. And stepfathers."

She recalled his attitude toward Parker Longrehn. He wouldn't give Parker the satisfaction of knowing he could affect his life. There were many more layers to laid-back, devil-may-care Cole Mitchell than she'd ever suspected. Or maybe that wasn't true. Maybe she'd suspected it but hadn't wanted to acknowledge it. Maybe she'd hidden behind resenting his job because it had kept her safe from the attraction she'd felt from their first encounter. If she didn't like him, then she couldn't possibly fall in love with him, right?

Except she had.

"I would insist on dragging you along to Connie's house, except her munchkin has the chicken pox. Since we seem to be stuck with one another for Christmas, why don't we go to Corfu?"

"What? Why?"

"Because it's there and we can. I want to go there with you. Christmas in Corfu has a nice ring, doesn't it?"

"But…" She couldn't come up with the rest, she just knew it didn't feel right. "I hadn't planned to go to Corfu."

"Neither had I. But then again, I didn't plan to fall in love with you, but it strikes me as a very good thing."

"I love to travel. But, you know, it's always scheduled. Anticipated. Part of business. I'm not packed. It'd cost a fortune. And who would watch for Mrs. Abramonoff's pears?"

He smiled, and if she hadn't been watching so closely she might've missed the flash of disappointment in his eyes. He leaned over and kissed her on her nose. "It's fine, babe. I don't really care where we are as long as I'm with you. And at the risk of coming across as an insensitive man, I'm kind of hungry. I missed lunch today and my dinner date stood me up." He grinned at her. "Mind if I heat up that chicken soup? Considering you're ill, I'll be glad to bring you a bowl in bed."

"Works for me."

Cole padded out of her bedroom and she heard him rustling around in the kitchen. She should be ecstatic…well, she would be ecstatic if she hadn't seen that quickly masked moment of disappointment in his eyes.

She had a lifetime of warm holiday memories surrounded by a family that adored her. Cole had been shuffled from one parent to another, and wanted by neither. Had anyone ever asked him what he'd like to do for Christmas? She'd bet her last dollar that had never happened. But he, who never got too close to anyone, had just told her what he wanted, and she'd shot it down for a host of ridiculous reasons that all went back to one thing—she didn't know how to have fun outside of work.

But by God she was about to learn. It was time for her to start building a Christmas tradition of her own and time for his Christmas tradition to take a step up.

She stood and pulled on her pink chenille robe—he'd seen her in it and out of it, so what the heck. She padded into the kitchen and found him testing the soup in a pan on the stove.

She wrapped her arms around him from behind and pressed a kiss to his naked back. He turned and nuzzled the sensitive spot beneath her ear. A delicate shiver chased over her skin. Of course, she seemed to have a multitude of sensitive spots with him.

"Sorry it's taking so long, but a microwave ruins the noodles," he said.

"Well, this sucks, but I'm sick."

He leaned back and peered at her. "What's the matter?"

"I've got the travel bug."

"What?"

"Someone mentioned Christmas in Corfu, and at first I thought it was crazy. But now I've caught the travel bug and I think there's only one cure for it."

"Are you sure?"

"Positive."

He picked her up and swung her around in a circle, looking for all the world like an elated little boy who'd just been presented a gift from a Santa he didn't believe in anymore.

Which reminded her... "When you came earlier, you had a present. Was that for me?" It wasn't as if she had a whole lot of gifts to look forward to.

Cole grinned at her. "It was your last Secret Santa gift. I volunteered to bring it over and check on you. It gave me a good reason to come by."

"Okay. At least it got you over here. Let me fire up my laptop and we'll book our tickets while we eat."

"Aren't you going to open your present?"

"Yeah. Later. I want to get the tickets booked first."

He picked up the box on the counter wrapped in Santa Claus paper topped with a big red bow and handed it to her. "Go ahead and open it now. Might as well get it out of the way."

She tore off the wrapping and lifted the box top. Nestled in white tissue paper was a pair of sheer red bikini panties...with a sprig of mistletoe embroidered on the front.

She looked up, laughing. "You. You're my Secret Santa."

He spread his hands, palms up. "Hey, you don't always have a sprig of mistletoe handy when you need it."

"I believe I'll have to pack this along with my massage oil for Corfu."

"Why don't you come sit on Santa's lap and tell him what else you'd like for Christmas."

"Well, Santa, I've been a very good girl all year—except

maybe I've been a little testy with this guy at work." She nuzzled his neck. "But I can't lie, Santa. I think I'm about to be very naughty and I think I deserve to get Cole in my stocking this year."

* * * * *

Experience entertaining women's fiction for every woman who has wondered "what's next?" in their lives.
Turn the page for a sneak preview
of a new book from Harlequin NEXT,
WHY IS MURDER ON THE MENU, ANYWAY?
by Stevi Mittman

On sale December 26, wherever books are sold.

Ambience is everything. Imagine eating a foie gras at a luncheonette counter or a side of coleslaw at Le Cirque. It's not a matter of food but one of atmosphere. Remember that when planning your dining room design.

—Tips from *Teddi.com*

"Now that's the kind of man you should be looking for," my mother, the self-appointed keeper of my shelf-life stamp, says. She points with her fork at a man in the corner of the Steak-Out Restaurant, a dive I've just been hired to redecorate. Making this restaurant look four-star will be hard, but not half as hard as getting through lunch without strangling the woman across the table from me. "*He* would make a good husband."

"Oh, you can tell that from across the room?" I ask, wondering how it is she can forget that when we had trouble getting rid of my last husband, she shot him. "Besides being ten minutes away from death if he actually eats all that steak, he's twenty years too old for me and—shallow woman that I am—twenty pounds too heavy. Besides, I am *so* not looking for another husband here. I'm looking to design a new image for this place, looking for some sense of ambience, some feeling, something I can build a proposal on for them."

My mother studies the man in the corner, tilting her head, the better to gauge his age, I suppose. I think she's grimacing, but with all the Botox and Restylane injected into that face, it's hard to tell. She takes another bite of her steak salad, chews slowly so that I don't miss the fact that the steak is a poor cut and tougher than it should be. "You're concentrating on the wrong kind of proposal," she says finally. "Just look at this place, Teddi. It's a dive. There are hardly any other diners. What does *that* tell you about the food?"

"That they cater to a dinner crowd and it's lunchtime," I tell her.

I don't know what I was thinking bringing her here with me. I suppose I thought it would be better than eating alone. There really are days when my common sense goes on vacation. Clearly, this is one of them. I mean, really, did I not resolve less than three weeks ago that I would not let my mother get to me anymore?

What good are New Year's resolutions, anyway?

Mario approaches the man's table and my mother studies him while they converse. Eventually Mario leaves the table with a huff, after which the diner glances up and meets my mother's gaze. I think she's smiling at him. That or she's got indigestion. They size each other up.

I concentrate on making sketches in my notebook and try to ignore the fact that my mother is flirting. At nearly seventy, she's developed an unhealthy interest in members of the opposite sex to whom she isn't married.

According to my father, who has broken the TMI rule and given me Too Much Information, she has no interest in sex with him. Better, I suppose, to be clued in on what they aren't doing in the bedroom than have to hear what they might be doing.

"He's not so old," my mother says, noticing that I have barely touched the Chinese chicken salad she warned me not to get. "He's got about as many years on you as you have on your little cop friend."

She does this to make me crazy. I know it, but it works all the same. "Drew Scoones is not my little 'friend.' He's a detective with whom I—"

"Screwed around," my mother says. I must look shocked, because my mother laughs at me and asks if I think she doesn't know the "lingo."

What I thought she didn't know was that Drew and I actually tangled in the sheets. And, since it's possible she's just fishing, I sidestep the issue and tell her that Drew is just a couple of years younger than me and that I don't need reminding. I dig into my salad with renewed vigor, determined to show my mother that Chinese chicken salad in a steak place was not the stupid choice it's proving to be.

After a few more minutes of my picking at the wilted leaves on my plate, the man my mother has me nearly engaged to pays his bill and heads past us toward the back of the restaurant. I watch my mother take in his shoes, his suit and the diamond pinkie ring that seems to be cutting off the circulation in his little finger.

"Such nice hands," she says after the man is out of sight. "Manicured." She and I both stare at my hands. I have two popped acrylics that are being held on at weird angles by bandages. My cuticles are ragged and there's marker decorating my right hand from measuring carelessly when I did a drawing for a customer.

Twenty minutes later she's disappointed that he managed to leave the restaurant without our noticing. He will join the list of the ones I let get away. I will hear about him twenty years from now when—according to my mother—my children will be grown and I will still be single, living pathetically alone with several dogs and cats.

After my ex, that sounds good to me.

The waitress tells us that our meal has been taken care of by the management and, after thanking Mario, the owner, complimenting him on the wonderful meal and assuring him that once I have redecorated his place people will be flocking here in droves (I actually use those words and ignore my mother when she rolls her eyes), my mother and I head for the restroom.

My father—unfortunately not with us today—has the patience of a saint. He got it over the years of living with my mother. She, perhaps as a result, figures he has the patience for both of them, and feels justified having none. For her, no rules apply, and a little thing like a picture of a man on the door to a public restroom is certainly no barrier to using the john. In all fairness, it does seem silly to stand and wait for the ladies' room if no one is using the men's room.

Still, it's the idea that rules don't apply to her, signs don't apply to her, conventions don't apply to her. She knocks on the door to the men's room. When no one answers she gestures to me to go in ahead. I tell her that I can certainly wait for the ladies' room to be free and she shrugs and goes in herself.

Not a minute later there is a bloodcurdling scream from behind the men's room door.

"Mom!" I yell. "Are you all right?"

Mario comes running over, the waitress on his heels. Two customers head our way while my mother continues to scream.

I try the door, but it is locked. I yell for her to open it and she fumbles with the knob. When she finally manages to unlock and open it, she is white behind her two streaks of blush, but she is on her feet and appears shaken but not stirred.

"What happened?" I ask her. So do Mario and the waitress and the few customers who have migrated to the back of the place.

She points toward the bathroom and I go in, thinking it serves her right for using the men's room. But I see nothing amiss.

She gestures toward the stall, and, like any self-respecting and suspicious woman, I poke the door open with one finger, expecting the worst.

What I find is worse than the worst.

The husband my mother picked out for me is sitting on the toilet. His pants are puddled around his ankles, his hands are hanging at his sides. Pinned to his chest is some sort of Health Department certificate.

Oh, and there is a large, round, bloodless bullet hole between his eyes.

Four Nassau County police officers are securing the area, waiting for the detectives and crime scene personnel to show up. They are trying, though not very hard, to comfort my mother, who in another era would be considered to be suffering from the vapors. Less tactful in the twenty-first century, I'd say she was losing it. That is, if I didn't know her better, know she was milking it for everything it was worth.

My mother loves attention. As it begins to flag, she swoons and claims to feel faint. Despite four No Smoking signs, my mother insists it's all right for her to light up because, after all, she's in shock. Not to mention that signs, as we know, don't apply to her.

When asked not to smoke, she collapses mournfully in a chair and lets her head loll to the side, all without mussing her hair.

Eventually, the detectives show up to find the four patrolmen all circled around her, debating whether to administer CPR, smelling salts or simply call the paramedics. I, however, know just what will snap her to attention.

"Detective Scoones," I say loudly. My mother parts the sea of cops.

"We have to stop meeting like this," he says lightly to me, but I can feel him checking me over with his eyes, making sure I'm all right while pretending not to care.

"What have you got in those pants?" my mother asks him, coming to her feet and staring at his crotch accusingly. "*Baydar?* Everywhere we Bayers are, you turn up. You don't expect me to buy that this is a coincidence, I hope."

Drew tells my mother that it's nice to see her, too, and asks if it's his fault that her daughter seems to attract disasters.

Charming to be made to feel like the bearer of a plague.

He asks how I am.

"Just peachy," I tell him. "I seem to be making a habit of finding dead bodies, my mother is driving me crazy and the catering hall I booked two freakin' years ago for Dana's bat mitzvah has just been shut down by the Board of Health!"

"Glad to see your luck's finally changing," he says, giving me a quick squeeze around the shoulders before turning his attention to the patrolmen, asking what they've got, whether they've taken any statements, moved anything, all the sort of stuff you see on TV, without any of the drama. That is, if you don't count my mother's threats to faint every few minutes when she senses no one's paying attention to her.

Mario tells his waitstaff to bring everyone espresso, which I decline because I'm wired enough. Drew pulls him aside and a minute later I'm handed a cup of coffee that smells divinely of Kahlúa.

The man knows me well. Too well.

His partner, whom I've met once or twice, says he'll interview the kitchen staff. Drew asks Mario if he minds if he takes statements from the patrons first and gets to him and the waitstaff afterward.

"No, no," Mario tells him. "Do the patrons first." Drew raises his eyebrow at me like he wants to know if I get the double entendre. I try to look bored.

"What is it with you and murder victims?" he asks me when we sit down at a table in the corner.

I search them out so that I can see you again, I almost say, but I'm afraid it will sound desperate instead of sarcastic.

My mother, lighting up and daring him with a look to tell her not to, reminds him that *she* was the one to find the body.

Drew asks what happened *this time*. My mother tells him how the man in the john was "taken" with me, couldn't take his eyes off me and blatantly flirted with both of us. To his credit, Drew doesn't laugh, but his smirk is undeniable to the trained eye. And I've had my eye trained on him for nearly a year now.

"While he was noticing you," he asks me, "did *you* notice anything about him? Was he waiting for anyone? Watching for anything?"

I tell him that he didn't appear to be waiting or watching. That he made no phone calls, was fairly intent on eating and did, indeed, flirt with my mother. This last bit Drew takes with a grain of salt, which was the way it was intended.

"And he had a short conversation with Mario," I tell him. "I think he might have been unhappy with the food, though he didn't send it back."

Drew asks what makes me think he was dissatisfied, and I tell him that the discussion seemed acrimonious and that Mario looked distressed when he left the table. Drew makes a note and says he'll look into it and asks about anyone else in the restaurant. Did I see anyone who didn't seem to belong, anyone who was watching the victim, anyone looking suspicious?

"Besides my mother?" I ask him, and Mom huffs and blows her cigarette smoke in my direction.

I tell him that there were several deliveries, the kitchen staff going in and out the back door to grab a smoke. He stops me and asks what I was doing checking out the back door of the restaurant.

Proudly—because, while he was off forgetting me, dropping by only once in a while to say hi to Jesse, my son, or drop something by for one of my daughters that he thought they might like, I was getting on with my life—I tell him that I'm decorating the place.

He looks genuinely impressed. "Commercial customers? That's great," he says. Okay, that's what he *ought* to say. What he actually says is "Whatever pays the bills."

"Howard Rosen, the famous restaurant critic, got her the job," my mother says. "You met him—the good-looking, distinguished gentleman with the *real* job, something to be proud of. I guess you've never read his reviews in *Newsday*."

Drew, without missing a beat, tells her that Howard's reviews are on the top of his list, as soon as he learns how to read.

"I only meant—" my mother starts, but both of us assure her that we know just what she meant.

"So," Drew says. "Deliveries?"

I tell him that Mario would know better than I, but that I saw vegetables come in, maybe fish and linens.

"This is the second restaurant job Howard's got her," my mother tells Drew.

"At least she's getting *something* out of the relationship," he says.

"If he were here," my mother says, ignoring the insinuation, "he'd be comforting her instead of interrogating her. He'd be making sure we're both all right after such an ordeal."

"I'm sure he would," Drew agrees, then looks me in the eyes as if he's measuring my tolerance for shock. Quietly he adds,

"But then maybe he doesn't know just what strong stuff your daughter's made of."

It's the closest thing to a tender moment I can expect from Drew Scoones. My mother breaks the spell. "She gets that from me," she says.

Both Drew and I take a minute, probably to pray that's all I inherited from her.

"I'm just trying to save you some time and effort," my mother tells him. "My money's on Howard."

Drew withers her with a look and mutters something that sounds suspiciously like "fool's gold." Then he excuses himself to go back to work.

I catch his sleeve and ask if it's all right for us to leave. He says sure, he knows where we live. I say goodbye to Mario. I assure him that I will have some sketches for him in a few days, all the while hoping that this murder doesn't cancel his redecorating plans. I need the money desperately, the alternative being borrowing from my parents and being strangled by the strings.

My mother is strangely quiet all the way to her house. She doesn't tell me what a loser Drew Scoones is—despite his good looks—and how I was obviously drooling over him. She doesn't ask me where Howard is taking me tonight or warn me not to tell my father about what happened because he will worry about us both and no doubt insist we see our respective psychiatrists.

She fidgets nervously, opening and closing her purse over and over again.

"You okay?" I ask her. After all, she's just found a dead man on the toilet, and tough as she is that's got to be upsetting.

When she doesn't answer me I pull over to the side of the road.

"Mom?" She refuses to meet my eyes. "You want me to take you to see Dr. Cohen?"

She looks out the window as if she's just realized we're on Broadway in Woodmere. "Aren't we near Marvin's Jewelers?" she asks, pulling something out of her purse.

"What have you got, Mother?" I ask, prying open her fingers to find the murdered man's ring.

"It was on the sink," she says in answer to my dropped jaw. "I was going to get his name and address and have you return it to him so that he could ask you out. I thought it was a sign that the two of you were meant to be together."

"He's dead, Mom. You understand that, right?" I ask. You never can tell when my mother is fine and when she's in la-la land.

"Well, I didn't know that," she shouts at me. "Not at the time."

I ask why she didn't give it to Drew, realize that she wouldn't give Drew the time in a clock shop and add, "...or one of the other policemen?"

"For heaven's sake," she tells me. "The man is dead, Teddi, and I took his ring. How would that look?"

Before I can tell her it looks just the way it is, she pulls out a cigarette and threatens to light it.

"I mean, really," she says, shaking her head like it's my brains that are loose. "What does he need with it now?"

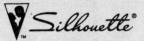

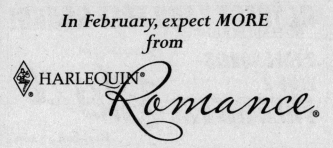

REQUEST YOUR FREE BOOKS!

2 FREE NOVELS
PLUS 2
FREE GIFTS!

 HARLEQUIN®

Red-hot reads!

Silhouette®

Desire

Don't miss
DAKOTA FORTUNES,
a six-book continuing series following
the Fortune family of South Dakota—
oil is in their blood and privilege
is their birthright.

This series kicks off with
USA TODAY bestselling author
PEGGY MORELAND'S
Merger of Fortunes
(SD #1771)
this January.

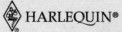

HARLEQUIN®

Blaze™

COMING NEXT MONTH

#297 BEYOND BREATHLESS Kathleen O'Reilly
The Red Choo Diaries, Bk. 1
When Manhattan trains quit and a sexy stranger offers to split the cost of a car, Jamie McNamara takes the deal. Now stuck in gridlock in a Hummer limo, she has hot-looking, hard-bodied Andrew Brooks across from her and nothing but time on her hands....

#298 LETTING LOOSE! Mara Fox
The Wrong Bed
He's buff. He's beautiful. He's taking off his clothes. And he's exactly what lawyer Tina Henderson needs. She's sure a wild night with a stripper will make her forget all about smooth attorney Tyler Walden. Only, there's more to "The Bandit" than meets the eye....

#299 UNTOUCHED Samantha Hunter
Extreme Blaze
Once Risa Remington had the uncanny ability to read minds, and a lot more.... Now she's lost her superpowers and the CIA's trust. The one thing she craves is human sexual contact. But is maverick agent Daniel MacAlister the right one to take her to bed?

#300 JACK & JILTED Cathy Yardley
Chloe Winton is one unmarried bride. Still, she asks, "Why let a perfectly good honeymoon go to waste?" So she doesn't. The private yacht that her former fiancé booked is ready and waiting. And so is its heart-stopping captain, Jack McCullough. Starry moonlit nights on the ocean make for quick bedfellows and he and Chloe are no exception, even with rocky waters ahead!

#301 RELEASE Jo Leigh
In Too Deep...
Seth Turner is a soldier without a battle. He's secreted in a safe house with gorgeous Dr. Harper Douglas, who's helping to heal his body. Talk about bedside manners... But can he fight the heated sexual attraction escalating between them?

#302 HER BOOK OF PLEASURE Marie Donovan
Rick Sokol discovers a pillow book of ancient erotic art, leading him to appraiser Megan O'Malley. The illustrated pages aren't the only thing Megan checks out, and soon she and Rick are creating a number of new positions of their own. But will their newfound intimacy survive when danger intrudes?

www.eHarlequin.com

HBCNM1206